Musings of a Romance Addict

Written by

Camille Dunhill

Cover by

Jonathan Tazzmore Productions

Photography by

Jack Schulman

BatCat Media Group

Makeup by

Beauty by Sharell

Musings of a Romance Addict

This book is a work of fiction. Any names, characters, companies, organizations, places, events, locales, and incidents are either used in a fictitious manner or are fictional. Any resemblance to actual persons, living or dead, actual companies or organizations, or actual events is purely coincidental.

Printed in the United States of America

ISBN - 978-0-9852196-4-2

Thanks to:

All of those handsome men and beautiful women who entered my life to contribute to my musings about Romance. I could not have done it without you.

Table of Contents

Prologue

My name is Stacey Donleigh and I'm a Romance Addict. I probably made that up, but since romance is a feeling of excitement and mystery associated with love, that's what I'm addicted to. And that's what I've been searching for. Apparently, it's not something you can find easily since I've been looking for it for years. So, I've decided to document my attempts and failures to find that elusive feeling.

But first, a little about me. I own a public relations firm in Palm Beach, Florida. I just turned 40. I'm tall and trim with auburn hair. I lived with a man for the past 10 years but we never married. He passed away two years ago.

After his death, I put myself on hold and stayed frozen in place. It wasn't so much that we had the greatest love since Elizabeth and Richard and I couldn't go on without him, but we had been together for a decade. There was a certain "comfort level." Well, maybe it wasn't always comfortable but it was all that we had.

I really wasn't interested in finding another relationship but my friends saw that I was just immersing myself in my work and had no social life and they were worried about me. They suggested that I join an online dating site because two of my best friends had found their significant others that way. So, I signed up just to give it a try.

What comes next is a story about my search for love and romance. It begins with my first encounter with online dating and continues as I discover a part of myself that I never knew existed.

I've written this book as a "Diary," so please forgive me for not giving you "Chapters" to read.

THE BEGINNING OF MY JOURNEY

CHRISTOPHER LOGAN

After being on a dating site for 2 days, I received a text from a man who said his "best friend" who was visiting him in Pennsylvania, saw my photos and just had to meet me. Would I please contact him? He said I would not be sorry. I was given the name, email and phone number of a man named Christopher Logan and I sent him a brief message.

He immediately got back to me and sent me some photos (he was adorable). Then, he began sending me the most romantic emails I ever received. Mind you, they were not X-rated, just very romantic! And as I mentioned, I had been searching for "Romance" most of my life!

Well, it had been so long since I had been swept off my feet, that I fell under his spell. He said he wanted to get to know me better before we actually met in person. While that should have been a red flag, I thought that it was sweet.

Christopher said he had been a widower for 5 years. His wife passed away from colon cancer. And he had not been with a woman since then (Wow! Another red flag—but I kept going).

After a few more days with dozens of terribly romantic emails and phone calls, I fell madly in love with Christopher (yes, hard to believe, even for me!). We spoke by phone at least four times a day. Each call was more intimate than the last one. The texts were instant reminders of the passion that was building between us. There was no way to resist the temptation!

We were scheduled to finally meet in person when he said he had to travel to New York on business, where he was making a presentation for 2 projects—one in China and one in Cape Town, South Africa.

When he returned from his trip to New York, he said that he won the Cape Town contract (for $3 Million) and had to leave for South Africa the next day. He sent me photos of him at the airport at 7:00 a.m. as he was getting ready to board his plane. By 4:00 p.m., he called me and said he had arrived in Cape Town. Now I know for a fact that it takes about 20 hours to fly to Cape Town and when I questioned him, he said he took a private jet (another red flag). Even a private jet couldn't get there in 8 hours!

He then contacted me to say that his cab was robbed on the way to his hotel in Cape Town and they stole everything, including his clothes and equipment for the project. He asked me to send him an

Apple Computer, iPhone and Canon camera and he would pay me back. Why would I want to do that? Well, before he left, he sent me a bank statement from Chase Bank that said he had $12 Million in the account (of course, it was a fake). He said after the robbery, he cancelled all of his credit cards and couldn't access his money.

I thought, "Excuse me…but if you have $12 Million in a Chase account, even if you have cancelled your credit cards, I do believe they can accommodate you with a line of credit. Also, why would I want to send computer equipment to Cape Town? I can't believe they don't have Apple products down there." All of these questions I posed to Christopher. He didn't have an answer, just an emotional outburst about how I was "breaking his heart" by not trusting him. By this time, the red flags, bells, whistles, everything were going off in my head. Plus, people around me were telling me about this thing called the "Romance Scam," which I was now living through. I researched it on the Internet and sure enough, it was a real thing!

When I refused to give in to Christopher's demands for equipment, money and credit card information, he finally gave up. But he did not disappear completely. He contacted me one more time, trying to get me to click on a fake link where he could infiltrate my files and compromise my information.

In less than 14 days, I had fallen in love, almost been scammed, and had my heart broken by a man who did not exist! All in the name of "Romance."

I later found out that these "Romance Scammers" work in teams of men and women, targeting people on dating sites. They use scripts and have a folder of photos of the person they are currently pretending to be in every imaginable situation—cleaning the pool, in the hospital, at the airport… They profess their love for the mark and tell them they want to marry them. All this takes place within a couple of weeks. For lonely men and women, it seems like a dream come true. Unfortunately for Christopher, the two concepts that made me run for the hills were "lend me money" and "marry me." Neither of those was EVER going to happen!

I saved all the emails between me and Christopher and used them as a reminder of how out of control I let the situation get. I started a Diary documenting each day and reminding me of my experiences. Little did I know that I would lose control and find my real self… I realized that under my sweet, controlled exterior, I was to become a romance addict.

***

WEDNESDAY

Good Morning Christopher,

Your friend Jason suggested that I send you an email. He said you live in my area. Why don't you get back to me with a little information about yourself?

Stacey

Dear Stacey,

Wow, I wasn't expecting my Friend to email you on my behalf. That was very sweet and lovely. It's so nice to hear from you. Thanks for your message. I was caught by surprise. Let me start by saying my name is Christopher Logan. I have to introduce myself to you in order for you to know who I am and what I do for a living. I'm an Engineer. I guess I should start by letting you know that I am still new to this kind of dating as well but I just needed to try something new. I am looking for a serious and long-term relationship with one special woman. I want a woman who is mature and also independent. A woman who is kind and generous. A woman who tells me, "Honey, you can do it," no matter what the situation may be. A woman who I can connect with emotionally and who shares the same interests. I don't need anyone to take advantage of my weaknesses or my strengths; I need someone who appreciates the good things in life and love. I would love to know more about you to see when we can both meet and see if the chemistry is there. So, tell me more about yourself. I mean those things you do like and want from a man you will want to be with for the rest of your life. What do you like doing in your free time and what you do for a living and your profession?

I got motivated by what you said on your profile, as I came across it and have always believed we are all looking for the same thing here. No one will waste time when there are a lot of things we need to do. I want someone who will walk through fire for me and I would do the same for them. (Not literally... but you know what I mean.) I believe relationships take work, too. I think it is easier to walk away than to stay and work it out. Personally, I think that if two people both want it to work, they need to always make a conscious effort to be thankful every day for the person that came into their life.

I was made to understand that most people on this dating site don't put their real information out there. I want you to be honest with me because I really admired your profile when I first saw it. I will appreciate your telling me your actual age, where you reside and more about yourself.
I think I have written enough, so I'll close this email now. I will be hoping to hear from you if you think I will be an ideal man for you.
Thanks.
Christopher Logan

Hi Christopher,

It was so nice to hear from you. Your friend Jason seems to think the world of you. I appreciate your giving me so much information about yourself and for sending photos. As I mentioned, I live in Palm Beach, Florida, where I have my own Public Relations firm. My long-time life partner passed away 2 years ago. He had a massive heart attack and died in my arms. I've been recovering and now feel that I am ready to move on with my life.

Aside from my business, I enjoy volunteering in my community—at the local hospital, at the animal shelter, and at the PBS station. I love to read—mysteries and thrillers. Also love flea markets, garage sales and estate sales. Cooking and entertaining are my ways to relax (some people may think that's crazy).

Stacey

Good Day Beautiful,

Thank you for the messages. First, I'm 6' tall and have been a widower for almost 5 years now. I'm a huge animal lover and have one awesome dog named Jackie. I love horses, fish, birds, dogs and all of God's creatures. I get to travel for vacation once in a while, which is quite interesting, but believe me, it's always better to have a travel partner. That way, you enjoy and see the world through both person's eyes. I have actually been single for five years when I lost my late wife to colon cancer. I haven't been able to put myself out there to date again or meet people since I am not the type of guy who goes to bars, clubs and all the other social and crowded places.

I guess I should start by making you know that I am still new to this kind of dating as well but just needed to try something. I would love to know more about you to see when we can both meet and see if the chemistry is there. So, tell me more about yourself. I mean those things you do and want from a man you will want to be with for the rest of your life.

Interests: I tend to have a variety of interests, such as the following: I enjoy the outdoors, I love spending time by the beach, as the water grounds me and provides me with inner peace and I enjoy a nice sunset, especially right by the water (romantic). I enjoy walking, swimming, anything with outdoor involvement and playing like a kid when am with my partner. I am very playful and have a free spirit. I enjoy a good movie, all types of music, reading, some sports, and different types of food. I am open to trying new things. The bottom line is I am active and have a tremendous amount of energy to expend.

I am a one-woman man, and I give myself completely to my partner, respect, care and support her through thick and thin. My mom is still alive and well. She lives in Germany and she is 82 years, while my dad passed on when I was still a kid. I don't pretend and do not have time to waste or waste people's time. I say what's on my mind and get straight to the point, not to the point of being rude - but certainly to the point of being honest.... I am open to trying new things and always love to learn. I am not a perfect man, and I am not looking for a perfect lady. We both can learn together, grow together and see perfection in everything we do, even our flaws.

I must confess I feel so comfortable and easy with you. There is this smile when I read your messages. It's a very important part of every relationship. It will be nice to hear back from you. I hope we'll be able to start getting to know each other more and communicate better, because I know every good and healthy relationship starts with good communication and understanding. I have so much to share with you but I should not reveal everything at once. You haven't yet answered my questions on what kind of relationship you're looking for—if it's a fling or long-term relationship. Have a wonderful day and I Hope to hear from you soon.
Sincerely,
Christopher Logan

***

THURSDAY

Good Morning Sunshine.

It's too early for good mornings, but you're already on my mind. So, "Good morning!" and I am sorry about the telephone connection last night. As I was trying to tell you, I am currently living in Wellington, FL, and I have been here for the past 5 years.

Always,

Christopher

Dearest Stacey,

How are you today? Hope you had a lovely night? Thank you for your nice and lovely email. I feel your pain. I really see that we share a lot of things in common. I am new to the online dating and it will be nice to be with someone like you. I would like to know more about you. Dearest, I want to know everything about you, your favorites...I want to see you, to touch you, so that I know you are real.

Thought I would share my "top nine" list. This is a list of qualities I came up with to measure a woman. They are a list of values I want in my partner. Here goes:

1. Freedom - I need someone who enjoys freedom, who has interests of their own and allows freedom in another.

2. Compassion/Kindness - The Dalai Lama says that compassion is the greatest power. So true.

3. Spontaneity - I love being spur of the moment, living in the moment.

Yesterday is history, tomorrow a mystery, and today a gift. That's why they call it the present.

4. Responsibility/Stability - I need to rely on the other person to be there for me and to have our life together.

5. Healthy - Body, mind and spirit.

6. Humorous - If you cannot find the humor in life, then what is the point?

7. Intelligence - Must I say more?

8. Passionate - I love a woman who is passionate about life, about the little things, about love.

9. Respectful - One must show respect for their partner.

Still looking for the person to fill all of these traits. I see so many of these qualities in you and want to know if you agree. I'm just thinking about you and can't wait to have my arms around you. As this is my first time trying this online dating, I am still skeptical about it, but I believe and hope you are for real. Have a lovely day.

Sweet Hugs and Kisses

Christopher

Hi Christopher,
I don’t know when we will finally meet in person but I hope that you are not building me up to be something that I cannot live up to. You seem sweet and kind and that is something that I had from my former partner. Not sure how I score on your “list of values.” You will have to decide when you meet me.
Stacey

Hi Gorgeous,
How are you? I hope you're having a good day. I am writing this email in response to your words saying if I am not building you to a situation you cannot live up to. I want you to understand that as a man, I lost my wife at a very crucial time and it broke my heart to pieces. It was hard for me to be able to be with another woman, but since I met you, you have been a wonderful person who has all the attributes of my kind of woman. Being single is one hard thing but I learned to be like that until the right person comes along and that is what I am seeing in you now. I am not trying to put you in any standard but to let you know the kind person I am and to be open as much as I can be to you.

You don't have to worry about impressing me. I just need you to be the best you can be and that will be enough for me. I am a simple person and I live the simplest life I can just to fit in whatever situation I find myself in. This is going to make it easy for me to blend with you. Like I said, I just need you to be the best and as natural as you can be and I will be okay. I would like to meet you at any time and place of your choice but I'd prefer we continue to know more about ourselves in the meantime and maybe next weekend we can make plans to spend time together over some coffee or wine.

Love,

Christopher

Hi Christopher,

I appreciate everything you have said. I am looking forward to meeting you in person. As I said before, you seem sweet and kind and it's been a long time since I've felt the warmth you have shown to me.

Stacey

***

FRIDAY

Hi Stacey, Good Morning,

First, I want to say that I love hearing from you. I love that you were open and honest with me and I really appreciate that. I think you are the kind of woman I might be looking for and with that, I would like us to take this a little further. I'm taking this opportunity to share more about myself with you and would love to meet with you sometime soon and make plans on how we'll meet. I think for now, it's better if we chat a little and know more about one another. I prefer to go slow but steady, so it enables me to get to know more about my partner.

Although I value my independence, I am looking for a sidekick, someone to laugh with, confide in and who confides in me. I realize that almost everything I do and everywhere I go would be best enjoyed with someone by my side as a lover and partner because, at the end of the day, life is a team sport. I'm looking for love, real love, head over heels, and a "can't-live-without-each-other kind of love." I want a woman who has a good heart and knows how to treat her man. I am gentle, I don't get ahead of myself, I am very calm...people think I'm charming too. I don't focus on looks, I like to have fun moderately, I love having conversations, I'm a free to talk person and a very good listener. My friends say I'm intelligent, poised, soft-spoken and hardworking. I tend to gravitate toward people who are quick-witted and a little sarcastic and really value a smart sense of humor. I have seen and done a great deal, both

personally and professionally, and I am unafraid to chase after my dreams.
I like to go swimming once in a while, enjoy dancing, taking pictures and having candlelight dinners. I love to open doors for my woman, kiss her on the head or cheek and be as romantic as possible, get her flowers for no reason, whisper sweet things in her ear, hold hands, cuddle, kiss, play in the bedroom, walk along the beach, take road trips, stay home, watch DVD movies, popcorn, dark chocolate, foreign cuisine. I wish I could roller skate but I would probably end up breaking a bone... lol. I love to give and be given body massages, gaze at the stars, go to the theater, the mall or theme parks. I am a sentimental type of guy. A lot of romance is always my thing. You can say I am a Pleaser, but I think I'm stuck with the old-fashioned values.

In a nutshell, I just want to spend the rest of my life enjoying the fruits of my labors. I want a woman who would be my best friend and everything. Someone to be with, love and be happy with as we both grow old and gray, doing nothing more than enjoying our lives and telling each other how much we love and appreciate each other. I can be a total package, and I am an honest and open person, always willing to learn and listen. Oh well, I think I have rambled enough. Enjoy the rest of your day and I look forward to hearing from you again.
Smiles,
C. Logan

Good Morning Christopher,

I really look forward to reading your emails. I thought my former partner was the most romantic man in the world but you are sure coming close. You say things that any woman would want to hear. I almost can't believe that you're real. After you called last night (by the way, don't call me that late again!), I couldn't get back to sleep thinking about you. I feel very drawn to you and I only met you 2 days ago (and not even in person!). That's a big "wow" for me. Anyway, I agree to take it slow and get to know more about one another.

In the meantime, here are some small factoids about me:

1. I love Christmas (I have been watching the Hallmark channel's "Christmas in July" movies all week long.)

2. I like to hold hands (it warms my heart when I see a couple, especially an older couple, walking side by side holding hands)

3. I don't like secrets (my partner did some work for a "government agency" and had to keep me in the dark about what he was doing—to protect me, I'm sure—but it did take its toll on me)

4. While I'm very independent, I enjoy when a "gentleman" opens a door and treats me with respect (since women demanded

"equality," I think men have started treating us like "one of the boys").

5. I like to dress up (I'm not a club-goer but even when I was at home, my partner and I would dress up for dinner.)
I would love to grow old with my "soul mate" (it's been very lonely since he passed away—I'm sure you know about that since your wife passed)

That's not the whole list but as we progress, more will be revealed. I have an early morning meeting, so I need to get ready. Have a wonderful day.
Stacey

Good Morning Sunshine,
Thanks for the email. I am really happy I got a response. I am hoping to meet you soon. I must confess that I love the way you express yourself in your messages and I would like to know if there is anything I haven't told you that you wish to know. Please feel free to ask. I love everything you write in your messages. I really get lonely at night, so I work for long hours so as not to think or feel bad about my present situation. I am sure I am very close to the end of the waiting. I feel that special woman that I am looking for is really close to me now. I am not trying to shop for women, as I hate

head games. I seek a long-term relationship, like I told you earlier. I am searching for that woman who would make me feel complete—a woman who would be there for me all the time, both in the happy and the sad moments of life. I have only loved once and I want to love again. Since my late wife passed away some years ago, I have never dated any women.

I want a woman who I would be able to share both my good and bad experiences with. A woman where we would both love each other for the rest of our lives. I can understand that you have been through a lot. For now, I would like to know what you like in a man. I mean what you expect from a man, how you expect him to behave and how you expect him to treat you. I think I have stated that I am looking for a long-term relationship and I am not ready to settle for less. I am not into casual relationships.

I enjoy going to the movies very much, live theater, karaoke. It's great! I enjoy walking in the park, it makes me think and appreciate nature. I like sports--watching Baseball and the NFL, favorite team is Pittsburgh Steelers. I play Golf.
What are your favorite things--cars, sports? I enjoy classics and country from the 80s & 90s, also do R&B music. My three favorite movies are Sound of Music, As Good as It Gets, and The Lake House. My favorite actor is Bruce Willis. I also like Sean Connery

but he's retired, so I'll stick with Willis, I guess, favorite actress, Julia Roberts, my favorite singer, Barry Manilow. If I were granted one wish, what I would ask for is a True Love.

Dislikes: I hate unfaithfulness but I am not jealous.

Basically, that's all on me for now unless you're willing to know more, then you can ask! Meanwhile, I'd love to know more about you also.
When is your birthday?
When dining out, what food do you enjoy?
How much do you enjoy a walk on the beach?
How much do you like reading?
Do you enjoy going to the movies?
Which sports do you most enjoy watching?
What type of music do you prefer?
Do you exercise regularly?
How often do you lose your temper?
What do you do when you're alone?
When you go anywhere, are you usually on time?
How often do you like to go out?

Well, that's all about me for now. Thanks for reading and hoping to hear from you soon.

C. Logan

Dear Christopher,

Here are my responses to your questions:

When is your birthday?

November 11 (Scorpio—when is yours?)

When dining out, what food do you enjoy?

Love Italian but I eat anything and will try anything once.

How much do you enjoy a walk on the beach?

I'm sorry to say that since I've been in Florida, I've only been to the beach a few times but I do love walking on the beach and looking for sea shells.

How much do you like reading?

I LOVE to read and go through at least one book a week.

Do you enjoy going to the movies?

I do like the movies. I take myself to the movies whenever there is something I want to see.

Which sports do you most enjoy watching?

The only sport that I like is football—I'm still a Washington fan (since I lived there for so long). I can't get into the Miami Dolphins (yet).

What type of music do you prefer?

I have a country music station set on my car radio—love that sound! I'm also into classical music and rock (especially the older rock).

Do you exercise regularly?

I have tai chi once a week and a personal trainer comes to my home twice a week.

How often do you lose your temper?

That's a good one! I don't lose my temper for no reason. But as soon as the explosion is over, I'm back to my calm self…

What do you do when you're alone?

I read, write, think…

When you go anywhere, are you usually on time?

Always…I'm even early…

How often do you like to go out?

It depends. With my own business, I have client meetings almost every day. Also, with my volunteer activities at the local hospital, animal shelter, and senior center, my schedule is pretty full.
Stacey

My Dear Stacey,
Thanks for the email. It's good to get an upfront and sincere response from you. Thank you so much for telling me about yourself. You sound so passionate and very loving. Those were questions I sit and think up. I didn't get them from anywhere. We need time to talk to each other and get to know much more about each other. We have to be so sure and certain of ourselves about making sure that this relationship is what we want out in life. Everything in life happens for a reason. My being lonely for a very long time makes me want a companion and a woman to share my feelings with. I'm in search of a soul mate to spend the rest of our lives together. I hope you know Love is not about finding the right person but creating the right relationship. It's not about how much love you have in the beginning but how much love you build till the end.

No one is perfect and we could only give it a trial. A relationship is all about TRUST, SINCERITY and HONESTY. All this must exist in a relationship before anything can come out of it. I'm a man of my word and will always stand by my word. I'm a caring and loving

man, open-minded and upfront in every aspect of a relationship. We shouldn't be scared to give this a trial and work on our hearts. Faith is the substance of things not seen but the evidence of things being hoped for. Why not put your Faith and Trust in the Lord? I am September 7th (Virgo).
C. Logan

Dear Christopher,
In reading your email, I'm not sure which one of us you think is "resisting" another relationship. To be honest, you frightened me initially because you came on so strong. But I believe your heart is in the right place. I am not a "player" and I want a lasting relationship with one person. Having been with my partner for so long, I can't imagine what it would be like with another man. But I am willing to try. I'm not trying to drive you away but I don't want either one of us to get hurt. In the 3 days we have been corresponding, I have come to look forward to hearing from you. I miss it when I don't hear from you. It sounds so crazy to me. I've never been this emotional in a long time.

I think that our getting to know one another BEFORE we even meet is a good idea. If we can spot any potential problems, we can decide if we want to take a chance. Nothing you have said or done so far (except for the late-night call!) has turned me off. As a matter of

fact, if I were writing a romance novel, I would include much of what you are saying in my book. The more I hear from you, the more I wonder if you are real. I feel such a connection to you that I don't know what to do with it. I feel like I've known you in another life. It makes me happy and sad at the same time. Don't give up on me.
Stacey

Dearest Stacey,
Thanks for the immediate response. I understand we need time to talk to each other and get to know much more about one another. I have been thinking about you since the first day that I heard from you. I can see we are looking for the same things. Love is a noble act of self-giving, offering trust, faith, and loyalty. The more you love, the more you lose a part of yourself, yet you don't become less of who you are, you end up being complete with your loved one. As food is needed for the body, the same way love is needed for the soul. Food strengthens the body, while love strengthens the soul. A person is incomplete without love. I don't believe in love at first sight anymore. I cried too much over it to believe in it. I think I need glasses to see accurately because I can never really see the right one for me. Well, I am very happy meeting you. I have been lonely for years just because I don't want to meet the wrong woman. I will be very happy to come over to you. I just hope you are not playing with my heart.

I want a woman who is loving and caring. A woman who would love me for me and always be there for me both in times of sorrow and in times of happiness. A woman who would give me a shoulder to cry on when I am sad and laugh with me when I am happy. I am a God-fearing man, a one-woman man. I don't play games and I feel we are both mature and we don't need to beat around the bush anymore. I believe one thing in life--that there is no one in life who is perfect, only that we need to make the best out of whatever we've got. It is quite obvious that we are looking for the same thing in a partner and here we are together. I feel it is the right time for me to quit my search and stay with you. I can imagine a better future ahead of us. I hope I am not getting too forward for you but I am speaking my mind. I feel it is high time for me to love and be loved again. What do you feel about that? Waiting to hear from you.
Christopher

Dear Christopher,
I think we need to stop torturing one another and find a time to meet in person. We need to look one another in the eye and see what happens. Are you doing anything on Sunday? Is there a place where we can go to talk? I would be happy to meet you. Let me know your thoughts.
Stacey

Hello Dearest Stacey,

I rushed to my computer to look for your message. I am really anxious to see what you have for me in the message, plus what I have in mind that I want to send to you. After reading your message over and over, I have been thinking about something and I am finding it difficult to put it into words as I am becoming anxious. It's quite obvious that we are looking for the same thing in a partner and here we are together. I feel it is the best time for us to find love and end loneliness. You may be wondering about what I have seen despite the fact that we have not met yet. What I have seen in you is internal beauty and that is what I have been looking for. Although physical attraction is necessary, it is not really important to me. I believe internal beauty is the best. I learned so many things from your previous messages that made me imagine what it would be like to be beside you. You may feel that we don't know much about each other but I feel the things we know are the basics and we can never know everything about each other. In life, we live to know more every day.

I feel this is the best time for me to love and be loved again. How about you? I imagine a brighter future for both of us. I hope I am not too forward or being pushy but I am only pouring out my thoughts. I'm the most excited soul on earth reading such a wonderful, very sweet and passionate letter from you. You indeed sound so wonderful and so compassionate. I never believed I could meet someone as sweet and great as you in my life...I fell for you right from the first day I saw your profile. You look so great and so passionate. I never believed I could be this lucky to meet someone like you... You make me so happy in just this little time and I will be so glad if you can have the same feelings as I do. I fell for you right from the start.

As I said before, I would not be free this weekend but I would like to see you next week before the weekend. I am so anxious to see you, to look into your eyes and see what it tells me. I am so much in love with your heart because every word you write touches my heart. I am so happy because it has been so long since I've had such feelings.
Lots of Love
C. Logan

Dear Christopher,
Let's plan on meeting sometime next week. We can coordinate our schedules so that we can spend some time together just talking. I'm very much looking forward to seeing you in person. I'm happy to talk with you by phone at any time--before 9 p.m.! :-). I want to keep our dialogue going by email, text or phone. I feel like a child at Christmas waiting for Santa Claus (I told you I was watching a

marathon of Hallmark Channels "Christmas in July" movies—so pardon the pun). Talk with you soon.

Stacey

***

SATURDAY

Dearest Stacey,

I see myself searching for your emails and believe me, I am getting so familiar with you. The bad things in life open your eyes to the good things you weren't paying attention to before. Love is not about finding the right person but creating the right relationship. It's not about how much love you have in the beginning but how much love you build in the end. If it is meant to be, our hearts will find each other when we meet. And if our hearts melt together, so will our bodies and souls. Then, every word and every touch will fuel our passion flame. I will be yours, you will be mine, and we will be one. What is more important to you—the love you share, the memories you have or the lover?

Ever since we started sending messages, I've been thinking about you so much and to be honest, I am thinking about you now. Wow! We're not so different after all. Here, I stand surrounded by people who've met online, people who've loved and lost, and people who are found and somehow, in a desperate world, found each other. So, what do I say that hasn't already been written or been already said? Hmmm, pretty tough! Okay... try this: I no longer need to hope for love by going to bars, church, chat rooms, etc. I don't have to search for love since I have found you. I prayed for a miracle, wished for an angel, and God brought me heaven here on earth, and that's you. Thanks for coming into my life.

Hugs and Kisses Good Morning, my sweet found love

C. Logan

Dear Christopher,

You are the most amazing man! I've said this before: I can't believe you're real. The things you say just warm my heart.

I guess it's taken both of us time to get over our losses. Once we did that, we were able to look beyond the sadness in our lives. And once you look for the goodness and kindness, it seems to come to you. With so much going on in the world, it's refreshing to have an "anchor" that can move you to a better place. I find myself missing you more each day. And THAT is amazing, considering I've never laid eyes on you.

I believe that the universe provides us with a "radar" where when we meet someone, we have one of 3 responses: 1. We instantly like them; 2. We instantly dislike them; or 3. We are completely neutral to them. It's like a magnet that pulls us together or repels us apart.

I hope all of this flirting that we are doing doesn't spoil the effect when we finally meet in person. I wouldn't want to see the look in your eyes if you were disappointed. Anyway, I love our communication and I so look forward to hearing from you.

Whatever you're doing today, I hope you are having a good time. Talk with you soon.

Stacey

Dearest Stacey,

I am happy to hear from you again. I just see myself searching for your emails. Ever since we started sending the messages to each other, I have been thinking about you and to be honest, you are always in my thoughts.

Since the first time that I viewed your profile, I have felt a great force on me and ever since then, I have been thinking about you. I thought you might be an end to my search or a realization of my dreams because you are just what I am looking for. I can feel that my dream is becoming a reality. This is what I have been searching for and I would not trade this for anything in the whole world, so I want to see where this will go and being a one-woman man, I will give this a total chance and I am sure it would take me where I want to be.

Love is like planting a seed and should grow as the relationship grows. Again, LOVE to me is the result of absolute trust, mutual respect for one another and passion. That feeling of wanting to be with your lover. It's Fireworks. It's the feeling that you would climb the highest mountain for, swim the deepest ocean for and the comfort of knowing he cares about you also. If you could see inside my soul, see inside my heart, you would know how I long to see you and sit with you. If you could see inside my head, if thoughts were things to see, you would know how I cherish you and how much you mean to me. You found me when I felt there was no more hope. Made me happy when I thought all happiness was gone. You mean so much to me and I really want to make you happy and make you feel like a QUEEN all the time. I really want to thank you for coming into my life. Bye, For Now, hope to hear from you soon.

Love,

Christopher

Dear Christopher,

You have been in my thoughts all day long. I imagine conversations with you—just sitting and talking in a park. It's so relaxing and comforting. We are not trying to solve the world's problems. We are just sharing our time. Miss you.

Stacey

Dearest Stacey,

I felt a great force on me when I heard from you and ever since then, I have been thinking about you. You are an end to my search and a realization of my dreams because you are just what I am looking for. When I hear from you, I feel you drawing closer and closer to me, and that's becoming true and I pray and hope it does. So, I want to see where this will go and being a one-woman man, I will give this my absolute 100% devotion and I am sure it will take me to where I want to be.

When I was a little boy, I dreamt of that one special person that I would share my dreams, happiness and energy with. I could not see her face but she was there. I always felt like she was out there, I just needed to find her. I visualized the bond we would have and the courage she would give me to endure life's obstacles. All these years I was with others, and feeling my way through life, learning lessons that later on would prepare me to become the man that I am now, I have felt alone and sad. Then, one day, my eyes opened and I became that little boy again, realizing that she is here now. Here in my world is the woman of my dreams.

Life is a journey meant to be shared and I would share my journey with no one apart from one special love, and that woman is you.

Awaiting to hear from you...

Christopher

Dear Christopher,

You have to realize that I am taking a leap of faith opening up to you without ever meeting you. I've never done anything like this before. As I mentioned to you, I have not been on a "date" in a long time. My partner was my world for a long time. But I am now ready to embark on a new journey and if you are "the one," I would be very pleased. I want to get to know you better and I want you to be patient with me.

As surprising as it sounds, I have developed feelings for you in just the few days that we have been in contact. That has NEVER happened before and it's a little scary for me. You seem so sure that I am "the one." Aside from our written and oral communications, you don't know that much about me. Again, that scares me. I am not trying to pull away from you—I don't think I could at this point. I care very much for you and want to get to know you better.

I'm hoping that we can get together next weekend. I am really looking forward to it.

Call me when you have read this. I miss you.

Stacey

***

SUNDAY

Dearest Stacey,

I am so afraid to love again. I am scared my heart might get broken again. Promise me that you would never hurt me. I am just so afraid to love again. But I am just totally afraid I will be lonely again. When my heart got broken the last time, I was just so afraid to cry because it was the wish of God. I want a lifetime with you and for the last time. I am not going to be afraid to love again. I believe in my heart that you are serious about us. I will be happy to be your man. I was afraid to love again, but God showed me the way, so I am letting him guide me in the right direction this time. So now I am not afraid to love you and Only You again.

Love always,

Christopher

Dearest Stacey,

The miracle of life shone in front of my eyes when you entered my life. Nothing can be compared to this feeling of filling up somebody's life. The excitement which tortures me while waiting for you to send me an email, the sweet emails that keep me awake even when I'm exhausted because I wouldn't miss a thing. The feeling that you know every corner of my heart. All these things are the most beautiful signs of my love for you. Every single word you say is a part of my soul when I am writing to you; you always make me feel needed. Most of all, you make me feel safe, emotionally and mentally. Thank you for being part of my life. I'm very happy with you and I could not ask for a better woman than you. Thank you for being an exceptional woman - you are one of a kind.

There is so much I want to tell you. A lot has been running through my head lately. I'm having trouble putting my thoughts into words, so you will have to bear with me through this. I keep thinking about the future, about life, and what I want out of it. I keep thinking about us and what this relationship means to me. I keep thinking about these things and I realize they go hand in hand. This relationship is my future; it's what I want out of life.

Here are a few things I wish to do with you at some point in this lifetime: Be your best friend, I want to grow old with you. I want to experience this crazy love forever and ever, and I really think I'm going to get it. I want us to walk through new houses, picking the one that would be just right for us. I want to see you walk around our house in a big T-shirt and catch me staring at how gorgeous you are. I want you to pull the covers off me at night and then I have to get even closer, if it's possible, to you to keep warm. I want to see you laugh like crazy at me when I do stupid stuff. Blindfold you and take you somewhere romantic. Spend my life making you happy. Spend my life making our family happy. Feel your heartbeat. Go roller skating together. Give you a backrub just because. ALWAYS being honest with each other. Go hiking/camping together. Have our first fight, make up and feel a stronger bond because we very successfully weathered the storm - together. Laugh at someone together. Share a plate of spaghetti. Go on a fun family vacation and bring back the kind of memories movies are made of. Treat you like my QUEEN. Envelope you in my soul. Look over at you during an office/military/family party and have you know without me saying a word - that I love you. Be able to say "I love you" in 89 different ways - in 89 different countries. Hold you when you're at your saddest and comfort you when you need it the most. Be the one you come to for that comfort and holding. Wipe away the days' stresses and issues with just one hug/kiss.

Get caught with you in the rain. Dance with you in the rain. Stargaze on a clear night. Watch the sunset together. Spend all day with you doing nothing. Moonlit walks on the beach. Be more proud of you than I already am at this very moment. Go on a carriage ride through the park. Do a crossword together. Go to brunch. Have a disagreement (it could/will only make us stronger). Go for a twilight horseback ride. Watch a bad movie together. Spend the rest of my life with you. Have our picture taken together? Eat ice cream with you. Make love to you passionately. I want to rub lotion all over your body because you were out in the sun too long. I want to hold you when you cry and smile with you when you smile. I want to fall asleep every night with you in my arms. I want you to fall asleep on my chest, listening to the beat of my heart and know it beats for you. I want you to be the first thing I see when I wake up and the last thing I see when I go to sleep. I want to see your bad morning hair; I think it will be so cute. I want to sit on the beach with you and watch the sunset, and I want all the people who pass us to envy the love that we obviously have for each other. I want to spend all night, and maybe the next day, making love to you with an undying passion (sorry to be so blunt). I want to sit there talking to you for hours about nothing at all but, at the same time, everything, or maybe we won't talk at all and just grin at each other, realizing how lucky we are. I want you to get mad at me for doing something stupid, and I want you to burst out laughing when you try to yell at me.

Lastly, I want us to run outside in the rain and act like total kids getting completely soaked, and when we come back in, stripping down to nothing as we stumble into the bedroom, or the kitchen counter, or the balcony, or the dining room table, or an office desk, or the shower, whichever one we feel like at the time. I want it to take your breath away every time I say, "I love you," because you know it's coming from the heart. I want us to sit down with a box of strawberries, a bottle of chocolate syrup, and a pint of mint chocolate ice cream; well, I'll let your imagination finish that one. I want to love you and be with you for at least forever, if not a little longer. I couldn't really express in words what I'm feeling right now, so I decided to share with you SOME of the images and thoughts that have been running through my head. I just want you to know that I have never found someone I wanted to spend the rest of my life with until I met you. I really am crazy about you. Everything about you. Spend all night thinking of 101 sweet things to do for you. Hold you and gaze into your eyes and realize how much I love you...and tell you.

Love Always,

C. Logan

My dear, dear Christopher,

I woke up early to see if there was an email from you and this one was just beautiful! There was nothing you said that I didn't want to do with you. It's like we're two sides of the same coin. I have never, never felt this way about a man before. I have constant butterflies in my stomach thinking about you. It seems like an eternity that we have known one another—but I realize it's only been 5 days!!! Can someone fall in love in just 5 days?

I've come to realize that my previous relationships don't even come close to what you are offering. I love the simplicity of those things that will make us happy. I don't have a "wish list," but if I did, I would wish for someone like you! I'm not looking for "things"—I have everything I need. But I have been missing unconditional love and that's what you are giving to me. As we get to know one another better, you will find out that "love" was something that was constantly withheld from me—by my parents, my family and some friends. I always had to be a "good girl" or "we won't love you."

I feel like you will allow me to be myself with you without judging me. That is a real gift.

I have been in such a depression for the last couple of years and I would wake up every morning, go through the motions of the day, and think, “I guess I’ll have to die alone.” My life seemed so meaningless. Yes, I have my business and my friends. But I was alone and had no one to share my life with. Before my beautiful dog Amber passed away, I would talk to her for hours. She was so sweet and understanding. After I lost her, I really went into a tailspin.

I may not go to church but I DO believe in God. And I do pray. And whenever I do pray, I don’t ask for anything specific. I just say, “God, please protect me and make something good happen to me.” I think he answered my prayers when he sent you. I’m ready to move on with my life. I want to do fun things. I want to make love again (it’s been way too long!)

I’m counting the hours until I see you in person. I keep imagining what our “reunion” will be like. I want to kiss you. I want to know what that will feel like (again, it’s been way too long since I’ve been kissed). I really do miss you!

Love,

Stacey

Dearest Stacey,

Give love a chance to swallow you up. Don't just think it will happen in an instant. It will surprise you before you know it, but it will be the most rewarding experience you will ever have. You know, when you're truly in love, when all you can do is just be speechless and stare at nothing because you're just amazed that you just found this incredible person. I'll surrender my world to you if that is the only way I could become a part of yours. The beating of my heart is a drum, and it's lost, and it's looking for a rhythm like you. We attract love by the emotions we display; we retain love by the emotions we possess. I don't need anyone to take advantage of my weaknesses or my strengths. I need someone who will appreciate me for everything that I am. Never turn your head from love and later wonder why you have such a stiff neck. Love is hard to find, but once you find it, you won't regret it. It may not be your first, but to be your last would be perfect. If I don't know what true love is, how will it ever find you. But I think you're perfect. Think of how amazing it will be to find the one who is yours. Don't let real love pass you by. Love happens whether or not you want it.

Love and friendship are what I feel with you. It is not just that we are lovers, we are also friends, and that is what makes our relationship much better. The greatest of lovers don't make the best of friends, remember that, and when there comes a time when you feel that things can't get any worse, think of me, for I can try my best to bring you all the happiness in the world. I want to grow to love you more and more every day, and I do not know right now what I would do without you. Sometimes, I would like to think my love for you is like a great dream. I don't want to wake up because I don't want to lose that love. I will be by your side whenever you need me and I hope I am and always will be in your heart and in your dreams forever.

Christopher

Dearest Stacey,

If I haven't told you - I am so lucky to have you in my life. I adore and love you so much! You are a wonderful woman and words cannot convey how much you mean to me. Just thinking about these feelings makes me tingle all over. To this day, I still have butterflies in my stomach. I feel like these feelings should be left for teenagers only - I don't know if you understand what I am saying: it feels great to actually love and be loved in return. I never feel less or more when I am writing to you; you always make me feel needed. Most of all, you make me feel safe, emotionally and mentally. Thank you for being part of my life. I'm very happy with you and I could not ask for a better woman than you. Thank you for being an exceptional woman - You are one of a kind.

Christopher

***

MONDAY

My Dear Christopher,

I love a man with a great sense of humor and who is intelligent—a man who has a great smile. He has to make me laugh. I like a man who is very ambitious and driven and, who has a good heart and makes me feel safe. I like a man who is very strong and independent and confident—that is very sexy—but at the same time, he's very kind to people.

Love is like a friendship caught on fire. In the beginning, a flame, very pretty, often hot and fierce, but still only light and flickering. As love grows older, our hearts mature and our love becomes coals, deep-burning and unquenchable.

Love is a really scary thing, and you never know what's going to happen. It's one of the most beautiful things in life, but it's one of the most terrifying. It's worth the fear because you have more knowledge, experience, you learn from people, and you have memories.

Unconditional love really exists in each of us. It is part of our deep inner being. It is not so much an active emotion as a state of being.

It's not "I love you" for this reason or that reason, not "I love you if you love me." It's love for no reason. Love without an object.

True love is not a strong, fiery, impetuous passion. It is, on the contrary, an element of calm and deep. It looks beyond mere externals and is attracted by qualities alone. It is wise and discriminating, and its devotion is real and abiding.

I hope you will think of me while you are away. I will be thinking good thoughts about you and missing you.

Love,

Stacey

Honey,

I should be able to come and visit you this Thursday but I will inform you once I am back from a meeting in New York. I have a business meeting I will be attending today in New York but I will keep you updated once am back. I would like to feel your strong body, knowing I will share it because you want me to and because our love knows no bounds. Yes, I would do anything for you because you raise in me all the buried passion I have neglected over the years of being lonely....and being alone.

Love Always, I trust you with my loving heart, and I will forever cherish our memories. I will never let our love die because what we have is ENDLESS LOVE.

Christopher

Dearest Stacey,

It seems like we've been together for so long that I think I've known you forever. I feel the nearness of you even though I know we are miles apart. I feel your touch, knowing we haven't been together. I feel your breath, knowing we haven't kissed. I have all these feelings because I am connected to you, not physically but mentally and wholeheartedly. I have you in my heart since the day we "met." I could feel my heart beating fast every time I see your messages for me and your outpouring of love just enveloping me with passions and emotions and I cannot help but shed a tear or two for all the wonderful things you say to me. I am looking forward to all those and we'll see to it that we do most, if not all, of the things that you want us to do together.

I love you. I love every little thing about you. I love your cute smile, your magical eyes, and the sound of your voice. I love your gentle touch, and I love the warmth I feel when I'm by your side. I can't stop thinking about you when we are apart. I need you by my side. You complete me. You mean the world to me. You are the best thing that has ever happened to me. You are the one I've always wished for. I never thought that I would ever meet someone as special as you. I love each and every moment I share with you.

Christopher

Dear Christopher,

I really hope we can get together on Thursday. How much time will you have to spend with me? I thought you might like to come to my house. I really hope we can make this happen. My thoughts are always with you.

Love,

Stacey

***

TUESDAY

My Strawberry,

How are you doing? Thank you so much for your lovely email. You are such an incredible woman and you are gifted with words. It's amazing how you combine words together to make great sense and express your inner feelings. I am here to guide you to everlasting peace and happiness. There is no one that I have communicated/connected with in such a long time like you. My Internet connection was somehow interrupted and I have been busy as a result to share the good news with you. I wish I could talk to you on the phone while I tell you all this. I really wish for that right now, just to hear the voice of the woman who drives me crazy.

The good news is that, I was provided with two contracts in Asia and Cape Town. They want me really badly but I have to accept one. There was a little confusion in deciding because the job in Asia will last about 4 weeks with a contract sum of $5.9 million, while Cape Town will last for 1 to 2 weeks with a contract sum of $3.1 million. I have decided to take the job in Cape Town because the period at which the job will be done is very short compared to the job in Asia. Should my schedule permit me, I will like to meet you before I leave in order to get to know one other better.

I believe this has come through for me because you came into my life. You are indeed a blessing to my life, and please, I want you to know that this will not disturb our communication/relationship in any way.

Will wait to hear what you think because I believe your opinion matters a lot regarding this issue. I don't know how this sounds to you but I know I see you now as a family, so you can tell me what you think, as I feel you are part of me. Do take care of yourself and enjoy the rest of your day. How I wish you were here to hold you in celebration of my new achievement. I know it will soon become a reality. Talk to you soon.

I LOVE YOU...Sweet Hugs and Kisses

Christopher

Good Morning, Dearest Christopher,

I couldn't sleep thinking about you. I'm so happy you were offered the contracts. Whichever one you take is fine with me BUT I will miss you so much. I hope the assignments are not going to be dangerous for you. Now that I've found you, I don't want to lose you. How soon would you have to leave? We can talk about it on Thursday (I hope that is still going to happen). I miss you more than

I can say.

I love you MORE…

Stacey

Hi, My Strawberry,

How are you? I trust you are doing great. Honey, I just received a message from the contract company in NY that I'm going to be travelling to Cape Town for the job sooner than I expected, so I have to get all my belongings ready for the trip. I know how hard this might sound to you but this contract is a very big one and it has everything to cover my retirement plans with you. I can't wait to finish the job and come back home to be with you. I can't wait for that. I want you to understand that my going over there won't affect our communication in any way because I am going with my laptop and you will be the first person I'm going to call and email once I get there. I really wish I could have you by my side all through my journey. I am missing you already, baby. I want you to be strong for me until I return and I want you to know, like I said in my messages, that I'm ready to bring you into my life and to add more joy and happiness into yours. Believe me that, it breaks my heart to not be able to see you before I go and I'm crying now because I've had plans on how we are going to spend our weekend together but I have no choice but to leave ASAP if I want to receive the upfront payment.

Honey, I hope you can understand the importance of me leaving and you do know I'll be coming back in no time. The approval letter states that I need to be in South Africa latest by tomorrow, so by Thursday this week, the job will be starting. That's not fair but they talked to me about the paycheck and how rewarding it is to act early, and I don't want to jeopardize that. Before you know it, I will be back and we can spend the rest of our life together. Baby, I really need you to be strong for me now because I will leave tomorrow morning and you will be my shield and love to keep me going over there. I give you my word that I shall compensate you one day with the thing that we both want the most. We'll be one family. A family that belongs to us, a family where we can share our ups and down and stay together till death do us apart. Honey, that's all I can give.

I really wish that you could be by my side all through my journey, knowing you in this short period of time has brought immense happiness into my life. However, knowing that you're going to love me so much is enough and if I can be your husband, then this would make me proud for the rest of my life. Remember, you need to take care of me until we're 80 or 90 years old, so you've got to take good care of yourself to do it. Ich liebe dich Schatz, means you're the only one that I want in English. I know deep down in my heart, you are the one for me and I don't ever want to lose that. Sweetheart, I LOVE YOU, AND I'M IN LOVE WITH YOU!!!

I know that you feel the same about me but you're just being protective of your heart and I give you my word, which is my bond, that you'll never regret falling in love with me. We have been dealing with the restless nights lately and waiting until we can be together finally. Just be patient and God will bring us together sooner than expected.

And you should have nothing to worry about, honey—it's just 14 days in South Africa.

Loving you with all my heart,

Christopher

Dearest Christopher,

I'm so disappointed that I won't see you before you leave but don't worry about me. You need to take care of yourself because I don't want anything to happen to you. Also, I need you to concentrate on your project and not be distracted by me. I will be there for you during the entire ordeal and when you return.

I love you with all my heart and I will miss you terribly. But knowing it's only for a short time will get us through it.

I love you MORE,

Stacey

***

WEDNESDAY

My Dear Christopher,

You haven't even been gone for one day and I miss you so much. I feel like there's a hole in my heart. I hope your flight went well and that your back pain didn't get worse. Hopefully, the communication channels between Florida and Cape Town allow us to continue our conversations. I can't believe it's only been one week since I sent you my first email! I feel like I've known you forever.

I feel like this past week may have been a dream and that I'm about to wake up to the reality of living without you in my life. You are a half a world away from me and the pull toward you is stronger than ever. Please be careful and take care of yourself. I couldn't bear to have anything happen to you.

I'm looking forward to getting reports on what it's like in Cape Town. Is there any place in the U.S. that it compares to? I'll be thinking of you all the time. Stay safe and come back to me.

All my love,

Stacey

Hello, My Darling,

Oh, how I really missed you! It seemed like forever without hearing from you or writing to you. I missed you so much that I was beginning to have a migraine. How are you doing today, Honey? It really warmed my heart to read your emails from a totally different environment.

I arrived at 9:07 pm on Thursday, South African time and I had some delays at the airport. I had to do some clearance at the airport because I shipped some of my equipment for the job, so that kind of delayed me a little when I arrived.

Baby, you won't believe what happened. We were robbed on our way to the guest house from the airport. The driver of the cab was shot and the robbers took everything we had on us--our luggage, our iPhones. The luggage contained our laptops, iPads, our clothes, our shoes, my camera, which I had my credit cards in the camera bag, including the beautiful postcards I got for you. They took everything from us. I thank God they did not shoot at us. I'm so upset and pissed!! I was so lucky the immigration officer was running a check on my passport and travel documents. If not, I would have also lost that too!! What a way to start my adventure out here but most importantly, I have quickly learned to be really careful out here and alert. The airport authority said these petty thefts are common here at the airport, but I should come back later today or tomorrow morning and check if my bag or property was found. I am too tired to go anywhere today, so I will be going back to the airport tomorrow morning to find out if they have seen my bag, or any of my belongings. If not, I will have to immediately call and get all my credit cards blocked, just to be on the safe side.

But baby, as we drove down to the hotel, I was wowed by the country's natural beauty. It is amazing and so beautiful with a lot of mountains and beaches. I hope to take some time out to enjoy and explore the city before I leave. I was also warned of the incessant knife attacks by the South African young lads and told to be careful when moving around, which I will, so you need not worry so much about me, baby, because I know my safety is your concern... (Smiles)

Furthermore, the job starts on Friday morning. I'll be heading to the campsite with others to go through the site and make sure everything is set and ready for the project to begin, but I honestly don't know how I would be able to pull through without my laptop and some of my electronics, as I would need to run programs for this project with it. I don't want to think too much about it now. I'll have to sleep and then think of what to do.

I'm really tired. I read articles from several magazines, I listened to some good music with my iPod and also dozed off a couple of times on the flight, but I must tell you, baby, that you were in my heart and mind all through the entire journey. I found myself wishing and daydreaming about us together and how lovely the experience would be to finally have you in my arms. Honey, I have been consumed by your love. I feel alive again. I hate to feel so far away from you but I also can't wait for these agonizing weeks to go by very fast and we can unite. I miss you so terribly and would hang on to our love as a source of strength. This is going to be a very busy week for me, but I want you to promise me you would never stop loving me and missing me. I will try to write as often as I have a chance to do so, okay? I had to quickly locate an Internet cafe here close to the hotel so I could write you and let you know I got to my destination safely and also tell you how much I missed you, baby. I have great feelings for you and I want to keep up the communication No Matter What.

I believe communication is a major part of our relationship ... Miles can separate us ...But our hearts are connected! My feelings for you have been growing since the very first day and I know that we would move higher in everything we do. Distance is just a mere thin line between two hearts, true love will find its path blindfolded. So, baby, this distance will soon disappear. I want to be with you and meet with you soon so that we can start off and plan our lives together, even now! I believe we have started and have a wonderful future together. I have been alone for so long and now that I have found you, my love, my loneliness is gone!

Real love is felt. I know what I feel for you, I hardly make mistakes in my choices and I know this is no different. Distance means so little when you love someone so much...You are sweet, loving, caring, beautiful, and you make me feel like the luckiest man in the world... I need you to know I am with you through everything, the bad and the good, the ups and downs. I've given you my heart and I hope that you won't break it. Keep it and give it some loving from time to time. I will never treat you badly; rather, I would share in your joy and pain.

I explained to the receptionist what had happened to me and luckily, she gave me a small phone I can use in the meantime. You can call or text me at +27 74 940 8792. Right now, I am still suffering from jet lag and I still need to go have some rest and unpack and also get ready for tomorrow. So, till I hear from you again, take good care of yourself and have a wonderful day ahead. I love you so much, Honey... Kisses and Hugs.

Love Always,

Christopher

Dear Christopher,

Oh, Christopher, my heart stopped when I read your email. You could have been killed! I can't lose you now. I guess there was nothing you could have done to prevent the attack. But you would think the authorities there would protect the visitors. I had no idea how much I love you until I saw the possibility that you could have been harmed. It never occurred to me that you were going to a dangerous place. I promise I will never stop loving you or missing you.

Are you going to be able to complete your project without the items that were stolen? Will it extend the time of your stay there? I hope not because I'm holding my breath until you return. I hope you do find the time to at least explore the country. But please be careful!

Please, darling, be very careful and take care of yourself. I won't sleep well until you're safely home and I can hold you in my arms. I will say a prayer that you are protected for the rest of your journey. I love you more than I can say. I want you in my life!

Love,

Stacey

Hello my sweetheart,

How are you doing? Remember I told you that I am giving you my heart to move on with you as my wife if you will accept me as your husband. I believe before we make the decision of spending our life together in good and bad situations, we have to stand for each other. I share a lot of things with you because I believe you are part of my life.

You can't have trust without faith. Faith is believing without seeing but most of all, Faith is LOVE. So, with faith (LOVE) comes the trust that is needed for a relationship. Where is your faith, my sweetheart?

Trust is the by-product of faith. It's the part that says, "I don't care what you say, I believe (have faith in love) in this person and you won't change my mind." So, if enduring pain, braving shame, despising oneself for the sake of affection and accepting misery without question is the definition of love, I hope and pray our love goes so deep as we endure pain. Have a lovely day, wishing you all the best. I miss you so much. Love you always.

Sweet Hugs and Kisses

Christopher

Christopher,

Something seems wrong. I thought you said the flight to Cape Town was more than 20 hours (I even checked it on the Internet). But if you flew out at 7 a.m. this morning, how could you already be there at 4:19 p.m. Florida time? If you are going to ask me to send you money, that's another red flag. I'm not sure what is going on but I have a bad feeling that I'm not being told the truth. I thought you were too good to be true. Please don't make that a fact. I just have a very bad "gut" feeling that this situation is not what it seems. I hope I'm wrong but right now, I have a serious trust issue with you.

Stacey

Dearest Stacey,

I just keep thinking of you even in this hard time of my life. Your memory still remains the first in my thoughts. Still thinking how it will be next to you at night and waking up beside you in the morning in a king size bed. Won't that be lovely? I have been thinking of a lot of things which I would like to do with you, and I know for sure that everything will come to reality soon.

I wish you could know how much I love and care for you.

Christopher

Dear Christopher,

First call: The phone cut off right after you said you had no money. I expected the next statement to be asking me to send you some.

Second call: I started to tell you that I told my trainer about you today and how much I cared for you in only one week. That's when the call cut off.

My trainer told me that it was impossible for someone to get that serious in such a short time. Then he pointed out that you didn't even meet me before you got serious. He questioned that you were even in South Africa. That's when I checked on the flight time and it didn't make sense. My trainer was just trying to protect me. He's dated a lot and he has told me stories about what men do and say to get women.

I lived with my partner for many years and he would make up stories or withhold the truth from me. I never knew when he was telling the truth, so I stopped asking and we drifted apart. I told you when we "met" that I had trust issues and today it became Deja vu.

I'm sorry to have hurt you because of the sins of another man. You don't deserve it. I also don't want to distract you from your work. I didn't mean to disrespect you. You have a right to be upset with me. I would understand if you didn't want to see me ever.

Again, I apologize if I have misjudged you.

Stacey

Dearest Stacey,

I love you, honey... and please don't ever compare me to another man and stop telling me about what your trainer said or what he thinks... please, I am sad but I can't ever forget about you.

I love you, baby... I have airtime but am angry, so if you want to talk to me try and call me, baby.

Christopher

***

THURSDAY

Dear Christopher,

I promised I would never hurt you and I did! I will never forget your voice when you said I broke your heart. That was not my intention. I apologize that I let someone's comments make me doubt you. I appreciate your wanting to get to know me better before we actually met in person but I'm not sure that wasn't a mistake. You were still "not real" to me.

I tried to explain to you that I am flawed. It has taken me a long time to trust anyone and I opened my heart to you. I was just coming out of my shell and then someone put doubts in my mind. It didn't take long before I just crawled back into my shell. Now, I feel like I can't trust my instincts.

I really love you and I don't want to lose you. I think we need to spend some time in person when you return to get to know one another on a "real" level. Written communications are fine but what you can see in the other's eyes tells more of a story.

So please, once again, accept my apology. I need you to concentrate on your work so that your trip is not delayed or extended. I am looking forward to "meeting" you and getting to know you as a flesh and blood person when you return.

Love,

Stacey

***

FRIDAY

Hello, my sweetheart,

How are you doing? Remember I told you that I am giving you my heart to move on with you as my life if you will accept me as your man? I believe before we make the decision of spending our life together, in good and bad situations, we have to stand for each other. I share a lot of things with you because I believe you are part of my life.

You can't have trust without faith. Faith is believing without seeing but most of all, Faith is LOVE. So, with faith (LOVE) comes the trust that is needed for a relationship. Where is your faith, my sweetheart?

I want you to see below my bank account statement, which I called my bank to suspend all my credit cards, so when you told me you hoped I would not ask you for money, I was ashamed of myself. As you can see, I have more than enough money to pay you back if I were to ask for help. I miss you so much, love you always.

Sweet Hugs and Kisses

Christopher

Hello, my sunshine,

How are you doing today? You have been all over my thoughts. There is no doubt you make me feel happy. It all began very funny -- our connection, exchanging emails online, confessing love, and then it happens. I developed an unbelievable feeling for you. Sometimes I try to imagine but for the fact that I know that you don't find love but love finds you instead. I totally accept this as a genuine love and God knows it will remain so. Darling, I think I am the luckiest person on earth to have you because you have shown me so much love that I have never had for a long time. You are very unique and you give me joy and laughter in a special way. I enjoy every moment I read your emails and when I am not talking or writing to you, I miss you like crazy. Sweetie, you don't have to doubt our feelings for each other, ours is from God.

Dear, I will propose to you officially when am back to the States. You are the sweetness of my heart and I will never take your love for granted. I will love you endlessly and overwhelm you with love and caring. There will never be a dull moment when we are together because when I am not happy, you will make me laugh and when you are not happy, I will make you laugh.

We shall be very good together and we shall be one big family.

Darling, I can't wait to hold and make sweet passionate love to you in my bed. We will never get tired of each other. Our love for each other will never die because we were destined to be together.

My Strawberry, you cannot believe what happened, the police authority called me to inform me that they found my bags. On getting there, I found the bags completely vandalized. They took our laptops, cameras, and my iPhone. They took my clothes too. I was so sad but I had to look for a way to send you an email.

Work commences fully today because I need to be done here in time and get back home to you, my Princess, I LOVE YOU. Have a great day, my darling, waiting for your reply.

Sweet Hugs and Kisses

Christopher

Dear Christopher,

I apologize for getting you upset. That was not my intention. That was a conversation that should have been done in person. Please do NOT come home. You made a commitment to this project and you need to fulfill that commitment. I will be waiting for you when you have completed it—no matter how long it takes.

This is no excuse as to how I reacted to you, but my lack of trust stems from my relationship with my partner. I told you he worked for a "government agency," so some of what he did was done in secret. I think I handled that very well, considering my background. I don't mean to give what some of my friends are saying any credence in our relationship. They don't want me to get hurt. I don't want to hurt you. That was NEVER my intention.

I didn't stop loving you in spite of what they were telling me. It makes me sick that we had a long-distance argument. I wonder how you can still love me with all of the emotions that I am putting you through. You understand unconditional love but that is something that I must learn.

Please, get your head back in the game—get your work done—and we can talk about this in person for as long as it takes. I can't stop loving you—so please take that option off the table.

No matter what happens, I could NEVER fall out of love with you. If we make it or if we don't, you are the love of my life and that will never change. Stay safe.

Love,

Stacey

Dearest Angel,

How are you? It truly seems like I've known you forever and I honestly can't imagine life without you now. There will be no looking back, no second thoughts and no regrets. I love you and only you ... and that love will only grow stronger. Sometimes, life hits you with unexpected things that take you totally by surprise. All I can say is you're the best surprise life has given me and your capacity for love, caring, and understanding never ceases to amaze me. I've truly been blessed by finding you and I'll never let you go.

Honey, after seeing the job I will be doing over here, I don't think I will spend up to 2 weeks if things go as planned. I'm here to renovate an old abandoned refinery and a bridge across the road.

The airline told me that there's no evidence that my packages are stolen, as they found my bags with some of my papers, so they are not going to replace it for me. I have done all that I could but all my efforts were abortive. Honey, I need to ask you for a very important and quick favor, but first, let me explain some things to you. I had to call a photographer this morning after I came back from the airport to take some pictures of the site so you can have a proper understanding of what I am talking about. Below, I have attached a few pictures of the site today, so you see the ground still needs clearing and filling to be able to hold a solid foundation, and that would probably take a couple of days to get done, so I would be needing my computer to run all the programs to the building once the foundation is set.

Please, I need you to also understand that this is not compulsory and if you don't feel comfortable helping me out, I would totally understand, as I would never base our relationship and my feelings for you on material things. Besides, I will refund you every penny you might spend in purchasing it as soon as I get back or figure out a way to solve this issue. It also took a lot of courage for me to come to you and ask for a favor, as I know we haven't even met yet and are still building our relationship. But on the other hand, I also couldn't lie to myself or let pride have the best of me, knowing I am a little stranded out here and need help getting those things. That is the only reason I came to you and am opening up. I emailed my bank to suspend all activities on my account until I can get my accessories back. I have attached a snapshot of my account so you can view yourself. I'll really appreciate it if you help me out and I give you my word that I'm going to pay you back every penny you're helping me with as soon as I can. Please, if you can Honey, I desperately need you to help me get a few of the items I lost. Just the basic things I need for work and to communicate with, items from Apple store or Best Buy and DHL or UPS them, to me here at the hotel ASAP. It is very difficult and impossible for me to carry out my work effectively without these items. Lucky for me, I have all my programs saved up in my iCloud account and would just download them as soon as the laptop gets here. Please I would like you to help me get the following items with their specifications:

1.) MacBook Touch Bar and Touch ID

2.) Apple iPhone X Max 256GB Silver

3.) Canon EOS 80D 24.2 MP SLR - EF-S 18-135mm IS USM Lens

Send them to me here, so I get them before the ground is set for solid foundation and casting. Please let me know if you can help me with this favor once you get this email so I will go and ask for the right postal address you can send it to, so it reaches me safely. Then will send it to you in the next email you will get from me.

Love

Christopher

Dear Christopher,

This is exactly what the "Romance Scam" warned about. I cannot do this favor for you. You may want to contact the company you work for and see if they can help you since you are their consultant.

I can't tell you the terrible feeling I got when you made this request.

I was so hoping you were a real person. I don't want to think of you being stranded but if we do this, our relationship would be over. You're talking about hundreds, if not thousands, of dollars' worth of merchandise. If you think by sending me a statement that says you have enough money to cover these expenses will work, that also can be faked. I am so disappointed. I was beginning to think that this was legitimate. I love you (or the person you pretend to be) but this is not something that I can do for you. So sorry.

Stacey

My Dearest Stacey,

I am shocked as what you have concluded about me, but all I can say if you think this is a scam or whatever you call it, I would say thank you but I would prove you wrong and it would hurt me that day to see your face. I would always love and think of you as long am here. I would find my way by whatever means.

Thanks

Christopher

***

SUNDAY

Dear Christopher,

Why did you call me yesterday? I could hardly understand a word you were saying because of the connection. What I did get was that you were upset at my calling you a scammer.

First of all, it wasn't just my friends who were warning me, it was also the articles on the Internet, and the dating site had a list of things to beware of. You did everything on the list!

Was that even YOUR photo? It now makes sense that you didn't want to meet me in person because then I would see that you were someone else.

If you really lived in Wellington, Florida (which is not far from me), you would have found the time to at least have coffee with me before you went off to Africa (BTW, I found out that anyone can get a Cape Town phone exchange for a small fee plus minutes. It can even be used while in the US.) All of the inconsistencies were too much to ignore. Are you really Christopher Logan?

Your job was to make me fall in love with you (good job, by the way—it worked) so that I would do anything for you—send you money, computer equipment, electronics… However, once the red flag went up with you asking me for what would amount to a large purchase, I was on total alert. And I almost became a victim. Even if you cancelled your credit cards, you could still have contacted your bank to allow the purchase. I can't believe they don't sell Apple computers and equipment in Cape Town! Also, you could have gone to your employer and they should have been able to help you. After all, if they were paying you so much to do the job, they could at least make sure you had the proper equipment.

You said that I broke YOUR heart…YOU are the one who broke MY heart. I so wanted you to be real. If you look at my past emails, you will see that I didn't believe you could be real. You were too good to be true. I guess I was on to something.

You have set back my emotional recovery more than I can say. Now, the next man I meet who professes his love for me will be met with skepticism. I opened my heart to you. You were in my thoughts day and night. You were the love of my life.

Now, I will look back on the last 10 days as a roller coaster ride that I need to get off of. It was wonderful. It made me feel alive. But it almost killed me.

I love Christopher Logan and his good heart. If he doesn't exist, I will mourn his death and keep the memories.

Stacey

***

MONDAY

Dearest Stacey,

I want to let you know that love is something eternal; the aspect may change but not the essence. Love asks me no questions and gives me endless support. Through love, I want to express the whole feelings of my heart for you, I love you so much.

Christopher

Dearest Stacey,

No matter how many times we fight or argue, I always want to work it out. You have touched me more profoundly than I ever thought you could. No one could ever take your place. You will always be in my heart. You are amazing in every way and I am better with you. You understand me like no one else can and I can truly relate to you in every way. I mean it when I say that I am yours, and you are mine. I love you and will always fight for you. I want to spend the rest of my life with my amazing Stacey.

Christopher

TUESDAY

Christopher,

I sent an email to your "friend" Jason in PA. He's the one who supposedly introduced us. I asked him about you (see below).

What can you tell me about your friend, Christopher Logan? After I contacted him, he left the country. I've never met him but he continues to write/email/text me. Any input would be appreciated. Many thanks. Stacey

Here is his response:

Hi, Stacey, I'm Jason. I didn't send that message. My account was hacked. The hacker sent it.

Jason

I think that says it all...

Stacey

Christopher,

In the last 18 days since your "friend" in PA introduced us, it has been a whirlwind. I love the "romance" you've introduced into my life (in spite of the fact that we have never met face to face). It was something that had been lacking for so long that it took my breath away.

But now that you have been away (with no chance of an in-person meeting), I've had time to think and decide what it is I really want from a partner.

I want a man who can take charge and find solutions to his problems on his own. I want a man who has his own resources: home, car, bank account, etc. I do not want to be thought of as Plan B when something goes wrong. I want a man who is honest and trustworthy. If my partner thinks he can "protect" me by not telling me certain things, he needs to decide if that will come back to bite him/me in the ass in the future (been there—done that).

One thing I don't think you ever understood about me—I'm NOT looking to get married (again, been there—done that). Whenever you tell me you want to get engaged/married when you return, I'm ready to run in the opposite direction. The 2 "M's" that I don't want to hear are marriage and money…

What I think about every day: I hope to God you are a real person. Are you really in South Africa? Do you really have a home in Wellington? Are you really an engineer? How long will you hold out before you write me off as a failure to fall for a scam (again, I apologize if this hurts you but I'm a "doubting Thomas").

In order for me to TRUST a complete stranger (again, sorry if this hurts your feelings), it takes time and a track record. Once I have been betrayed, that trust may never return.

I already told you where my lack of trust comes from and you should not have to pay for the sins of another but I can't afford to go through that agony again!

I hope you are safe and I hope you are real. You're not going to scam me again…go away!

Stacey

***

That was the last of my communiques with Christopher Logan. In less than two weeks, I fell in love with a complete stranger who I had NEVER met. Again, the romance he showed me fed right into my addiction.

But I continued on my journey to find romance. And my quest continued.

MATTHEW

I have been a busy little girl post-Christopher Logan. First, I retrieved the "50 Shades of Grey" trilogy from the library and am halfway through reading the second book. Needless to say, I'm horny as hell. Christopher Logan started this with his romantic emails, phone calls and texts—and for that, I am grateful. But now he is totally out of the picture.

My first date after the Christopher Logan debacle was with Matthew. He had been pursuing me on the dating site very vigorously, and I had been ignoring him. But I finally decided, "What the hell… what's the point of this dating exercise if I'm not going to participate?"

So, I scheduled a dinner date with him. He was tall, dark with beautiful blue eyes, and handsome (no, not just handsome…he was gorgeous!). I met him at an upscale Italian restaurant. He had been using terms of endearment with me in his emails even before we met— "Stacey, love," "Darling," "Baby". Again, Christopher Logan got me used to this, and I missed it!

"Geez, between Christopher's memories and the Christian Grey books, I'm a hot mess!!"

Matthew was a perfect gentleman, impeccably dressed—a cross between what I imagined Christopher Logan to be (except that Matthew is real) and Christian Grey!

He told me he's a chemical engineer with a major drug company, lives in Boca, and has been divorced for 3 years.

He asked, "So tell me, Stacey, what is a beautiful woman like you doing on a dating site?"

I responded, "My partner passed away two years ago, and I really couldn't move forward until now. I'm not even sure that I'm ready now. I'm not looking for a serious relationship…just a friendship. After only two days on the site, I had a very bad experience."

He asked me what happened.

I told Matthew about my experience with Christopher Logan, and he held my hand and listened intently. Afterward, he kissed me on my cheek and drew me closer to him in the booth. He was warm and smelled like heaven. I got butterflies in my stomach.

Then he told me that something like that had also happened to him. He said he met a woman online who was writing very romantic things to him. She said she was in Rome and was traveling when she was robbed and ended up losing all her money and credit cards.

She asked him if he could help her by sending $1000 to her hotel, and she promised to pay him back. What could he do? She was a damsel in distress. So, he sent her the money.

I asked him what happened afterwards and he said he never heard from her again. He said he knew nothing about this "Romance

Scam" until I told him about my experience. He just thought it was an isolated incident.

I asked what's a handsome man like him doing on a dating site. He said that because of his work, he travels a lot, and it is difficult for him to find the time to date.

After dinner, Matthew walked me to my car and kissed me. The kiss (a toe-curling kiss!) was so great we got into my car and started making out!

Startled by the tidal wave of emotions, I thought, "Whew!"

I stopped everything before things got out of control and said I had to get home. I invited Mathew over to my house the next night for wine and cheese (and probably whatever!). When I got home, I found this text from Matthew: "Good night, love."

So romantic…so Christopher Logan.

***

STACEY

I canceled my second date with Matthew. He was supposed to come to my house for wine and cheese after work but had to go to Miami on business, so he said he wouldn't get there until much later. I told him I was tired and needed to get to sleep early because I had an early morning meeting, so I suggested that he take a rain check. There was something so familiar about Matthew. He reminded me of Christopher Logan in so many ways.

A few days later, Matthew called me and asked me out again. This time we were going to the theater. I let him pick me up at home even though my friends said it was still too early to let him know where I lived.

He looked more than delicious, and again, he smelled like heaven! What is it about this guy? After just one date, I was ready to make love to him.

After the theater, we went for a light supper and continued our conversation from our first date.

Matthew drove me home, and I asked him to come in for a glass of wine. We barely got in the front door when he pulled me into his arms and gave me another toe-curling kiss! I could hardly stand up. He carried me to my bedroom, gently laid me on the bed, and continued kissing me. I could feel that he was beyond excited and was ready for whatever would come next. Then all of a sudden, he stopped. He kissed me on my forehead, ran his finger over my lips, and said he should probably go. He didn't want to rush me.

My emotions were conflicted between what my head said and what my heart wanted and my blossoming orgasm that had just been thwarted! I wanted him so badly, but it felt too soon to do all this. After all, I just wanted a "friend," not a "lover."

We both got off the bed very slowly, gathered our wits about us, and I walked him to the front door. My stomach was flipping, but I knew I had to put on the brakes. I was still so vulnerable from Christopher Logan. Maybe I was projecting my feelings for Christopher to Matthew.

He apologized and said that he knew I had just come off a very bad experience and he wanted to make sure I was ready if and when we did take the next steps.

My head was screaming, *"But I want you NOW."* I gathered myself, thanked him for the lovely evening, and said I hoped we could do it again.

After Matthew left, I returned to my bedroom and imagined what could have happened in my bed. I was beyond excited and couldn't sleep for the rest of the night.

Unfortunately, my relationship with Matthew fizzled out, and it was time to move on.

***

LOGAN

My next encounter was with Logan. Can you imagine that I would find a man with Christopher's last name? He was a yacht captain—handsome, smart, sexy and single. We flirted by text for quite a while before we decided to meet. When we finally met, he was everything I was looking for.

After a few dates, we tried to have sex, but it was futile. I had not had sex with my former partner for years because he was ill, so my "lady parts" were not working. It was like I was "revirginized." I made up that word but you get the point. I got very upset with myself and told Logan that I couldn't satisfy him sexually, so we should not see one another again. He laughed at me and said that was ridiculous.

I went to my gynecologist and explained the problem to her, and she recommended a vaginal dilator which would solve the problem. I did, and it did, so that I could move forward.

When Logan and I finally had sex, it was amazing! He brought me to sexual heights I had never dreamed of. We did things I did not even know about. I was spoiled for any other man.

Logan was scheduled for a 10-day business trip to the Midwest. He called me from the airport before he left. All seemed well. We did not exchange phone calls or texts for one week after he left.

I was annoyed at not hearing from Logan, but I didn't want to appear "clingy," so I just played it cool, waiting for him to contact me. I had been so crazy about him before he left. He was all I could think of.

One week after he left, Logan called me with a "Hi, Sweetie. How are you? I've been so busy on this trip."

I thought I would not give him the satisfaction of knowing that I missed him; even though all I could think about was him. He gave me no indication at all that I had been in his thoughts during his entire trip.

I am an independent woman, but this relationship with Logan was chipping away at my self-confidence.

I had several other men pursuing me, but I kept putting them off because of my feelings for Logan. As childish as it may seem, it was now time to have "revenge sex" with other men.

I had gone out with an Italian, who was smitten with me and would have taken me to his bed in an instant. But I wanted to wait a little longer with him.

Logan was such a great lover—the best I ever had (so far). If Logan goes out of my life, where will I ever find a man who could bring me to those sexual heights again and who I can play out my fantasies with?

When Logan returned from his trip, he called me to see when he could come over. He said he was "horny." I decided to act as if nothing was wrong and when he arrived, I acted normal. But this time, I wasn't wearing a sexy outfit as he had come to expect whenever he visited me.

I was going to start thinking like a man. I'll just have sex with him and have my multiple orgasms and not get emotionally involved. I'll use him just like he's using me.

Those 10 days apart from Logan with "radio silence" had broken the spell (or so I thought). If he had contacted me just once in a while during his trip, I would have been his slave. But with the spell broken, I was able to think clearly. I felt like I was a "booty call." It made me feel angry and cheap.

While I had learned much from Logan, I was furious that he didn't take me out on "dates." I had become his sex toy, and while I was getting a lot out of it myself, I had time to decide that I wanted more out of a relationship. That was a real wake-up call.

When I signed up on the dating site, I made it clear in my profile that I was only interested in "friendship." However, Logan had broken through that hard shell and made me realize that I wanted more than a friend. In his mind, I was still a friend, but in my mind, I wanted a lover and someone to spend time with…possibly a lifetime.

***

DANTE

Then there was Dante. He was sweet and adorable and made me feel special.

Dante invited me to the theater, and I had him come to my house for a quick meal before we left. After the theater, Dante brought me back to my house and came in for a drink. One thing led to another, and we found ourselves in bed.

This was only the second time since my partner passed away that I found myself in bed with a man. Logan had been the only one.

Once more, Dante fizzled out, and I moved on.

***

VICTOR

Victor the Russian invited me to his house to meet him (yes, I actually went). He lives in an upscale community not far from me. His house was like a museum—filled with gorgeous antiques and paintings. He had a table set up in the family room with beautiful china and silver flatware, flowers and a candle. He served smoked salmon, sliced cheese, raspberries and dates. He offered wine, but I stuck to mineral water. He played his white grand piano (wow!).

We talked and got to know one another. He had a girlfriend (a

Russian named Valentina), and they recently broke up. He was a perfect gentleman. And as a "parting gift," he gave me a large, beautiful oil painting. I absolutely refused to take it but he wouldn't take no for an answer and he carried it to my car and put it in the back seat. He was a very sweet man, and I like him as a friend. He wants to go to an auction house where he says they will have some fabulous pieces. Don't know if I'll go. I didn't get any sparks from him, but I think he fits into the category of the Italian—a gentleman I can go out with occasionally. We shall see.

***

RECAP: I had lunch again with the Russian on Friday (he brought me a dozen roses). Tonight, I'm having dinner with Brad, the pilot (more about Brad later). Jordan the Brit (again, details to follow) wants to have lunch this week. The Italian invited me to get together this weekend. My dance instructor wants to give me "private lessons." Bob in California is calling at least twice a day. Is your head spinning yet? And finally, Logan (the one I'm crazy about) has been MIA (again). He did post that he was at the Super Bowl in Miami. I have to get that man out of my head!!

To be honest, when I saw on Facebook that Logan was at the Super Bowl in Miami, and I hadn't heard a peep from him since January, I was furious, jealous, and angry. That's when I texted all the other guys I had put on hold to get them started again. I know it's terrible, but I can't control myself when I think about Logan being with someone else. I keep hoping I can find another guy who can replace him, but so far, no one has been up to the task (and that doesn't even count if they are good in bed). I know what you're thinking, but please don't say, "I deserve it." I know Karma is a bitch, and I'm too old for this. I was going along so nicely before Logan came into my life…giving up on my Libido…ready to settle into the life of a nun… but Logan opened Pandora's box, and now I'm horny ALL THE TIME!!! Haven't been able to find someone to scratch that itch. God help me!!

***

BRAD

Had dinner with Brad the Pilot last night. We went to a cute restaurant in Lake Worth—an Irish/Australian pub (who knew?). After dinner, we walked up and down the avenue. He held my hand. Then, as we were heading to our cars, he said he had to ask me a question (that's not good). He said, "Will you be my Valentine?" (What is this? 6th grade?). I just looked at him. He explained that he wanted to take me to a special Valentine's lunch at the Flagler Museum (tickets required), and they sold out quickly. I figured that since it was lunch, I could still have dinner with someone else (I'm a bitch!). He's cute, but again, no chemistry on my side (yet). He kissed me when he walked me to my car…still nothing. If he asks me to "go steady," I'm out of there!!

LOGAN

Logan texted me yesterday and wanted to come over. We caught up on what he's been doing. Then we went into the bedroom and had mad, passionate sex for 2 hours!! Boy, did I miss him. He finally had to leave to go to West Palm Beach for work on the yacht.

BOB

Two minutes after Logan left, the phone rang, and it was Bob from California. I met Bob online, but he had had an accident before he contacted me and was recuperating at his son's house in California. I never met him in person. We communicated via text and phone. I finally disillusioned him from my spending a week in California to perhaps spending just a long weekend. I'll take it slowly, eventually getting it to no time in California.

BRAD

Had coffee with Brad, the Pilot, this morning. He was nice enough but NO chemistry yet. He walked me to my car and then asked me to go to the movies and dinner tomorrow (but "don't give me an answer now, just think about it…") Don't know what I'll do.

LOGAN

I had lunch with Logan on Friday. He contacted me, and we met at a restaurant, had a nice lunch and returned to our respective homes. It's funny…all these months, I've been wanting to go on a "date" with him, and when he asked me out, I was disappointed that there would not be any "fun." Go figure.

BOB

Bob continues to call me every day, and last night, he said that his son wanted to send me a ticket to visit them in California. I guess he wanted to see what I was about to get his dad so anxious to return to Florida. I don't think that will happen because my work schedule is full, and Bob's son leaves for Thailand in a few weeks. A very strange turn of events.

PETER

I had coffee with a photojournalist, Peter, last week. He's very sweet. Calls me pet names. Did a cartoon of me for the newspaper. He wants to stay in touch.

BOBBY

Got a call last night from Bobby, who has a TV show. He and I are Facebook friends (never met him). He said he thought I was an "amazing" woman. I asked him how could he know that since we've never met. And he said that by reading my posts on FB and how I respond to his posts, he just knows… He asked me out to dinner, and I told him I was busy for a couple of weeks. He said he would get back to me.

***

While this is all very flattering, you know what I'm going to say… why can't Logan be smitten with me??? And maybe, just maybe, BECAUSE he's acting very cool, it presents a challenge that I have never had before. If he did act crazy for me, I probably wouldn't be so interested.

JEFFREY

Had a great time dancing with Jeffrey last night. He's in my dance class, and he's very good. We went to a place called the Pavilion. The band played the "oldies" from the 60s. Two other ladies from our dance class were also there. It was like "old home week."

On my way to the Pavilion, my phone pinged, and it was a text from…wait for it…Logan… He said he just gotten into town and was "toast." I'm pretty busy this week with Wes (a new guy) tomorrow for coffee and Peter (a journalist) on Wednesday for coffee… and I'm sure Jeffrey will find another "dance" we can go to this week… And then there's Bob in California…at least one call daily. Don't know how long I can keep juggling my social life, but honestly… I'm having a ball!! Will keep you posted.

***

JORDAN

Well, I had a busy weekend. On Saturday, I met a new man—Jordan, from England. He had a wonderful accent and a terrific sense of humor. We decided to meet at the Delray Green Market and we spent 3 hours sampling the food and talking. There was also an art show going on, so that was a bonus. One of the booths we visited had Chinese food, and Jordan spoke to the woman in the booth in Chinese! They carried on a conversation for quite a while. I was so impressed! Jordan has his own company and is an artist for fun. Later that day, he sent me the following text: "Miss your company already…what have you done to me…?" I texted him back: "I'm a witch." Then yesterday, he sent me the following texts: "Are you spoken for his evening or can you meet me for a quiet dinner?" I texted him: "Thank you for the invitation but I'm having dinner at my sister's tonight. May I have a rain check?" (This was a lie—I was having dinner with Brad.) Jordan texted me back: "Witches don't fly in the rain. I will hide my pent-up feelings for you until another day." (Whatever that means!)

BRAD

On Sunday, I had Brad the Pilot over for dinner. This was our third date—1. Coffee; 2. Dinner. I ordered Chinese food and set a beautiful table with my Blue Willow china, crystal, silver… He had just returned from a few days "glamping" in his 35-foot RV. The thing is a bus! After dinner, we adjourned to my bedroom and went "all the way." He is almost as good a kisser as Logan. (You know; I compare everyone to Logan!) His techniques were a little rough, but he can be taught to slow down.

BOB

And then there's ever-present Bob in California…Still calls at least twice a day (bless his heart!). We had a conversation the other day about his coming home to Florida. He said he wanted to see me every night. Whoa, Nelly!!! That can't happen. It would definitely put a cramp in my social life! I told him in the nicest way (without revealing my true motive) that I was very busy with work and couldn't see him every night. I didn't want to move in with him or have him move in with me, and we had to take it slow and get to know one another IN PERSON for a while before we made any plans to "go steady." He said we had both lived with partners and I told him that my partner and I had separate places for years before we moved in together. Jeez, what is it with men… He seemed to back off and said he would do whatever I wanted.

RECAP: Today, I'm meeting another new guy—Billy—for drinks in Delray. Don't know too much about him. He looks cute. I'll let you know.

Tomorrow I'm having coffee with Peter—the cartoonist for the newspaper. He keeps pursuing me but doesn't move beyond coffee.

He's sweet, smart, and an artist, and I think he will stay in the "friend" category.

Well, that's all for the moment. I may have told you that Brad the Pilot is taking me to the Flagler Museum for tea on Friday (Valentine's Day). I'm holding the evening open to see if any of the other guys would like to take me to dinner (I'm such a whore!). Will keep you posted.

***

BILLY

Normally, I would wait and give you a rundown of several dating expeditions, but yesterday I met Billy. He was adorable! Smart! Sexy! Handsome! Tall! Trim! Beautiful blue eyes! Wore Ralph Lauren shoes… There was nothing about him that I could pick apart!!! He was the complete package. And…God help me…I felt sparks… this is the first time in dozens of dates that just being with someone made me tingle. We met for drinks (I had club soda, and he had red wine) and talked for about 2 hours. I REALLY hope he will contact me again. I'm not going to pursue him. If he doesn't call, I'll just chalk it up to a fun date that went nowhere… Guess what? It went nowhere…tsk, tsk.

JUSTIN

My dance instructor, Justin, came over this afternoon to give me a private lesson. He brought me a rose plant. He selected some music and we started dancing and before we knew it, we were kissing. He and I have had this amazing chemistry since I first met him. We went into the bedroom and had orgasmic sex for 2 hours! He just left. We did use condoms, and we did it twice. Since he was young (probably in his 30s), he recovered quickly and was ready to go again. I'm so glad I got that vaginal dilator. He just slipped right in. He may be a good replacement for Logan.

***

RECAP: Since I had the Vertigo episode on Thursday, I canceled my date with Jordan the Brit. We will reschedule.

Below is the text that Logan sent to me yesterday. He did not call me last night (a big surprise). I think that since I didn't get back to him immediately (and not at all), he thought he might run into a hailstorm of recriminations.

I am not dead. HAPPY VALENTINES DAY. There has been a lot going on; Vince is in the hospital. I took off for S America and Mexico. Had some health issues, so flew to LA. Went to check in for a few days. Will call you later today and go over it with you. I am sorry I have not called or written, but just been dealing with things. Happy Valentine's Day. Hugs. Logan

So, this morning, I sent him the following text, trying to keep it light (and not act like a jealous girlfriend ready to scold him):

Welcome back! I'm so glad you're not dead. I worry about you when you go on your "Missions," and there is radio silence for an extended period of time. Wouldn't want anything to happen to the hero of my book...

We'll see if/when I get a response to that…

***

LOGAN

Yesterday I snapped and decided to bring closure to my "relationship" with Logan, so I sent him the following text:

Hi Logan, I know I will regret this...but here goes... Last week, you said you would "call later today...." Still waiting for the call...That being said, I'm going to make it easy for you. If you never want to see me again, just say so. It's okay.

In response, I received this text from him:

I am sorry I am just going through some issues right now. I have been working in Mexico and South America. I was in LA in the hospital for a bit for some tests. I will call this evening. I hope to be back on Thursday or Friday. It's not you, dear. I am sorry will explain later. xoxo

Right after the text came in, he called me (I was at the Rec Center waiting for my tai chi class). He explained that Vince, his friend and

Captain of the yacht, was in the hospital dying of cancer, and Logan, as co-Captain, had been called to travel to Venezuela and Mexico with the yacht.

He said he's been feeling very depressed and didn't want to talk to anyone. Logan flew to LA to have some tests in the hospital, and they found he has prostate cancer, and there's nothing they can do at this point. He had been complaining about numbness in his feet and was diagnosed with peripheral neuropathy and pre-diabetes. I guess all of that bad health news sent him into a tailspin. He said his sisters also suffer from depression.

He apologized up and down and said he just couldn't talk to anyone. He was going to fly home from LA either last night or today and would contact me when he returned.

Right now, I just want to be his friend and let him know that I am here to listen to him and his concerns. I don't think sex will even be an issue. I found myself crying, thinking about him being gone. God help me—I love this man!

***

This week started out with a bang (literally). But first… on Monday, I was volunteering at the hospital, and a patient came in for tests, and I was his "escort" to the Lab and then to the MRI department. When I picked him up to take him back to the lobby, he asked me out on a date for dinner. (Bless his heart—he was a widower and probably in his 80s.) I told him I was flattered, but I had a boyfriend. That didn't seem to matter to him. He then asked if I could have lunch...then coffee...again, I said no. When he was leaving the hospital, he passed by the desk where I was sitting and came over and shook my hand...but he wouldn't let go...said he had to see me again...One of the other volunteers (the man who has been asking me out since I started working there to no avail) came over and disentangled this man's hand from mine and tried to lead him away... One of the female volunteers who witnessed this scene said that she wouldn't have believed it if she hadn't seen it with her own eyes. She said I must be sending out major pheromones. Carl, another volunteer, said it was because I looked the man right in the eyes, smiled, and was nice to him (typical man—it's my fault). I said I was not trying to seduce the poor man. I'll probably never see him again, but he was very sweet.

***

JUSTIN

Yesterday, my dance instructor texted me and asked to come over to my house for a dance lesson. I made sure I used the code word—Clubhouse—which meant that was where the lesson would take place (not at my house). We did have a private lesson at the Clubhouse, and after, he asked to come into my house for some "private time." What the heck! We played for about an hour, and during that time, my phone was ringing off the hook. When I checked my messages, there was one from Bob from California (of course) and one from Brad the Pilot. I called them both back, and Brad wanted to get together this weekend after his sister and her husband left.

I have a meeting tonight with a client and Peter the Cartoonist will be there. He wanted to have coffee tomorrow.

JORDAN

I thought last week would be quiet, but it ended with a bang (several, actually). Jordan, the Brit, texted me about getting together for a Scrabble game, so I invited him over on Tuesday. I ordered Chinese take-out, and we played Scrabble (not a euphemism for sex). After I lost the game to him, we sat and watched TV for a while. Wound up just kissing on the sofa (that's all!). He left—game over—not really.

He called me on Thursday because he missed me (very sweet). Then he texted me on Friday and asked if I was going to the Delray Green Market on Saturday and if he could buy me breakfast. We met at the Green Market for breakfast then he had to leave for 2 client meetings.

He said he wanted to get together for lunch. I told him I could pick up some delicious things at the Market, and he could come over for lunch. He showed up at 12:30, and I had a lovely spread set out. We had lunch then he asked if he could swim in my pool (mind you, the pool temp is about 60 degrees). He said he swims in his pool twice daily, and it's not heated. He loves the cold water. He had a gym bag in his car with his swimsuit and towel and he changed in my room, then he proceeded to go into my pool. After his swim, he took a hot shower in my bathroom. Came out with a towel wrapped around him.

Fast forward…the towel winds up on the floor, and he winds up on my bed (naked). He takes me down on the bed, removes my slacks, and opens my blouse. The kissing ensues, but he won't let me touch him (there). We don't consummate the sex act, but he did pull a "Christian Grey" and played, bringing me to the brink of orgasm and then backing off—leaving me slightly frustrated… At 4 p.m., he asked if we could have tea (typical Brit), so we did. After tea, he asked what was on TV—I had been watching a Sex and the City marathon, so when he turned on the TV, that appeared. I said I would change it but he said he liked the show (what!?!?). We watched for several episodes, and he laughed at all the right places. Then I said we could watch something else…we wound up watching Two and a Half Men. He also likes that. So, we watched 2 shows—women's point of view and men's point of view… That was very metrosexual of him, at 7 p.m. I told him I was tired, and he suggested a "sleepover."… I said that wouldn't happen and escorted him and his gym bag out the door. He left like a gentleman.

***

BRAD

At the beginning of the week, I invited Brad the Pilot to our community brunch at the Country Club on Sunday as my guest. He didn't want to wait that long, so he invited me to dinner at a German restaurant in Boca on Friday night. When he dropped me off after our date, he came in for more time with me… You can guess where that went… On Sunday, he picked me up, and we went to the Country Club for brunch…again, after brunch you can guess where that went…when we were playing in bed, my cell phone rang. I thought perhaps it was Jordan checking in with me. When Brad left, I checked my voicemail…wait for it… it was a message from Logan! He left a 1-minute message…cheery and perky… telling me he was in San Diego and was planning to fly back to Florida on Wednesday. He just left that hanging in the air…no "Can I see you?"…Just giving me a heads up…

BOB

Bob in California continues to call every day. He called me Sunday at 10:30 p.m. to say he missed me and would try to get a flight to Florida on March 18 (geez, Louise!). With all the airlines cutting back on their flights because of Covid, I don't know how realistic that might be.

Anyway, I have nothing on my calendar this week (I said that same thing last week and look what happened).

***

Wednesdays must be the "witching hour" for the boys. Far enough from the past weekend but close enough to the upcoming weekend to get their bids in for a date. But first of all, let me say that I woke up Wednesday morning with another Vertigo episode (that figures into my responses to the "boys.")

Jordan, the Brit, sent me a text last night wanting to meet for "drinks or dinner one evening." I told him I wasn't feeling well, and we went back and forth with this response:

I'm no doctor, but your blood pressure may be off. Too low or too high...lack of sleep pushes the pressure up. Look after yourself...I wouldn't want to lose you. Not yet, anyway...

Brad, the Pilot, called during my text exchange with Jordan. He wanted to get together as well. Gave him the same story as Jordan.

He was so worried about me that he said he would drive down on Thursday, bring me some food, and take care of me. How sweet is that! I said that wouldn't be necessary, but he insisted that he text me the next day to decide if I needed his "medical attention."

***

Brian, my friend from Virginia, called after Brad to catch up on his "sister's" (that's me) social life. We've been friends for decades. He said he would order 5 gallons of chicken soup from Amazon and deliver it to me (LOL)! We talked for an hour.

Peter, the artist, texted me to have our weekly coffee meeting then he sent me this text:

I apologize for manipulating some of your time without at some point asking you to give me some idea of what representation with you is like and the cost - for reference. You are wonderful company - but we are both professionals, and these things can and do overlap.

Many thanks

Bob called to tell me how excited he was that he would probably see me next week. He's even going to let his son Bobby be in charge of getting his furniture, etc., into the POD and sent back to Florida.

This morning, I canceled my ballroom dance class with Justin and got this response from him:

Good morning, darling. Feel better. I miss you

What started out as Stacey sowing her wild oats has turned into a circus. I didn't count on the "boys" getting so caught up in a romantic "relationship." This is a total role reversal from everything I've ever known. I've turned into the guy (I just want to have fun—no strings attached), and the guys have turned into the girls (I want a serious relationship). Who could have predicted this? But at least I'm getting some "Romance" out of this. So, I win!!

***

On Tuesday, Logan called me from California, and we talked for about a half hour. He was all chatty and "sweetie" and "honey" you know what that does to me…

***

RECAP: Not having enough activity in my life (LOL), I returned online and found 3 new men to contact—Rock, Elliott and Jeff. I spoke with Elliott and Jeff today, and Rock will call me in the next couple of days. They seem promising...

Brad, the pilot, called me, and we talked about his wanting to visit me…

Justin, my dance instructor, has been texting me, telling me he misses me and loves me…

Jordan, the Brit, has been texting about coming over to swim in my pool (possibly a euphemism).

The Italian sent me Easter greetings and said he missed me…

Peter, the artist, texted me with Easter greetings as well…

And last but not least…Victor, the Russian, called me today. He said he was depressed. His daughter and grandson had been staying with him, and they were leaving in a couple of days to go to their apartment in Miami. He wants me to keep in touch…

Well, if I weren't in self-isolation from the Pandemic, I could be screwing my brains out. I sure hope this thing ends soon. I'm so horny I'm going crazy…

***

I was getting bored, so I decided to have some fun with a few of the "boys." I sent the following text to Jordan (the Brit), Brad (the Pilot), and Justin (the Dance Instructor) this morning.

A big snake was swimming in my pool last night (not a euphemism). Don't know what it was. I left it alone, and when I returned, it was at my patio door trying to get in (again, not a euphemism). I wonder...was it a sign???

Look at their responses…

Jordan was the first to answer with a big *YES*…

Justin said:

Good morning to you. Black snakes are typical in Florida. They eat everything but shouldn't eat my MJ. My pool's open. I see snakes sometimes here, too. What were you wearing?

(BTW, he calls me MJ because he said I look like Spiderman's girlfriend, MJ. P.S. My response to his question about what I was wearing was "Nothing")

And, of course, we have Brad (Catholic) wait for it:

Perhaps you should say a prayer to Saint Christopher.

If this quarantine doesn't end soon, who knows what kind of trouble I will get into...

***

Chanel hosted a Girl's Night Out/Pool Party yesterday. Chanel is the stylist/owner of House of Vermehr, a Palm Beach boutique beauty and fashion showroom. She's a beautiful platinum blonde with a sparkling personality. Her parties are on the wish list for everyone in Palm Beach.

The party started at 1 p.m. Chanel had her patio furniture stationed at 6 foot intervals so we could talk and not be too close to one another (remember this was during Covid). BTW her patio is spectacular...looks like a tropical resort. Anyway, the party was going along nicely, then about 5 p.m. Samantha started acting funny.

Samantha is also a blonde. She's tall slim, and owns and trains horses.

Samantha had been drinking all day and had not had anything to eat, so she was probably dehydrated. She disappeared into the house, and we later found her passed out on Chanel's bed! We called Samantha's husband and he came to get her to take her home. Shortly after that, the party ended (around 7 p.m.). A good time was had by all.

During the party, Brad the Pilot texted me to say he called and left a message on my home phone and to call him when I got a chance. I texted him when I got home, and he called me, and we talked for a while. He wants to see me and has marked on his calendar that on May 1, we will see one another. We'll see about that.

I also received a text from Peter, the Cartoonist. He told me that he included my "Toon" in his new book "*Glorious Women of NYC and the World*." These aren't actually cartoons. Peter takes your picture and then digitizes it. Apparently, he is famous for his digital cartoons and has regular columns in several newspapers. I was very flattered (I didn't even have to sleep with him).

And finally, I received the following email from Victor the Russian:

Dear Stacey, I was glad to receive a message from you. Your message warmed me, and I began to feel better. I know that you are a true friend. I like you and hope that over time I will replace the word I like with love. But we will be patient. My day is spent reading, playing the piano, exercising, swimming and doing all kinds of meditation. I am glad that you are ok, keep it up. I will call you. Truly yours, Victor.

Each day I wake up, I have no idea what will happen… it's like I'm watching a movie and can't wait until the end to see how it turns out...

Jordan came over last night for drinks and snacks. I had food in the living room where we could sit 6' apart (during Covid, remember). He had cranberry juice, and I had white wine. We sat and talked for about a half hour, then he got up and came over to the loveseat I was sitting on and, kneeled in front of me and began kissing me. Well, that lasted all 5 minutes, and then we wound up in the bedroom tearing one another's clothes off. I must say he is a very good lover (not Logan-good, but multiple orgasms good). He's also a good kisser. The nicest thing he said to me when we were lying in bed was that I looked 18 years old. (The lights in the bedroom were out, we had only ambient light, and he wasn't wearing his glasses… but I took the compliment anyway!) After 3-1/2 hours of lovemaking (with a brief retreat to go to the living room for more food and beverage, we went back to the bedroom).

BTW, this was our FIRST time…usually, it takes time to get to know a partner and make it good, but Jordan gets points for hitting a home run on the first try. He told me that he wanted to "bed" me the first time we met for dinner. We had many dates after that, and he was very patient waiting for the big day… Anyway, I got my rocks off (because I was so horny, I was going crazy) and it felt very good.

BRAD

Brad the Pilot is coming over on Friday with lunch/dinner, depending on when he shows up, and I have a surprise planned for him. No, Jordan did not wear me out. He only made me more eager to continue. What's with this libido? Thank you, Logan, for waking it up!

***

Yesterday, I went to see my sister to return some books I read and pick up some more to add to my pile (she has a library in her clubhouse). We had lunch, and then she asked me if I would stay and go through some old photos with her that she wanted to discard but needed help. We worked on it until 5 p.m. and found some old photos. She gave me a bunch to take home. I texted some of the photos to some boys (Jordan, Brad, and Justin, the Dance Instructor). That's the prologue, which I will explain later.

***

Brian (my longtime friend from Virginia) called me last night (he's made it a habit to call me on Wednesdays after 7 p.m.). I gave him a quick rundown of my meeting with Jordan the night before (left out the juicy details, which he used to call TMI… but now he seems to want more info). He still wants to punch these guys and hurt them (in a brotherly way, of course).

During my call with Brian (on my landline), my cell phone rang. It was Jordan. I picked it up and asked if I could call him right back. In the meantime, I didn't put Brian on mute; he was saying hello to Jordan. I'm not sure if Jordan heard or not.

JORDAN

After I got off the phone with Brian, I called Jordan back. Now, this is where sending the photos comes into the story. Jordan loved the photos and sent me the following text:

"That's exactly what you looked like last night when I remarked that you looked like a compliant submissive of 18. Perhaps I can paint you from one of these photos one day?"

Jordan is also an artist. We spoke for a while, and he discussed the possibility of my coming over to pose for the portrait. We'll see what happens.

During my call with Jordan (on my cell phone), Brad called on my landline. I ended the call with Jordan (told him my sister was on the other line—I'm going to hell!), then picked up the call from Brad. Are you getting this? Brian suggested I use a whiteboard to keep track of all this.

BRAD

Brad wanted to confirm coming over on Friday and said he would send me some menus to choose from today. He commented on the photos of me that I sent. BTW, I also sent him the photo of my Zoom meeting with my high school class. He sent me the following text:

"The photos of you are very cute. I especially like the one of you in the white sweater sitting in the chair. BTW, I can't believe you went to school with all those old ladies."

Even with the self-quarantine, I seem to be getting myself into tight spots (no pun intended), but I am still having a good time. Can't wait to see what happens with Brad tomorrow… Will keep you posted.

Brad came over yesterday at 2 p.m. We hadn't seen one another since the lockdown began. He arrived with Thai food and a bouquet of flowers (he's always so thoughtful). I greeted him at the door in my "naughty schoolgirl costume." After he started breathing again, he came in, put the food and the flowers in the kitchen and marched me to the bedroom. Sounds pretty sexy, huh? Unfortunately, Brad's techniques are not the best. It's not that he doesn't try. Maybe he tries too hard. I try to act like I'm in the throes of passion, but it's just not there. All I could think about was Logan and Jordan (kill me now!).

During my "sporting event," with Brad, Jordan called on my cell phone (I didn't take it, but I did call him back when Brad left at 8 p.m.). Jordan wanted to know when he could see me again, and I said this weekend. He was going to see his daughter on Saturday, but he was available on Sunday. I asked what time he could come over and he said 7 p.m. I said no, that wouldn't work—I wanted to see him sooner. So, he'll be here tomorrow at 4 p.m. He wanted to bring dinner (these guys are so thoughtful—they all want to feed me). I told him I would make something. I plan to wear the same schoolgirl outfit and see how Jordan reacts. I feel like these poor guys are lab rats, and I'm bringing them into my laboratory to do tests on them. I'm sure my encounter with Jordan will yield some VERY interesting and different results (again, lab rats!).

I'm washing my sheets now. I had to get the laboratory ready for my next victim. Will keep you posted.

***

JORDAN

Jordan came over yesterday at 4 p.m. I greeted him at the door in my naughty schoolgirl outfit (just like I did with Brad). Unlike Brad, he has more self-control…and after he put his eyes back into their sockets, we went into the kitchen where he left the bottle of wine he brought. We continued to talk (in the kitchen) and embellish the fantasy of the schoolgirl and the older man. He's very good at improv… I poured wine for us, and we continued to talk (kissing every chance we got). He wanted to go for a swim (talk about self-control!), so he put on his swimsuit and joined the 2 ducks that had been inhabiting my pool all day. They were happy to share with Jordan. He moved very slowly so they wouldn't be frightened.

While he was swimming, I was cooking dinner (Chicken Marsala and Arugula Salad). After his swim, he got dressed, and we had dinner. After dinner, we moved the party into the bedroom (it's about freakin' time!) and then the fun started. Jordan is very adept at sex and very uninhibited. He is like Christian Grey. He was seduced when he was 15 by an older woman in England, where he was staying during his boarding school break, and she taught him quite well. We "played" for hours, and multiple orgasms later (mine, not his) … we were both fried. He kept cuddling with me (some men don't like to do that, but Jordan does). It was very comfortable. At 8:30 p.m. I told him I was tired, and he left. My insides were still tingling, and it was difficult to sleep thinking about the erotic nature of his visit.

One thing he said during our lovemaking was, "I think this could turn into love…" That threw me for a loop. He said the "L" word. I thought only women felt the need to be in love after such sexual escapades… I need to cool him off a little. I'm not ready for that kind of relationship.

During our acrobatics, I heard my phone ping with a text. Guess who? Of course, Brad, the pilot, was texting me, asking how I was. I texted him back after Jordan left and told him I had a friend over for dinner and didn't hear my phone (I am SO going to hell!).

This week's calendar is blank so far. I think I got my fill (pun intended) last week and can probably hold off for a while (I do have my vibrator for emergencies).

***

BTW, Logan called from California on Saturday with the same "Honey," "Sweetie," etc. The real test will be when he returns to Florida. Will he want to come over, and if so, will he want to fuck? I'm not sure how I feel about that. I've developed my "surrogates" who can satisfy me. It would be a shame to screw up (pun intended) the works with a session with Mr. Perfect! We shall see…

BOBBY

I just got a phone call from a man—Bobby—he has a TV show and is one of my friends on Facebook (I've never met him). He's been in the hospital for the last month with Covid and is now in rehab in West Palm Beach. He wanted to let me know that he wanted to put together some sort of TV fundraiser and wanted me to help him with the marketing. I asked him how he was feeling, and he said, "I want to do a gorgeous woman." I laughed, and then he said he was talking about me. He made a few more "colorful" remarks (it could have been the drugs talking). Now, mind you, he has never met me. He follows me on Facebook and sees my photos there. He says he's in love with me and can't wait to meet me. WTF!!!

Men are so funny…they can fall in love at the drop of a hat… and HE'S NEVER MET ME!!! (Sound familiar?—LOL.) I'll let you know if anything comes out of this TV fundraiser, but I'm hoping by the time he completes rehab, he will have forgotten all about me. Will keep you posted.

I have some nerve criticizing Bobby for falling in love with me, even though we've never met. Remember Christopher Logan, missy?

***

JORDAN

Jordan, the Brit, came over at 4 p.m. on Saturday for dinner. I made stuffed chicken breasts with cauliflower risotto. I did not wear a costume…just jeans and a sweater. I had wine, and Jordan had lemonade that he brought. He gave me a warm hug and a kiss when he entered, and then we went to the kitchen for drinks. He sat at my kitchen table while I prepared the meal. I couldn't keep my hands off him. I kept walking over to him and straddling his leg, holding his face and kissing him (he's a very good kisser). After dinner, we went into my "playroom," where we stayed until he left at 9 p.m.! He's an amazing lover—very thoughtful, gentle and sexy. He knows how to push my buttons and left me a tingling hot mess… He wants to make our "dates" regular (I'm all for that!). He keeps asking me if I'm "seeing anyone," and I keep dodging the question. I don't think men want an honest answer to that question.

BRAD

Fast forward to Sunday…Brad, the pilot, came over at 2 p.m. for a late lunch. I had made Tuscan White Bean soup and Arugula salad with cookies and grapes for dessert (very Italian). We had drinks—he had mineral water with cranberry juice, and I had wine (the guys seem to want to stay sober while I feel the need to get slightly tipsy). After lunch, we sat in the TV room and began watching an Alfred Hitchcock movie (The Birds). After that, we watched the movie

Vertigo (for which we moved into the bedroom). Anyway, once in the bedroom, he takes off his clothes, and I take off mine… I really like Brad, but he is not a very good lover. He gives quick, hard, wet kisses. Then he tries to get hard, thinks he's done it, and begins pounding into my body. Mind you, he's not anywhere near my G-spot, so it's kind of a wasted effort. But I go along with it just to get it over with. After his "attempt," we played the Vertigo movie. He left after that.

After Brad left and I was cleaning up the kitchen, the phone rang, and it was…wait for it…Bob. He must have me lojacked to know when I am there… He had texted me on Wednesday, then called me on FaceTime on Thursday, telling me he wanted to pursue our "friendship." I told him we could begin with an occasional phone call (which I guess he interpreted as a daily phone call—geez). Anyway, I finally broke down and said I would come to his home tomorrow for lunch on the patio (no sex, no kissing, etc.). Yeah, yeah, whatever… That will be another update for you.

***

Logan called me on Tuesday, and we spoke for about a half hour. He's still off the San Diego coast. Doesn't know when he will return. I'm getting better at not letting his calls mess up my head as long as they used to—by the next day, I'm back to normal.

BOB

I went to Bob's house for lunch today. I arrived a little after 11 a.m. He greeted me at the door, and we went into the house. He walked me into his bedroom and sat on the bed. I thought, "This is not going to happen…" He beckoned me to lay down next to him, and reluctantly I did. The next thing I know, he's all over me, kissing me and petting me and…God help me, I'm enjoying it (I'm going to hell). He was quite large for a man his size, and he was quite adept at sex. He caused multiple orgasms with his tongue, his fingers, and his penis. OMG! After playing around for a while, we went out to get Thai food for lunch and brought it back to his house. After lunch, I came home. I hate to admit it, but he was very good in bed, and he did turn me on. The main problem I see is that now that he's had sex with me, he thinks I belong to him… I thought only women thought like that. This has been the pattern of all the men I've recently slept with. This is going to get complicated. He will begin calling me again every day, and I guess he will want to see me for an encore. What is wrong with me!?!?!? My raging hormones have taken over my body, and I feel like an out-of-control teenager…

***

Well, this shelter-in-place thing has taken its toll on my AmEx credit card… I miss guys coming to my house, so the Amazon deliveries have really helped with my social life…the only thing is that they ring the bell and walk away…what's that about?

***

JORDAN

Jordan, the Brit, came over on Saturday at 4 p.m. He brought some raspberries, blackberries, whipped cream and sexy lingerie (stockings with seams and a fishnet body suit). I was not wearing a costume—just black slacks and a blouse. I made us dinner of crusted salmon and riced veggies. He had lemonade (which he brought), and I had a glass of wine. As usual, there was lots of kissing as I prepared dinner. After dinner, we went into my Playroom and did what came naturally. He really is SO good. Multiple orgasms later (by the tongue, fingers and penis), I was spent.

We took a break in the kitchen for our berries and whipped cream dessert. During our break, Amazon delivered a package…it was my bondage starter kit. I opened it, and we went through the contents, deciding what to play with. I eliminated the ball in the mouth contraption, nipple clamps (yikes!), the dog collar and leash, and the rope (not sure what to do with that). We returned to the Playroom and started playing with the rest of these new toys. He put the cuffs on my wrists (behind my back) and another set on my ankles. Then he connected them with the "X" contraption so that I couldn't move at all. I was totally under his control…this is where the "trust" factor comes in… I certainly would NOT do this with a man I didn't trust. He then smacked me on the ass with the flogger (it didn't hurt…felt kind of good) and then began tormenting me with the feather toy. OMG, I was beside myself. Finally, he got my vibrator and finished the job…by that time, I must have had 20 orgasms…

He definitely is Christian Grey, and now I know why Christian had to carry Anastasia Steele to her own room when they were finished playing…Couldn't walk…couldn't speak.

As is often the case, I received a text and a voice message during Jordan's visit…no, it wasn't Bob… it was Peter, the Cartoonist, checking in on me… Jordan and I ended our amazing evening at 9 p.m. Even Logan didn't last that long!

BRAD

Brad, the pilot came over on Sunday at 2 p.m. Again, no costume for me. He brought Papa John's pizza and brownies. It was yummy! He had lemonade (which Jordan had brought), and I had wine. After we ate, we watched a movie in the TV room. When that movie was over, we went into my Playroom (for what I knew would be some very unsatisfying sex). We selected a movie to watch then he leaned over and kissed me. I already told you that his kisses are wet and sloppy French kisses (the NEW way to kiss is more with a closed mouth, no tongue, and just nibbling at the upper and lower lips—I find it very sensual—both Jordan and Logan kiss like that and it's such a turn on!!). As he's trying to do his thing, I'm giving directions—"Not so much tongue, gentler, that hurts, no I don't want to put my legs above my head" (like that). I figured he would only keep going if I didn't do something—so I gave him a blow job, got him satisfied, and we went back to the movie… He left at 8 p.m. AND…of course, while he was here, I got 2 phone messages and a text—no, not from Bob…they were from Jordan. He wanted to say goodnight and thank me for Saturday. He really is so sweet.

***

Bob called on Monday (as if nothing happened). Asked if I was still seeing my "friend." He said the polo matches would begin in Wellington and he would like to take me. I told him I wasn't ready to go out in crowds and I was busy with my friend. We'll see if he calls again.

***

Brian called on Wednesday (for his weekly call). We spoke for an hour (as usual). I have not been giving him details of my dating experiences because he said it was TMI (too much information). Now, it seems he's curious and he's asking for more "information."

I filled him in (not in the detail I share with you) and he seemed okay hearing about things. Then, he called me on Friday night to continue the conversation. He said that he and his friend John would be available to "talk" to any of my suitors if they did anything to hurt me. I believe they would. He said because of the meds he's taking for his prostate problem, his libido has disappeared. But I think my stories are at least making him feel more "normal" in that department. Whatever I can do to help…

***

I already told you that Logan called on Thursday to let me know he's home and he wants to visit me next week. We'll see how that goes. I haven't had sex with him since January and have not seen him in person for over 2 months…

***

JORDAN

Jordan came over yesterday at 3 p.m. He sent me a restaurant menu where he would pick up our dinner so I could select my choices. Unfortunately, the restaurant didn't open until 4 p.m., so he went next door to Whole Foods and got dinner: Turkey meatloaf, tiny roasted potatoes, 2 salads… and for dessert—Creme Brûlée (which was delicious). I greeted him at the door in my new "dominatrix" costume over my new "Bustier" with fishnet stockings. It had the desired effect. He didn't even put down the bags of food before he took me in his arms and kissed me (as only he can). We went to the kitchen, and I unpacked the dinner, fixed him a drink (lemonade for him, of course), and talked briefly. I told him I was hungry, so we had dinner.

After we ate and I put the leftovers in the fridge, we retired to my Playroom. He unzipped my dress and found a way to get me out of my bustier and stockings, and we began our lovemaking. He began with his tongue, sending me into an orgasmic orbit…then he inserted his fingers for another round of orgasms, and finally, the piece de resistance—his penis. OMG, I was in heaven. I didn't do these things when I was younger; now it's SOP. We took a break to have our Creme Brûlée then returned to the Playroom. He's unbelievable in bed… never stops…makes sure I am totally satisfied. Well, to repay the favor, I gave him several blow jobs, and I had him moaning and sighing. He said he never had anyone give him such pleasure down there in his life.

We did do some talking between our marathon sex session, and come to find out he was born in England; his father took the family to Borneo when he was young for his job. As he got older, he was sent back to England to boarding school (that's where he met "Mrs. Robinson," who taught him about sex during a school break). After that, he went to Australia, where they had family, and he graduated from the University of Sydney. After that, he had several jobs in Asia, where he met his wife (she was English). They married and had 2 children—a boy and a girl. After 12 years, they divorced. His daughter now lives in Miami, and the son lives in Ft. Lauderdale. He does not see his ex-wife. After that, he had a 12-year relationship with a woman with a child. The reason they broke up was because she wanted to get married, and he didn't. She is now married to someone else. Whew!

I think he's a damn interesting guy! We didn't use any of my new bondage toys this time, but he did bring a couple of "penis rings" that we tried. They are flexible rings that fit over the penis. They have little bumps on them so that when you have intercourse, they stimulate the woman. Pretty cool! He discussed having an overnight, but I said I wasn't ready. He's very understanding. Never pushes me to do anything. He feels that if the woman isn't comfortable with something, she shouldn't do it. Love that about him! Of course, I had a text message on my phone while Jordan was here. It was from Peter, the cartoonist. He wanted to keep in touch and let me know he was thinking about me. He's very sweet too. Jordan left at 8:30 p.m., and I was totally spent. I'm still tingly down there this morning. He sure knows how to make a girl happy.

I have nothing scheduled for this week. Maybe Jordan will come over (he said he can't wait for a week to see me again). Maybe Logan will show up. We shall see…

***

File this under the "you're not going to believe this" category...

LOGAN

My cell phone rang at 2 p.m. today. It was Logan. We spoke for about a minute, and I asked him where he was. He said he was IN MY DRIVEWAY!!! (When I gave him the universal gate code to get into the community, I never thought he would use it without calling first...shows how wrong I can be...) Anyway, I went to the door, and he stood there in all his handsome glory. He said he would stay 6 feet away from me because of Covid (I guess he was testing the waters to see how I would react to seeing him). I invited him in, and he gave me a huge hug.

We entered the kitchen, where I gave him some of Jordan's lemonade. We talked for a little while then he asked to see some of my new "outfits." We went into my Playroom, and I thought he was going to join me in my closet to see my outfits, but instead, he laid down on the bed (I guess he was waiting for me to put on a fashion show for him—which I didn't—I just brought out a couple of outfits that he had not yet seen). One thing led to another, and...you guessed it... we spent the next 3 hours having amazing sex.

BTW my lady parts seem to be just fine. He did it with his fingers and his huge penis. I had forgotten how large he was. He said he wanted to come back to play some fantasy games with me. Oh

Lordy, don't know how much of this my heart can take. Twenty orgasms later, and I'm having trouble walking… I'm not going to let him make me crazy. If he calls, he calls…if he doesn't, he doesn't. But I must say it was great seeing him.

***

BRAD

I went to dinner with Brad, the pilot, on Friday night. He picked me up at 6:30 p.m. We went to City Oyster, a very nice restaurant in Delray. I hadn't been to a restaurant in 2 months, so I wasn't sure what to expect. (This was during Covid.) When we arrived in Delray, Atlantic Avenue was like Mardi Gras. People were all over the sidewalks, restaurants were full, and most people were not wearing masks. Brad and I had our masks on. We had a 7 p.m. reservation, so we were seated immediately. The restaurant had put up Lucite dividers between the banquets, and the wait staff all wore masks and gloves.

Dinner was delicious, but I admit I was nervous since most of the patrons were hugging, kissing, and touching their friends. After dinner, we returned to my house and Brad just assumed he was invited in (which was fine). We sat in the TV room talking, and I could see he was just itching to start kissing me. Before that happened, I told him about my little "accident" and the chemical burn from removing the hair on my lady parts. I did it very discreetly since he seems to be somewhat of a prude when it comes to sex or cursing. It wasn't long after my revelation that he decided to leave.

***

BOB

On Saturday afternoon, Bob called me AGAIN (he had called me on Friday asking me to come for lunch, and I declined). I told him AGAIN that I was seeing someone, and he said it didn't matter. I said, "You don't mind knowing that I'm having sex with another man?" He said no. (What is it with men? Do they just like challenges? Is everything a contest with them?) He said he was not going to give up trying, and since we had sex, he had a taste of what he wanted. You know what… I don't care… if I feel like going to an equestrian event with him…so what? It's not like I'm married and cheating on my spouse… We shall see what happens…

***

JORDAN

Now for the Big Event—Jordan the Brit—AKA "Christian Grey." (WARNING: The following content is rated MA—Mature Audiences only.) Jordan arrived at 3 p.m. on Saturday, toting wine and lemonade. I had ordered Chinese takeout for dinner. We hugged and kissed and went into the kitchen for our drinks. I wore my white skin-tight designer jeans and a silk off-the-shoulder blouse. That was not the main entree—it was what I was wearing underneath that outfit—black lace crotchless panties and a black lace bra.

We had our drinks, and Jordan said he wasn't hungry right then, so we talked. He told me about living in Borneo as a child. His father was part of the British police force. They had caged monkeys, actually orangutans, at their compound. So, he grew up with them as part of the family (WOW!). He was sent to England to boarding school when he was 7 and didn't get to see his parents sometimes for 2 years. After school, he went to Australia, where he learned to fly planes. He was about to be drafted to go to Vietnam when the war ended. (I had no idea that Australia was sending troops to Viet Nam.) We started talking about the improvements he made to his home, and he said most of the big stuff was done. Now, he had to clean out his garage (pronounced gaar-age). He said he had a plane with folded wings that he had to get out and try to sell. WTF? Again, Christian Grey was flying his own plane.

I had cut up some mangoes that Samantha gave me, and he said he would like to have them now. After we finished our mangoes, we decided to go into my Playroom and have dinner later. We both undressed—I kept my lingerie on—and I pushed him down on my bed, tied his arms above his head and began my role-play. I played with his penis in my mouth, almost bringing him to climax, then I'd back off and ask him for the nuclear codes. He caught on immediately, and we improvised the script. I got out my flogger from my Bondage Starter Kit and softly whipped his penis. He was in agony (I'm a real Bitch!). When we finished that role-play, I untied him, and we had amazing sex in every position possible. Finally, after a few hours of this, I told him I was hungry, and we took a break to have dinner.

After dinner, we returned to the Playroom, and I told him about my fantasy. I said that I wanted my hands tied above my head and attached to the over-the-door hook on my bedroom door. In that position, I would stand on my tip toes (my doors are very high). I said he could do whatever he wanted with 2 caveats—no taking pictures or video, AND when I said Stop or Red, he would Stop. He agreed, and we began the fantasy.

He tied my wrists together, pulled my arms over my head and tied them to the door hook, bringing the excess rope down to the door handle to secure it (the rope was quite long). In that position, I could see my reflection in the floor-to-ceiling mirror on the wall beside my bed. I must say stretching out my body like that, lifted my tits, featured my abs and made me look great! Jordan then began teasing me with the flogger and his hands, and finally, he got out my vibrator and started using it on every part of my body. I could see myself in the mirror in ecstasy, and Jordan was having a good time.

After he thought I had enough, he untied the rope from the door handle and led me over to the bed with my hands still tied together. He sat me on the edge of the bed and pushed me down (again, hands still tied over my head). While he was fondling my breasts with one hand, he had my vibrator in the other in that special place. I was writhing around on the bed, moaning and screaming as one orgasm followed the next. I asked him to stop, but he was having too good a time watching what he was doing to me. Finally, he stopped, and my lady parts were throbbing in agony. They were so sensitive that just touching them with his fingers gave me another orgasm. This guy is good!!! He finally untied me, and we lay on the bed in each other's arms, basking in the afterglow of amazing sex.

He asked, "Do you want to do this again next week?" I immediately answered, "YES." …he said, "You can think about it," then laughed at my immediate response. He left at 9 p.m., both of us tired and happy. I was still so turned on I slept in the nude (which I never do), but it seemed so fitting after what my body had been through.

Of course, during our sex marathon, my cell phone rang…It was this man who had a TV show, Bobby. We're friends on Facebook, and he has wanted to go out with me for some time. He said as soon as things let up a little with Covid, he wanted to see me. Oh boy…

Well, as I say at the close of all of these musings, there's nothing on my calendar for next week except Jordan on Saturday. We shall see what happens. I'm so curious—it's like I'm watching someone else's life.

***

Anyway, things seem to be heating up with the Brit… I don't know how they got the reputation for being "cold" because Jordan is one of the hottest numbers on the planet…must be his being a world traveler and individualist.

Can't wait to see what other tricks he has up his sleeve…

***

Last week didn't turn out to be as quiet as anticipated…Better get yourself a large cup of coffee because this will be a LONG update...

JORDAN

Jordan came over on Wednesday at 6:00 p.m. for dinner. We were scheduled to meet on Saturday, but he said he couldn't wait that long to see me. (BTW, he changed our next date from Saturday to Sunday because he had a birthday party to go to for an 82-year-old friend.) I made tomatoes stuffed with chicken salad with strawberries and cookies for dessert (Jordan also brought 2 slices of cake). I wore black slacks and a black blouse over very sexy underwear. Before Jordan arrived at about 5:30, Bob called with a "How are you? Still, seeing that guy?" I told him I had someone coming over for dinner and had to get ready (you'd think that would discourage him—but who knows?). After dinner, Jordan and I went into my Playroom and, you know, the drill (tongue, fingers, penis—multiple orgasms—cuddling—repeat). We played until he left at 10:00 p.m. My vagina hasn't had this much of a workout in decades. It was cozy with a thunder and lightning storm going on outside (after we had just finished a thunder and lightning storm inside).

***

LOGAN

Logan called on Thursday. Said he would stop by on Friday…and sure enough, he did. But before Logan showed up at 3:30 p.m., Brad, the pilot, called and asked me for dinner on Saturday. He's taking me to a restaurant in Boca. He's picking me up at 6 p.m. on Saturday… Back to Logan… I didn't know what to expect from the mercurial Logan, but I gave him his favorite Strawberry Water, and we went to my Playroom.

I wore my red/black lace bustier and matching thong panties under black slacks and a black blouse (the outfit I wore for Jordan). Looked very conservative. We stood in the Playroom kissing and getting very turned on, and then he ripped open my blouse (don't worry, it had snap closings), and he saw my lace bustier and went crazy with lust. Then he pulled down my slacks and saw the tiny thong, and it was "game on." He dropped his trousers (he was going Commando—no underwear—very sexy), threw his t-shirt on the floor, turned me around and bent me over the bed (with my undies still on) while he stood behind me. He pushed aside my thong and went to work on me. Meanwhile, I'm standing on my toes with the top half of my body spread across the bed (I'm on my stomach), writhing in ecstasy while he plays with my breasts while fucking me from behind! OMG, I can't believe we got so hot with virtually no foreplay.

We went at it (it seemed like forever with multiple orgasms on my part) and then took a break and cuddled (he likes doing that). He began opening up to me about his second wife and how he met her, how they got married (her idea, not his), how she got pregnant (had an abortion both agreed upon), how she lied and cheated on him with her current husband, how he never cheated on her (she was such an adventurous sex partner, he didn't need anyone else to satisfy him). It must have been like a catharsis for him.

When he finished, he said he had never told any of that stuff to anyone else and thanked me for listening. I felt like his shrink, but I'm glad he could get it out. He told me what he really liked about me was that he could tell me anything, and I did not judge him, and that I was a sexy, sensual, passionate and willing partner in bed who turned him on. He even got excited about my teaching him about Bondage (I can't believe he didn't try that before).

I asked him why his marriage with his first wife fell apart, and he said she was a great mother to his kids but they didn't have any passion in the bedroom—so he found it with other women. Then we went back to making love (I used to call it fucking with him, but something happened after he bared his soul to me, and he became different). We did the whole repertoire—tongue, fingers, penis (and oh my, what a penis—now that I have had so many lovers, he deserves the grand prize for size, girth and function!). When he goes inside of me, I feel like he's up to my throat…

As we cuddled for another break, he asked me what I was doing on Saturday. I said I was going to dinner with some friends (almost the truth—I'm having dinner with Brad). He asked me where we were going, and I said PF Chang's in Boca. He said that was a horrible restaurant and we should try Mario's or Alexander's next door. Then he asked me about Sunday. I said I was going to my sister's for dinner and some movies (that's my day with Jordan). He asked how long I would be at my sister's and I told him all day. Then he asked about Monday. I said I was available on Monday (we'll see if he follows through on that).

That was very strange since he's never tried to "book" me for a future date while we were on a "date." He would usually go into "hiding" for a while after we had a sex session. We shall see. He left at 8 p.m. I hope you noticed the time frame… fucking for almost 5 hours! We beat Jordan's time this week of 4 hours! I'm surprised I can walk today.

BRAD

Brad picked me up on Saturday at 6 p.m. We went to PF Changs in Boca. When we got there the place was packed with a 30-minute wait. BTW, we wore masks even though many of the people did not (remember it was during Covid). While Brad stood in line to get us on the waitlist, I walked over to Mario's next door and got us immediate seating. It's a beautiful Italian restaurant—first class (one of the restaurants Logan recommended).

I went to retrieve Brad at PF Changs and said I got us a table next door with no wait. He looked at me like I was an alien (not sure he was ready for a "take charge" lady). We had a lovely dinner (the portions were huge, so we took home half of our meals). When we got home, I invited him in. I gave him mineral water and cookies, and he asked what was on TV.

I said I had been watching the "50 Shades of Grey" marathon (for the 5th time) and did he want to see that. He reluctantly said OKAY. He was not enjoying watching the movie, so I changed it to something else. If either Logan or Jordan were watching that movie with me, they would have had me on the floor naked, ravaging me after just a couple of the sex scenes, but Brad seems like a bit of a prude… At about 9:30, he said he had an upset stomach and was going home (no sex, thank the Lord).

I gave him an antacid for the road and escorted him out. Whew!

Another thing about Brad (aside from his not getting high ratings in the bedroom) is that he's not a very good conversationalist—driving to and from the restaurant and sitting in front of the TV, I was the one doing all the talking. It's a lot of work! With ALL the other "boys," we talk and communicate and have interesting conversations.

At 9:35, after Brad was gone, I heard my phone ping for a text. It was Peter, the cartoonist, saying, "Thinking of you. A sea of change? Will chat soon. Stay safe and smile often." He's very sweet (I never slept with him—only coffee dates once a week). Then at 11 p.m. I was awakened by a ping on my phone.

It was Logan. He said, "Did u have a good dinner." I responded, "Yes, Wound up at Mario's. Great suggestion. Sleep well." Then he responded, "Lol, glad you went there." I was astonished to hear from him following up on something we discussed. He never ceases to amaze me. Again, I'm keeping my heart tucked away in a safe… in a vault… in a volcano… He's my kryptonite!

***

BOB

Oh, BTW, Bob called me Saturday afternoon to chat. He keeps reviewing the dozens of texts we shared over the 8 months we corresponded when he was in California and doesn't understand how we're not together… Bless his heart… I guess until he finds someone else, he's not going away…

***

JORDAN

Jordan came over on Sunday at 3 p.m. I told him I had a "scenario" to play out with him, so he was somewhat prepared that this wouldn't be an ordinary date. I dressed up in my flight attendant uniform with fishnet stockings and greeted him at the door. This is how the dialogue went:

Good afternoon, Mr. Jordan. Welcome to Oasis Airlines. I will be your flight attendant. My name is Ms. Pussy. Please follow me to the VIP lounge. Your flight to Bogota is scheduled to leave in 1 hour, but since this is a private plane and you are the only passenger, we may leave whenever you like. Your luggage has been stowed in the cargo hold, and we have stocked the Galley with your favorite food and beverages. If there is ANYTHING I can do for you—anything at all—please don't hesitate to ask. Do you have any questions?"

He went right along with the role-play, and it didn't take long before we were in my Playroom, and he was undressing me. Standing behind me, he started caressing me and kissing my neck from behind. It was so hot because I could see what he was doing in the full-length mirror beside my bed.

After I couldn't take much more, he put me down on the bed and began with his tongue… OMG, he knows how to push my buttons. After multiple orgasms that way, he inserted his fingers and did it again… finally, I was begging him to fuck me with his penis. We went at it for long enough, and we were exhausted. We finally took a break (I needed it more than Jordan) so that I could prepare dinner. I made salmon with a vegetable.

I had sliced mangos, grapes and cake for dessert. He wore one of my turquoise bathrobes. Then he selected a nightgown for me from my "slut collection"—he wanted something "diaphanous," which I was happy to provide. He wanted to be able to see through it while I prepared dinner. After dinner, we returned to the Playroom and continued with our sex marathon. He is VERY good… Before he left at 9 p.m., he scheduled our next date for next Saturday at 3 p.m. BTW, he broke Logan's record—6 hours! Haven't had this much action "down there" in decades!!!

While we were playing, I heard my phone ping with several texts, but I waited until Jordan left to check them. All I could think of was, "Who in God's name is texting me now?" The first text was from the Italian asking how I was and telling me he missed me. The second text was from—wait for it—Bob. He said, "Can you talk?" the third text was from Peter, the cartoonist, just saying he missed me. I'll get back to all of them today…

I did send this text to Jordan this morning:

Dear Mr. Jordan, We hope you enjoyed your flight to Bogota yesterday. Please don't hesitate to ask if there is anything else we can do for you. On behalf of the flight crew and Oasis Airlines, we wish you success in all your ventures.

Sincerely,

Ms. Pussy.

***

LOGAN

Logan came over on Monday at 2:30. He wanted to show me an erotic movie—The Story of O—Google it for the plot. He brought over his portable Blu-ray player so we could watch the movie (it's a laptop, but all you use it for is movies.). I asked him where he wanted to watch it, and he said, "Let's go lay on the bed." I had made the bed that morning and put all the pillows and bolsters on it—knowing it might be where we would see the movie. The other option would have been to plug the Player into my big TV, but that would have been a pain in the ass.

The movie was like "50 Shades of Grey" on steroids. It included S&M, total nudity, bondage, and whatever else that lifestyle includes. I think he wanted to see if I was repulsed or excited. I fell into the excited category… Just watching the movie, it was all the self-control I could muster not to attack Logan! After it was over, we talked for a short while about what we saw.

He asked me to put on something sexy (I chose a sheer black negligee that exposed my breasts), and one thing led to another, and voila—we were at it (again, he was going Commando—no underwear—guess he anticipated my reaction and came prepared). While I was giving him oral sex, he was talking dirty to me. Good Lord, he should write a book with the scenarios he came up with.

Come to find out, he did those things. He kept telling me how much he liked my adventurousness with sex and willingness to try new things, and he loved it! He said you don't find many women who are so sensual. He's excited about experimenting with Bondage and using all my new toys. (It's one of the few things he hasn't already done! So, it appears I can teach HIM something!). We continued to play—tongue, fingers, penis, even my vibrator, with so many orgasms I stopped counting—until he left at 7:00 p.m.

I swear, I don't know how I can do all these things and still be able to walk the next day! He left me his Blu-ray player. I said not to. He said he wanted me to be able to watch the movie several more times. I guess that means he won't disappear for another 3 months.

As an aside—I was comparing Logan to Jordan. They are both tall (6' 2"), about the same age, have nice hair, and are very sexy and great in bed. They are both successful entrepreneurs. They are world travelers. Another thing about these men is that they will pleasure me in every way possible until I have multiple orgasms, and I have to beg them to stop.

I believe it gives them a great deal of pleasure and satisfaction knowing how much control they have over me (they like being the "Dominant" to my "Submissive.") Both of them had "sexual adventures" with their women (Logan with wife #2 and Jordan with is 12-year relationship lady). And they both went to sex clubs in Fort Lauderdale.

I could write a scenario where they were both at the same club on the same night, and they switched their partners… Wouldn't that be something if Jordan fucked Logan's wife… Jezus, where is my mind going? One of my fantasies is having Logan and Jordan in bed with me (a "Stacy Sandwich"). My main concern would be that I would lose both of them as lovers, and I don't want that to happen. I think I'm falling down the rabbit hole, and I'm following Alice's adventures in Wonderland—only it's an erotic Wonderland!

***

It's Tuesday, and Logan called me on his way to the VA hospital for some tests. He asked me about the movie he had left, and I told him I was watching it right now, and it was so hot. We spoke briefly, and then he said he was getting so excited about me and that movie that he had a hard-on. Anyway, a short time later, he texted me and said he was on his way over.

I decided to give him a fantasy visit, so I put on a different black sheer negligee with a "submissive" collar with a leash and prepared for his arrival. When he arrived at 11:30 a.m., I greeted him at the door, his eyes popped out of his head, and he couldn't get his shoes off fast enough (it's funny, all my "boys" leave their shoes at the front door) with an erection that I could see from a mile away!

He led me by my leash into the Playroom where I had the rope and flogger hanging on the door. He tied my hands over my head and then attached them to the hook on the bedroom door and started smacking me across my ass with the flogger (it didn't hurt—just made some noise). He got so turned on that it wasn't long before he took me down from the door, bent me across the bed, still standing on the floor, lifted my nightgown and fucked me from behind with my hands still tied up over my head. The more I moaned and screamed, the more excited he got! He was having such a good time with the scenario that his hard-on just kept going.

He said he'd never done bondage or S&M before, and this was something new to him. I can't tell you how turned on we both were. My orgasms just kept coming (pun intended), and his hard-on never stopped. He also had 2 orgasms inside me—this was a first! He usually never ejaculates. Then he told me a fantasy about what he wanted to do with me.

He said that he owned me—I belonged to him—and he was going to send a friend over, and I had to do whatever this friend wanted sexually, or I would be punished by him (mind you, this is the plot of "The Story of O"—now I have become his O). We were engrossed in our fantasies and fucking until he left at 2:00 p.m.

While all this is my dream come true—Logan being in my life—I can see problems down the line. He's been here 2 days in a row, and I think he feels he can continue coming over more often. He seems to be addicted to these new sexual adventures with me. The teacher has now become the student. But I don't want to worry about him and Jordan bumping into one another.

While Logan was here, I received a text from Jordan and a phone call from Bob. It's amazing—I could be home all day without anyone calling. The minute I have a guest, the phones ring off the hook. It's like my house is bugged…

***

LOGAN

Logan called, texted, and emailed me today (he's been a busy boy). He REALLY wanted to come over! He's so excited about this S&M Bondage stuff—he's spent the day doing "research" on it. He sent me a couple of articles to read, which were very interesting. He also ordered some books on being the "Master." I ordered a "Harem Slave" costume, a purple teddy and thigh highs and a bed restraint kit to be tied to. We were both going crazy on Amazon with our credit cards. Anyway, he didn't drop in today, so that was a good thing. He did say he wanted to come over tomorrow to play. It should be interesting…now that he's got some new ideas, we shall see what his imagination conjures up!

JUSTIN

Justin, my dance instructor, came over at 3:30 p.m. for my lesson. He's so adorable. Black hair a small mustache with a soul patch (I usually don't like soul patches—but it looks good on him). He's about 5'10" and very trim. I wasn't sure if I had to wear a mask for the lesson (remember Covid). When Jordan had his private lesson, his instructor made him wear a mask.

But Justin and I did not wear masks. We French kissed and hugged a lot! He's a very sexy man, and the chemistry between us is amazing, but I controlled myself. After my one-hour lesson (the Rumba), he suggested that we do "more," but I told him we would be good. He accepted that like a gentleman. I scheduled my next lesson next Wednesday at his house. Maybe I'll feel more comfortable doing "more" at his place without the threat of Logan stopping by.

***

While I was relaxing watching TV tonight, Bob called. I accepted his offer to use his gym and made a date for Friday morning to meet at his house. Then Logan called, and we talked for about a half hour. He said he ordered the "50 Shades" trilogy movies (uncut), and we could watch them together. Plus, he said he's been ordering some things for me (I can't wait to see what he got me). He said he was so excited about finding someone who he could "play" with because he had been so depressed lately.

And finally, Jordan called to confirm our date on Saturday afternoon. Whew!

***

LOGAN

To say this day was surprising would be an understatement. That being said…

Logan arrived at 2:00 p.m. (he was here a little early). I told him to expect a fantasy, and he was prepared. I greeted him at the door, wearing my black mink coat. Underneath, I had on a very sheer print nightie with nothing underneath (the print obscured that fact until a tactile inspection had to be made to determine nudity), high heels, and a pearl and diamond choker. I handed him a card that I made that said:

Welcome to the Oasis Gentlemen's Club

Your hostess today will be

Anastasia

She will be at your service for all of your desires.

We hope you enjoy your stay with us.

Madame Camille

I walked him to the "Salon" (the living room), where we could get acquainted. We chatted for a short while. He asked me to stand and take off my coat. Then he asked me to turn around. At that point, the tactile inspection of my body began. He suggested that we go into the mini salon (the Playroom), where he proceeded to tie my hands together in front and then tie me to the hook on the door. He kept touching me and exploring my body, driving me crazy. Then he got the flogger and pulled up my nightie, and smacked my ass (it didn't hurt, but it was very sexy).

After he had his pleasure with this endeavor but wouldn't let me climax, he took me to the bed and blindfolded me, with my hands still tied in front of me. He made me stand and laid me across the bed on my stomach as he had in the past. He went from pleasure to pain implements until I was so aroused, I could hardly breathe (again not allowing me to climax).

He then turned me over and began a series of ministrations with his tongue and fingers, and finally, after I could stand it no longer, he penetrated me, and the orgasms were mind-blowing. He had built up the sexual tension to the breaking point where neither one of us seemed to have any control. The playing went on and on, and I completely lost track of time.

Finally, he took off my blindfold, and we both lay on the bed, where he took me in his arms and gave me a grape (I had a dish beside the bed with grapes and cookies). He told me that I was his sex slave and he would take care of me.

During our break, he started asking me questions about if I was seeing anyone. I was so surprised, I became speechless. He then knew I was hiding something. He finally broke me down, and I said I had seen other men in his absence. He asked me why I didn't say something. I said it was because he was probably doing the same thing on the yacht—fucking anything that walked. He said he had many temptations but did not succumb (I don't know if I believe that). Then he wanted me to tell him about the men. I believe he is a voyeur.

Logan: *How many men have you dated since you met me?*

Stacey: *Six*

Logan: *Six!? Why so many?*

Stacey: *We've had this conversation before. You took my virginity for the second time in my life and got my Libido supercharged. Then you come over for an occasional booty call and then disappear for weeks at a time. A girl has needs...I have needs.*

Logan: *Tell me about these men.*

Stacey: (With much reluctance) *I've dated men from 55 to 85 years old.*

Logan: *Tell me what you did with them and what they did with you.*

Stacey: (Again, reluctantly, I tell him broadly about the men—no names—just basic details of our dates.) *Are you upset with me? Do you want to break up with me?*

Logan: *No, I'm not upset with you, and I'm not breaking up with you. I'm just upset that you felt you had to lie to me. I'm okay with anything you do if you don't lie to me. When is your next date?*

Stacey: *Saturday.*

Logan: *What time?*

Stacey: *3:00 p.m. He's coming for dinner.*

Logan: *You're feeding him? Do these guys ever give you things?*

Stacey: *Yes, they always bring something—flowers, candy, food.*

Logan: *Did you wear any of your "outfits" with them?*

Stacey: *I did wear the sailor outfit twice—once on New Year's Eve and then when I went to brunch. I also wore the police outfit to a Halloween party. I wore the naughty schoolgirl outfit once.*

Logan: *Good Lord, the naughty schoolgirl outfit? Did you have pigtails? That's the outfit I wanted you to wear for me...now it doesn't have the same meaning since another man has already enjoyed it.*

Stacey: *I'm so sorry. I didn't want to hurt you. It was just "revenge sex" since I thought you were out playing around, too, and you left me alone for so long.*

Logan: *It's okay. But you know, this will now work both ways. You will tell me when you see someone, and I will tell you.*

Stacey: *I don't want to know when you see another woman. You may not be jealous, but I am!*

I guess having this conversation about my dates got him so hot he took me again and again and again. We went on for hours. I think he likes to think of me with other men. It seems to turn him on. Also, my stock in trade went way up when he thought so many men wanted me… He went back to his "Story of O" fantasy and said he was my Master, I belonged to him, and he wanted to know about all of my sexual encounters.

While we were playing, the doorbell rang. It was the postman delivering my mail and a package. I ignored it until we took another break. It was my Cowgirl Costume. So, on one of our breaks, I went to the front door and retrieved the mail. He asked me to put it on and model it for him, which I did (he is my Master, and I cannot disobey him, LOL). We took some pictures.

After an unsettling and amazing afternoon, Logan left at 8:00 p.m. I was exhausted!

At 9:51 p.m., my phone pinged with a text from him:

Thank you for a wonderful afternoon of pleasure.

I responded:

Back at you, Babe.

Then, his final note:

Night hugs and kisses.

The good thing about our conversation yesterday was that I didn't have to figure out lies to tell Logan since he asked me to be honest with him. I was concerned about keeping my stories straight with all of these guys. So now, if he asks to see me, I can tell him I have "plans." He will probably want details because he seems to get off on that. Strange guy.

***

BOB

Bob invited me to his house to use his gym (since my gym is still closed due to Covid). I arrived there around 10:00 a.m. in my exercise clothes, and we walked to the gym. There was a guard at the door who asked to see our IDs. She said I couldn't go in because I was not a member, but Bob could. Bob was a little pissed (as was I), and we walked back to his house. He said he would try to get me a pass by saying I lived with him. I told him to please not do that.

When we got back to his house, we went into his bedroom. He lay down on the bed, and I just stood there. I told him that nothing was going to happen. He asked me to lay beside him, and he would be good. I did, and he started to get all "handsy," and I told him to stop.

I reminded him that I was seeing someone else, but he didn't care…he said he loved me and we should be together (oh boy!). He wanted to fuck me, but I resisted and told him NO! Finally, I said I had to get back to work and left. Good Lord, this guy is like crazy glue… Meanwhile, while I was there, I had 3 texts from Logan on my phone… Again, do these guys have me lojacked?

Then I received the following text from Bob at 5:32 p.m.:

Enjoyed our get-together. Sorry about the gym. I'm glad we've decided to stay in touch and see each other. We are good friends. Let's be there for each. Don't forget the Tango. Love ya.

LOGAN

While I was with Bob, Logan texted me asking if he could bring over the "50 Shades Freed" video he just got. I said OKAY. I was still shy about his knowing about my escapades for the last few months. He arrived at 3:00 p.m. with the video. Since I expected this to be a drop-off and leave visit, I wore jeans and a T-shirt. He also wore torn jeans and a T-shirt (God, he's so sexy!). I later found out he was going Commando (no underwear), so he was not going to make this a "drop off and leave" visit.

I had just gotten another package (the bed restraint kit), which was sitting on the kitchen counter. When he saw it, he said, "Let's go install it." So off to my Playroom we went (this is such dangerous territory for us). We figured out how to install the thing, and he said, "Let's see how it works." So, he restrained me with the cuffs—wrists and ankles—and took a look at me. I was still fully clothed with my jeans and t-shirt so I thought this was safe enough (no way to get my clothes off in that state).

Well, I guess Logan's hormones took over, and he began touching and caressing me, and I was helpless to stop him (but truth be told, I didn't want to). He pulled up my t-shirt and began fondling my breasts. Then he opened my jeans, pulled them down, and played with my lady parts. By this time, I'm writhing in the bed, unable to move.

He was kissing and sucking and touching, and I was just moaning and screaming with pleasure. He got out my vibrator and used it wherever it felt good. He finally undid my ankle restraints and removed my jeans and panties (my wrists were still tied up). Then he climbed on the bed and started teasing me and kissing me and finally fucking me. We went on like this for I don't know how long, and then he untied my wrist restraints, and we kissed and cuddled. We lay on the bed talking for a while, and then the sparks began to fly again, and we started down the road to extreme pleasure once more. When we took another break, he told me how rare it was to find a woman like me—attractive, sexy, businesswoman, intelligent, who really liked sex.

He said he'd dated many women, but none had all of these qualities in one package. He told me to hide the bed restraints and take the rope and flogger off the door so my date on Saturday wouldn't get any ideas. He says he is not jealous, but I think he has a bit of a jealous streak.

He finally said he had to leave, and we walked into the living room, where he sat down on the loveseat, and I sat next to him. We started talking about everything. We talked on the sofa for hours. He sat there, and I laid down with my legs over his lap, and he was stroking my legs.

At 8:00 p.m., he finally decided to leave. We walked slowly to the door, still kissing, and I could tell he didn't want to leave. His parting shot was to tell me not to have too good a time with my date on Saturday, and he wanted a "full report" (like that's going to happen!). As he went out the door, he said, "Love you," and I said, "Love you too" back to him.

I checked my weekly calendar and saw that Logan came over on Monday, Tuesday, Thursday and Friday (he called on Wednesday). At least he knows to call or text first before he comes over. Can't wait to see him again after he knows that I was fucking another guy… I'm such a whore!

LOGAN

Logan came over on Sunday afternoon. He texted me earlier saying he had the new "50 Shades Darker" video and wanted to bring it over. I asked him if this would be a "drive-by" or if he wanted a fantasy. He chose the fantasy. When he arrived at 2:00 p.m., he looked delicious (even in blue jeans and a T-shirt)! I was wearing my black "leather" dress with fishnet stockings and my hair in my long ponytail hairpiece.

In the goodie bag that he brought, he not only had the "50 Shades" video but also a riding crop (wow!), a leather bondage contraption, and a book (*Dom's Guide to Submissive Training*). Some guys bring candy and flowers, but bondage stuff is good, too.

We sat in the Salon (the living room) and talked while he shared the contents of his bag. He admitted that he loved my outfit, and it turned him on. After a while, we moved into my Playroom, where I had it set up with glasses of strawberry water (his favorite) and a bowl of grapes and cookies.

He tied my hands in front of me and tied the rope to the hook on my Playroom door. He proceeded to unzip my dress until it was wide open. Then he started touching my entire body and running the riding crop over me. He made me turn around and told me to open my legs where his crop found my pleasure center. He fondled my breasts and kissed my neck but wouldn't let me have an orgasm. I was going crazy.

After what seemed like an eternity, he untied me and took me to the bed, where he sat me down. By now, my dress was on the floor and I was wearing only my bra and fishnet pantyhose. He stood over me and started playing with my body. I was writhing in pleasure on the bed, but he would not let me climax. He then made me kneel on the floor, unzipped his jeans, and let me give him oral sex.

This went on and on until he finally took pity on me and removed my pantyhose (I had nothing underneath), sat me on the bed and fucked me until I couldn't breathe. The heightened sexual tension of his not letting me climax earlier gave me a series of ongoing orgasms that wouldn't seem to stop.

We took a break and decided to watch the "50 Shades" movie on my TV in the bedroom. We were both laying on my bed naked, caressing one another all over. During the movie, we would just lose it and attack one another with passion and abandon that it was like a tsunami hit the beach. (Geez, where has this passion been all my life?) We talked and fucked and watched the movie and went on like that all afternoon. What a splendid way to spend a Sunday afternoon! He left at 6:00 p.m., leaving me in a wanton state of sexual destruction (what a way to go!).

At about 8:00 p.m., he called me to say he had a great time. I was still in a semi-conscious euphoric state and felt like my lady parts had been pleasured beyond belief. I will need a few days to recover, but I continue reliving the memories with all the vivid details as if they were currently happening. Lord help me… I can't believe I'm going down this garden path…

I sent Logan the Update above. This is his response:

WOW, I sure like reading about our exploits the next day. It is like re-living it all over again. Each time, a new chapter in the book builds on the previous visit. I woke up again this morning in a complete state of arousal. I am starting to think we may need morning emergency visits.

I, as well as you, run the encounters over and over in my head and want to come up with new ways to push our adventures. With each visit, you learn to please your master more and become a more willing submissive slave to sex, pain and pleasure. It is funny how the two go hand in hand. I loved using the riding crop on you as you counted the self-imposed strokes across your bottom. I also love seeing you tied to the door, then as I touch you, feel the wetness build while you hang helpless.

I am starting to feel that at some point in each day, I need to see, pleasure and or punish you in some way.

Commanding you and your body gives me pleasure. Like having you watch TV impaled on top of me, grinding your body with me inside you. You stretched across the bed, giving me full access to your body as you licked, sucked, grasped and buried your face enjoying your Master's pleasure. Grasping my legs until you again find your own pleasure in doing so.

I know you will continue to learn, develop and think of new ways to please.

I am ready for another round. Great Story

Love Logan

***

I was awakened at 4:00 a.m. this morning in a heightened state of arousal by an erotic dream that seemed so real I thought I would have an orgasm. I replayed it in my mind and had to put it to paper:

I've fallen deeply into the world of BDSM with my Master. I will do anything for him. He wants to set up an engagement with one of his friends whereby I would pleasure them both by doing whatever they wanted. I must admit, I have a little trepidation about doing this (since I've never done it before), but I care more about pleasing my Master than anything else.

At the appointed day and time, my Master brings Mr. X to my home. I have been told to create a fantasy, so I greet them at the door in my Harem Slave outfit with my hair tied up in my long ponytail hairpiece. Refreshments and beverages are set up in the Galley. I hand them the welcome card for the Oasis Gentlemen's Club and escort them to the Salon. They sit, and I am asked to kneel at the feet of my Master. He pats my head and calls me a "Good Girl." It pleases me to be given that praise.

While Master and Mr. X are talking, I stay silent unless asked a question. They leave me in the Salon, tied to a table, while they go to the Galley for food and beverages. When they return, Master takes me by my leash to the Playroom, where he ties my hands in front of me and then ties the rope to the hook on the door. I am now hanging there, helpless, waiting for the next step.

This is the first time I have ever done something like this with a stranger, and I must admit that I am getting excited and wondering what will happen next.

Master tells Mr. X that he can touch me and do whatever he would like to me while I am restrained. Mr. X runs his hands over my body and then under my skirt. He pulls my bra down and fondles my breasts. He then puts his fingers into my sex and moves them around. I'm getting so aroused, but I cannot climax, or Master will punish me. They both have their way with me until I am barely able to stand.

Master then unties me from the door and removes the rope from my wrists. He walks me to the bed, blindfolds me and puts cuffs on my wrists behind my back. He lays me down on the bed and tells Mr. X that he can do anything he would like to me—remove my clothing, give me oral sex, fondle my body, or fuck me. I feel hands all over my body but do not know whether they belong to Master or Mr. X. I'm so aroused I can hardly breathe. Again, Master says that I may not have an orgasm. I'm writhing on the bed, barely able to contain myself, totally helpless.

I do not know how long this goes on because I've lost track of time and have been in a supercharged state of excitement, barely staying conscious. Finally, when they have had enough fun playing with me and touching and using every inch of my body, they unshackle my wrists (while I'm still blindfolded), and I realize by touching them that both men are naked. They join me on the bed, and one of them enters my sex, and the other is by my head, where I begin sucking his manhood.

Their hands are all over me, and since I am unshackled, I can touch them both. They are moaning and seem to be enjoying the pleasures I am giving them. When they are through using my body, Master takes Mr. X out of the Playroom to conclude their business.

As I lay there, I find myself totally without remorse. Master returns to the Playroom and tells me I've been a "Good Girl." My heart soars that I have made him happy. He takes off my blindfold, gets on the bed and caresses me. He kisses me, fondles my body, and enters me, and I have the most cataclysmic orgasm I have ever had. He says he's proud of me, and Mr. X had such a good time he wants to come back for an encore.

I do love pleasing my Master, but I wonder sometimes how he can share me with other men with such abandon...

***

What is written below actually happened…until the "Intruder" enters the picture…

Yesterday, I watched "50 Shades Freed" and "9-1/2 Weeks" … clearly, I overstimulated my libido.

I woke up at 3:00 a.m. this morning with my loins on fire (in a good way). I tried to get back to sleep, but all I could think about was the women in those 2 films being ravaged by the men. I saw their breasts and their bodies and the men going down on them and making them scream with passion. I began touching myself and running my hands all over my body. That just turned me on even more. I was out of control.

I pushed aside my covers, took off my nightgown and panties, got my vibrator and began to pleasure myself. I covered my private parts with lubricant and began rubbing the vibrator over my clit and then over the rest of my body. I had my legs spread wide open. I was one slippery mess… While I had the vibrator in my right hand, my left hand was caressing my breasts and pinching my nipples. Good Lord, I was turning myself on… all the while picturing my lover between my legs.

I played with myself slowly because I wanted it to last. I screamed with passion when my orgasm finally arrived. Then I turned down the speed on the vibrator and continued to have a series of slower, smaller orgasms… I'm such a greedy bitch… one is never enough!

After I was sated, I lay there in the dark, trying to recover. It was then that my fantasy mind took over…

I looked up, and a man was standing beside my bed, totally naked in the dark. He looked down at me and told me not to make a sound. He had been watching me the entire time I was masturbating. The first thing I thought about was how he got into my house at 3:00 a.m. and what did he want.

He got on the bed on top of me and held my arms over my head with one hand while he played with my clit with the other. I was squirming and writhing and moving under him. His cock was rock-hard pressed against my body. Then he entered me, and I screamed. He told me to be quiet, or he would hurt me. But I wasn't screaming because I was afraid. I was screaming because I was so excited that I was on the verge of having another orgasm. He started pumping inside me, and then he realized that his attempt at raping me was failing because I was cooperating and enjoying it. He was so turned on that he let my arms go. I embraced him and began kissing him. He was such a good kisser—nibbling at my upper and lower lips very slowly. When he opened his mouth to French kiss me, it was like he was sucking my soul into his body. He had his hands all over me, touching every inch of my body. I was in a frenzy beyond belief! I then had such an orgasm that I thought my head would blow off.

Shortly after that, he had a massive orgasm inside me and let out a howl of delight. I ran my fingers through his hair then I continued down his body. He had a beautiful body. I kept touching every inch of him as he moaned with pleasure. I finally touched his manhood, and he got hard again. I put his cock in my mouth and he came again—all over my face. I was covered in lubricant and cum and sweat... We were so turned on that we spent the next few hours having mad, passionate sex. We tried every position and each one brought more pleasure to both of us. I finally must have passed out from all of the exhilaration.

When I awoke later in the morning, the "Intruder" was gone. I wondered if I had just imagined what happened or if it had been real. I felt "down there" and it was still wet with cum (his or mine—I don't know). Did it really happen? I'm beginning to realize that my fantasy world and my real world are colliding...

Logan's response to the above fantasy:

HOLY SHIT!!! I think you should put your other career on hold and write sex novels for women. Your sex urges and impulses are taking over your life. Lol. However, I think that is pretty hot and sexy. If I did not know better, I would say you made it up in your mind and like MOST women, only wished this had all happened.

If you're going to use the lube all over your body each morning, I am going to need to bring more. Screaming that early in the morning is different than the afternoon. It may rouse the neighbors and bring the cops. If intruders are going to be cumming and going at all hours, please leave a sign at the front with Oasis Club pricing and a TIP Jar. Pussy Cost Money!!! I most certainly think you have earned yourself a couple of grapes.

I am very impressed with your writing skills and your clarity of events. I think I should have perhaps stopped over in any case if you were on the verge of this much excitement and have gotten my share.

I love the fact that you got so much pleasure from this morning. You're going to really have to start going to bed at 6 from now on if you intend to get any sleep at all.

I also like that you share your sexual adventures and pleasures with your Master. It shows a good degree of trust and continues to show me the extent of your growing sexuality. Almost each day, it builds in you as your desire to please and be of service to me and other men continues to grow. A sexual implement, if you will. Each day, losing the old Stacey and building a new Stacey, bathing in sexual desires all day and now even into the night.

Yes, like a Caterpillar into a Butterfly, you are evolving, day by day, week by week. The Master likes to see this.

What a fun evening you had last night. I think, you will be touching yourself most of the day today. Thinking and re-living this adventure. I think you're enjoying slowly becoming a Cum Loving Cock Pleasing Wanton Slut ~~~~ How wonderful.

I love waking up to your sexual dreams and stories. Keep 'em coming.

Love Your Master

***

I was having another very vivid dream this morning. It was 3:00 a.m. (again). I thought I heard someone knocking on my door. I kept saying, "Come in, come in…." but they just kept knocking. I woke up with a start and then I went to my front door and turned on the light to see if anyone was there. Then I went to the back door—no one was there either. My heart was racing and I wasn't sure if I was still dreaming.

I got back into bed. My loins were still hot and ready for action from my "experiences" the day before. I was still so turned on. Just clenching "down there" almost brought me to orgasm (even without touching myself). I tried to get back to sleep, but all I could think of was Christian Grey's "Red Room of Pain." Then I decided that I would make my Playroom "Stacey's Purple Room of Pleasure."

I got up, turned on the light and went over to my little table chock full of instruments of pleasure and pain. Then I realized that I could do what Christian Grey did and put them in drawers. I looked at the tortoise shell dresser and realized that all of the drawers were empty (what a waste!). I began carefully placing the “toys” from my little table into the top drawer so they could be seen and accessed with ease. Then I put Mr. Buzzy (my vibrator) in the second drawer all by himself (because he’s so special!). I still have room to store any other “toys" I may acquire in the remaining drawers. This way, my maid can do her job without touching my things and thinking that her mistress is some sort of a pervert since all of the evidence is out of sight.

Also, when visitors come over, I’d rather they didn’t see the “tools” of my craft…

I kept the little table where it was and put the lavage bowl with its contents on it for easy access. I can’t seem to turn my brain off… all I can think of is sex.

***

MONDAY

Logan came over for another marathon sex session (2:30 to 6:00 p.m.). Nothing you haven't heard before…

***

TUESDAY

Peter, the cartoonist, called to tell me he missed me and I suggested that we schedule a Zoom meeting so we could talk "face-to-face." I will set that up.

Brad, the pilot, called and left a message that he wanted to talk to me. I scheduled a Zoom call with him for Wednesday evening.

Logan called and wanted to come over (it was almost 7 p.m. and I was ready for bed—no makeup, etc.), so I told him no.

***

WEDNESDAY

I had a dance lesson with Justin at 3:30 at his home. He owns a house with a pool in a gated community. He has an enormous dog named Beemer (like the car). He gave me a tour of his house and the yard and showed me his pet turtle (it too was enormous—in a fish tank with an enormous goldfish).

I told him I wanted to learn the Tango, so that's what we did. He put on the music and he started teaching me the moves. He held me close in his arms and then began kissing me. I stopped doing that (after all, I was paying $75 for a lesson). When the hour was up, he put on some other dance music, took me into his arms, and said that I was so huggable. Even though he's young, sparks fly when we're together. We slowly danced and kept kissing (just like at the high school prom). By this time, I could feel that his manhood was hard as a rock pressing up against me. He wanted to take me into his bedroom, but I told him I had things to do. To be honest, the only reason I didn't go to bed with him was because I was afraid that Logan might stop over later and he would "smell" that I had been with another man… We scheduled another lesson next Wednesday at 3:30. After that, I think I'm going to go to a lesson every other week.

***

I had a Zoom call with Brad at 8:00 p.m. He was in South Carolina on his way to Virginia for his older brother's birthday party. He wanted to get together when he returned. I told him I was taking private dance classes and was doing a "self-quarantine" for several days afterward. That should give me some time before I schedule something with him.

***

THURSDAY

Logan came over at 2:30 p.m. He brought a duffle bag chock full of goodies—vibrators, lotions, implements, etc. The damn thing weighed a ton. He's been online all week buying these things. He's really getting into this BDSM stuff… He also brought me a white men's dress shirt because I said I liked it when Anastasia (50 Shades) was walking around in Christian's white dress shirt. I told him I just wanted an old, scruffy shirt BUT what he brought was a brand new, never worn Perry Ellis shirt! I said I couldn't take it, but he insisted and said that he had dozens of them.

We sat in the living room and talked for a while. The next thing I know, we have clothes scattered all over the living room rug and we're heading to my Playroom (big surprise!). We tried some of the new items he brought—the best being "Mr. Buzzy"—it's an enormous vibrator that you plug in. I can't even begin to describe it, but he handed it to me and he turned it on the lowest speed (it's multi-speed). I started by sitting on the bench at the bottom of my bed and inserting it into myself. Before I knew it, I slid off the bench and was writhing on the carpet, having multiple orgasms while holding this contraption. Logan was standing over me, getting all excited as I squirmed around on the rug, moaning and screaming. When I pulled it out, he had to carry me to the bed so I could recover.

We played and talked and played some more. He finally left at 6:30 p.m. (I walked him to the door in my Perry Ellis men's shirt with nothing underneath!) I was exhausted!

***

FRIDAY

After seeing Logan's "Duffle Bag of Pleasure and Pain", I decided that I needed to organize my toys so that other "visitors" and my maid didn't have to encounter them.

I hadn't planned on seeing Logan today, but he texted me and asked me if I wanted help re-installing the Bed Restraint gizmo on the bed. I said I would like to do it after I changed my sheets. He came over at noon (with 2 bags of Pepperidge Farm cookies). I had just received a bunch of things that I ordered online in the mail—6 beautiful lace push-up bras and 6 lacy boy shorts. Plus, my Harem Slave outfit. Of course, he asked me to model everything for him.

We both planned on this being a "drive by" visit, but again, one thing led to another, and… He left at 2:30 p.m.

He asked several times if I was having my "Saturday visitor," but I neither confirmed nor denied it. I basically ignored the question. He then asked me point blank who was coming over and I just said it was "the Brit." I didn't tell him what time or anything else about the man. He said that he would be spending Saturday with his daughter for Father's Day and on Sunday, he would be with his son. So, I assume that I won't see him until at least Monday which is fine with me because I don't know that I can take a daily dose of this intense sexual activity (who am I kidding… I've been enjoying fucking my brains out). Anyway, I was hoping to have today to rest so I would be ready for Jordan on Saturday, but I guess I'll just have to soldier on… (I know, you have no pity for me, LOL).

STILL FRIDAY (WARNING: This next section is rated R, possibly X)

Logan called around 5 p.m. He said he was still horny from this morning and was thinking about coming over and fucking me again. We talked for a short while, then I told him he could come over. Twice in one day, Mamma Mia!!!!

Logan arrived at 6:00 p.m. I was wearing a black lace bra and panties with a white button-front sweater that was scooped so low in the front that my black bra was peaking over the top. (He likes not knowing which of my many personas will be on the other side of the door when he visits or which sexy outfit I will be wearing! The anticipation turns him on.) Only the first 2 buttons of the sweater were done, so my black lace panties were showing. When he came in the door, he took in everything I was wearing/not wearing and gave me a big hug and kiss. (Love his kisses…they touch my soul… the best kisser ever!!)

We went to the kitchen, where I gave him some Strawberry water…I was already having a glass of white wine. We took our drinks into the living room and sat on the loveseat. I sat sideways with my legs on his lap. We talked while he kept stroking my legs.

After a short while, we went into my Playroom. I asked him to help me get into the leather strappy bondage vest that he gave me. I removed my sweater and he put the vest on me over my bra and panties and secured all the buckles in the back (that's why I needed help). The vest was all open straps which made the bra very accessible. Then he tied my wrists in front of me and tied my arms to the hook on the door. As I was hanging there, he pulled down the front of my bra, leaving my breasts exposed. Then he disappeared for a minute and returned with 2 ice cubes. He began running them over my nipples, which became so hard I couldn't believe it. Then he would suck my nipples and continue until the ice was almost melted. Not only the ice was melting…I was melting…I could hardly stand up…my legs had turned to jelly; I was so turned on.

He removed my panties as I stood there, untied me from the door and walked me over to the edge of the bed. He bent me over the bed and proceeded to spank my bare bottom with the belt. It did hurt, but that only turned me on more. He kept asking me if I wanted him to stop and I said, "No sir." He stopped for a moment and stroked his lubricated fingers around my clit. When I was writhing with pleasure and having multiple orgasms, he entered me from behind, occasionally striking me with the belt. I was swimming between the pain/pleasure shores—never in my life thinking I could be so turned on by such a scenario. When he pulled out of me, I fell to my knees, turned toward him, standing over me, and began sucking his enormous cock. He stroked my head and told me that I had been a "good girl." He told me to go get Mr. Buzzy (the super vibrator). I said I couldn't walk because I was so weak, so he got the instrument. I was still kneeling on the floor, trying to catch my breath.

He told me to get on the bed and lie down and gave the vibrator to me. I placed it on my sex and, slowly inserted it and brought myself to climax again and again. As he stood there watching me, I could see his cock getting larger. Clearly, he was getting as turned on watching me as I was playing with myself. After I had enough of the vibrator, he took it away and fucked me again while I lay on my back at the edge of the bed as he stood in front of me. The pleasure train kept rolling and I thought my head would explode.

When he finished with me in that position, he got on the bed beside me and, held me in his arms and told me again what a "good girl" I had been. I can't explain how his praise of me makes me feel. It's like getting a good report card and going to the head of the class.

We talked and continued to play until he left at 8:00 p.m. It was some of the most intense 2 hours I had ever experienced. Instead of quelling my need for sex, it just exacerbated my desires. Never in my life have I been in such a heightened state of arousal…all the time… Each time we get together, we push the envelope further… It keeps getting better and better… I will never be able to go back to "vanilla sex."

***

SATURDAY

Jordan came over at 3:00 p.m. He had asked for a "Gunsmoke" fantasy and I was happy to oblige. I was wearing my cowgirl outfit and hat and handed him an "invitation" (see below).

Welcome to the Long Branch Saloon

Your hostess today will be

Miss Kitty

She will be at your service for all of your desires.

We hope you enjoy your visit with us.

He brought lunch—Greek Salad, Green Salad, Crab Salad and Shrimp Salad. We went into the kitchen and I gave him some lemonade, and I had a glass of wine. We talked for a while (Jordan never likes to rush things). He asked me if I had plans for next Sunday. I said I had a birthday party to go to for one of my friend's granddaughters at 5 p.m. He said he wanted to introduce me to his daughter in Miami. It was going to be her daughter's birthday on Sunday. He said he could pick me up at 9 a.m., drive to Miami for lunch, and have me back in time for my second party. I thought, "What the hell, why not?"

We eventually worked our way into my Playroom and did what came naturally. I realized during our love-making that he may have a bit of BDSM tendencies in him. He would smack my ass with his hand (hard) when he was caressing me (I happen to like that). He liked to hold my hands above my head with one of his hands while he touched my body, so I couldn't stop him. I think many men would love to have a BDSM relationship but are afraid to ask a woman for fear of being thought of as a pervert. I asked him about his going to the adult clubs in Fort Lauderdale with his former girlfriend. I swear, he and Logan are very similar. I was afraid to let him know that I had a drawer full of BDSM implements because I didn't need 2 "Masters" tying me up and telling me what to do.

We took a break to have dessert. He went into my closet and got the blue terry bathrobe that I usually give him to wear (he's becoming very familiar with my things), and I put on Logan's white dress shirt. He looked at me and said, "A man's shirt. I like that." I said I liked wearing men's shirts. Then he said the next time he came over, he would bring me some shirts. Geez, maybe I should ask these guys for something other than used clothing!

After dessert, we relaxed in the TV room. I sat down with my legs on his lap while he stroked my legs. We then headed back to the Playroom for the final round of sex and cuddling. He left at 8:30 p.m.

While he was getting ready to leave, my phone pinged with a text. It was from Logan. He wanted to come over in the morning to see me before he met his son. I told him I would love that. Here is a man who was MIA more than he was in my life, and now he's always around. Mind you…I'm not complaining… I'm still crazy about him… but I don't want to get hurt if/when he gets tired of all this...

***

SUNDAY

Logan arrived at 10:30 a.m. I wore a black Calvin Klein dress with a black lace bra and panties. We sat and talked for a while in the living room, then went into the Playroom (leaving my dress on the loveseat). He blindfolded, handcuffed, and tied me to the bed on my stomach. Then he proceeded to use the belt on my ass. I don't know why that turns me on so much (picture Anastasia in 50 Shades in the same scene). Anyway, we played and talked and laughed and just had fun. I had multiple orgasms and was quite spent. He left at 1:00 p.m. to go to his son's house for a BBQ.

I have nothing planned for the upcoming week except my dance lesson with Justin on Wednesday. We shall see…

This will be short and sweet:

Logan came over on Monday, Wednesday and Friday this week. As usual, we had amazing sex!!! The days he didn't come over, he called.

Bob called on Friday and Saturday. He wants to see me. He's being very persistent.

Jordan came over on Saturday for dinner and a swim. He's picking me up at 9 a.m. this morning to go to Miami to meet his daughter and granddaughter (who is having her 6th birthday).

I have another children's birthday party this afternoon—one of the ladies in my "Witches" group—her granddaughter is turning 12. That starts at 5 p.m. Jordan promised to get me back from Miami by 4 p.m. so I could get to my next party.

Logan knows I was seeing "the Brit" on Saturday and said he was okay with that. He also knows about the 2 children's parties (although I didn't tell him that one was in Miami with "the Brit.") Anyway, he wanted me to text him and let him know when he could come over after the 5 p.m. party.

I have to be honest with you…the whole time I was with Jordan yesterday, I couldn't stop thinking about Logan. Jordan and I had "vanilla sex," but my mind and heart weren't really into it. I've become "addicted" to Logan… he's like a drug… I can't let him know how I feel, or I may scare him away.

***

MONDAY

I received a text from my former personal trainer, Mike, on Sunday evening. He wanted to know how I was doing. I told him I really missed my exercise sessions and asked if his gym was open. He said yes, and we went back and forth, texting. I decided to visit his gym this morning to see if I liked it and if I wanted to join.

I met Mike at his gym at 11 a.m., and he gave me a tour. The place was HUGE. Tons of machines and locker rooms with showers, which are very professional. There were so many machines that social distancing was not a problem. However, people were not wearing masks. I signed up for Tuesdays and Thursdays at 8 a.m. with Mike as my personal trainer.

Logan texted and emailed that he was horny (so was I) and perhaps we could get together later. He came over at 4:30 p.m. and we went into the Playroom. We both stripped down and he tied my hands and tied me to the door. He did the ice cube trick on my breasts and I was melting (along with the ice cubes). We did every position and wound up on the bed in each other's arms, talking about everything. He left at 7:30 p.m. Whew! I can't get enough of this.

***

TUESDAY

I had my first session with Mike, my personal trainer. He put me through the paces and introduced me to some folks at the gym. He said he could fix me up with any of these guys, and I said I would pass. Told him I was seeing someone, and we were into BDSM. I think he was a little surprised since he's known me for about 10 years, and I was such a "goody two shoes."

When I got home, I went into my pool (for the first time in about 5 years). I was naked, and it was so exciting. Did about 30 minutes of aquatic exercises (hoping that would calm down my libido).

Logan called to catch up and let me know he would be over on Wednesday.

***

WEDNESDAY

Logan came over at noon. I greeted him at the door in my Harem Slave outfit. The only thing was when I tried on the costume, the bra was too small and I was falling out of it. So... I moved the bra UNDER my breasts (like the outfits in The Story of O), and it looked very sexy with my breasts exposed. I had the gold collar and leash around my neck and handed the leash to Logan as he led me into the Salon (living room). He sat on the love seat and I knelt in front of him. He patted me on the head and said I was a "good girl," then unzipped his pants and let me suck his cock. It was exciting for both of us, and he eventually led me into the Playroom to continue the fantasy. He removed my harem skirt and sat me on the bed, then pushed me back and fucked me. He had my legs on his shoulders as he stood by my bed and just pounded me until we both had orgasms.

Then he got out Mr. Buzzy (the gigantic vibrator) and had me lay on the bed and use it on myself while he watched. When I removed it, he fucked me again, and I had several massive orgasms. He then laid down on the bed, and I was sideways sucking his cock, and he was patting my ass. I get so excited doing that—then I bury my head in his private parts and suck and lick and can't get enough!

He left at 2 p.m. and I was totally spent.

***

THURSDAY

Jordan called at 7 a.m. on my landline to see if I was okay. He had been trying to call on my cell phone but couldn't get through. Turns out his phone was in FaceTime audio mode so it wasn't ringing on my end. I told him all was okay and I was on my way to the gym. When I called him back from the gym, he confirmed our date on Sunday to visit his daughter in Miami, then asked me if I was free on Saturday. I said I was free (after all, Logan still has to ask me out on a real date), so he will come over at 3 p.m. on Saturday. I said I would cook.

This was my second session at the gym with Mike. The mandatory face mask rule was in effect. The trainers had to wear the masks all day, but the members could remove the masks when they were working out. They cleaned each piece of equipment before each use. There were not a lot of people in the gym, so social distancing was not a problem.

When I got home, I stripped down naked and did 30 minutes of aquatic exercises in the pool. I think I'm going to make this a regular thing. The pool temperature is perfect and I can go in 7 days a week. Part of my regimen is to get my body into shape after 3 months of being quarantined.

Bob called to check-in. Told him about my joining the gym and my dance lessons. I think he was a little disappointed that I was getting active again… He said he wanted to see me.

Got a text from Brad, the pilot. He's still in NY and probably won't be back until July.

Finally, Logan called to chat and tell me about all of the new "toys" he has been getting that he wants to try out on me. He's coming over tomorrow to try them out.

***

FRIDAY

Logan came over at 11:30 a.m. He brought his duffle bag full of "toys." I was wearing a sheer print nightie over my new lace bra and panties (oh yeah, and my gold collar and leash). Just as he arrived, the mailman had started delivering mail in the community. Logan thought it would be fun for me to go out and get the mail from him in the outfit that I was wearing. Unfortunately, when the mailman got to my house, he just put the mail in the box and took off. I think the fact that Logan's car was in the driveway may have put him off. But I did go out and get the mail in that outfit. My neighbors must really wonder what's going on.

We performed the "opening ritual"— Logan sitting on the loveseat in the Salon while I kneel at his feet. I unbutton his shirt and, caress his chest and lick his nipples. Then I unzip his pants and free his beautiful cock and suck and lick it until he pats me on the head and tells me I'm a "good girl."

We then head into the Playroom, where all the fun begins… My little black slut dress had come in the mail. I tried it on and it really looked good (it barely covered my pussy and was so tight it looked like it was painted on). I said this would be the perfect dress to wear out on a date. I wouldn't wear any panties, so my pussy would be completely accessible to my Master.

I removed my undies and Master tied my hands and then tied me to the door (this is one of my favorite parts). He had a bowl of ice ready and waiting and began rubbing my nipples with the ice so they were standing at attention. Then he would suck on my nipples and continue with the ice and the sucking until I was going out of my mind. Then he put nipple clamps on me (they were vibrating clamps, so it was a little shocking). The sensation on my nipples ran down my entire body. He removed the clamps from my nipples and put them on my pussy and continued with the "shock treatment." I thought I would pass out from the pleasure/pain that I was receiving. I could barely stand up. If my hands weren't tied to the door, I would have melted into the carpet.

He finally untied my arms and walked me to the bed, where he sat me down, facing him and pushed me back on the bed. Without any ceremony, he spread my legs and entered me with his beautiful cock—my motto is "get it up, get it hard, get it in," which he does extremely well and often.

Now, it was time to bring out more of the new toys for a test drive. He had a set of plastic balls to insert into my vagina that had a push button to vibrate them. OMG, I thought I would die when I put them in and he turned on the vibration! While I was enjoying the experience with the vibrating balls, he was standing beside the bed with his cock in my face. I couldn't resist—I had to take it in my mouth. As I was sucking on this man's beautiful cock, the vibrating ball that was deep into me began to hurt. It seems that something in my kissing his manhood caused my vagina to contract, and I couldn't get the ball out of me. He stopped the vibrations, and we finally extricated the ball from my pussy. BTW, we did try this trick later on with the same results. So bottom line, I can't suck his cock when something is inside me, or I will not be able to release the object without help. Good to know!

We took a break and went into the pool naked. We hugged and kissed and touched—it was amazing. I stood in front of one of the jets in the pool (it was pussy height) and almost had an orgasm from the pressure. He then fucked me. This is the first time that I ever did it in the pool. We talked and laughed and fucked in the water again. Then we kept kissing (he is the best kisser in the world!!!).

After our refreshing swim, we went back to the Playroom to continue with our experiments. We tried another vibrator that sounded like an MRI machine. I had several orgasms playing with that toy. He showed me a "50 Shades" vibrator that has a remote control. You insert the vibrator into your pussy, then when your partner pushes the remote control… well, you can guess what happens. It would be so hot to do it while sitting in a restaurant having dinner. I want to wear it under my slutty black dress.

After hours of playing, Logan laid down on the bed, and I was in my favorite position laying across the bed, sucking on his cock and burying my head in his manhood. I want to devour this man. I have never been so turned on in my life as I am with him. We then continued resting, talking, kissing, more fucking, etc. etc. I couldn't get enough.

He left at 4 p.m., and I could barely stand…some of the best hours of my life so far have been spent with this handsome, sexy man…He brings out every ounce of sexuality that I had no idea existed within me… thank you so much, Logan.

***

Bob called this evening. He wants to keep seeing me. I again (for the millionth time) told him I was seeing someone else, but it didn't make any difference to him. He said we had a "connection," and we were more than friends. He keeps re-reading the texts we shared while he was in California and thinks we share some sort of a bond. I'm not going to argue with the man. If he wants to remain friends, I can do that. I just don't want him to think it will go any further.

***

SATURDAY

Jordan arrived at 3:00 p.m. I was wearing my white jeans and navy lace top (no fantasy this week). He brought…wait for it… his Scrabble game (and a Dictionary). We had drinks—Jordan had lemonade, and I had white wine—and sat in the TV room. We talked for a while then I asked if he was ready for me to prepare supper. Jordan likes to take it slow. I made chicken cordon bleu with rice. After we ate, we relaxed for a while and then decided to go into the pool. We went into my Playroom and got out of our clothes, then went into the pool naked. We floated around and he fondled me and kissed me. It wasn't the same as with Logan.

We came back inside and had dessert—cream pie, cookies and grapes. Then we went into the Playroom. He tried to go down on me, but I pushed him away and told him no. Then he got on the bed and started kissing me and playing with me. We finally had vanilla sex. Again, all I could think of was Logan. This went on for a while, then at 8 p.m., he said it was "the witching hour" and got dressed to leave.

While Jordan was here, my landline rang, but I had turned it off from getting messages, so it just continued to ring. Then my cell phone pinged with a text. It was Bob calling to talk. He said he tried to call my landline, but it kept ringing and sounded like it was going to my fax. He had just called the night before. Bless his heart… he just doesn't give up.

***

SUNDAY

Jordan picked me up at 9 a.m. We were going to see his daughter in Miami. It was his granddaughter's birthday. When we got to Miami, his granddaughter was not there. She was with her Grandmother. Jordan's daughter has a roommate who is from Barcelona. She's 26, a part-time nanny, and is HOT. His daughter is also hot—in her early 30s, big breasts, thin, great ass! I hate to admit this, but I was picturing myself playing with each of them (I am turning into a complete horn dog).

Jordan's daughter said her daughter's party was on Saturday, and she had all this food left over, so she put out a spread for Jordan and me. Father and daughter bantered with one another—it was clear that there was some animosity toward her father. But I really liked her, and we seemed to get along just fine.

Jordan mentioned that I might like to have some marijuana (which she grows and sells). While I would have loved to try it, I didn't want to be impaired since I still had an entire day of activities planned. We all took a walk around the neighborhood (which was very pretty and quiet) with her dog, Shadow. When we came back, just before we were going to leave, a song came on the music system, and Jordan grabbed me and started dancing with me. Then I told him he should dance with his daughter (which he did). They seemed to be having a good time.

We left, and on the way home, Jordan made a stop at his house in Boca before dropping me off. I know he said he was a painter (not a house painter). His home was filled with paintings that he did—portraits, seascapes, townscapes… I was VERY impressed. He's extremely talented!

He dropped me off at my house about 3 p.m., which gave me a couple of hours before I had to go to the birthday party down the street.

***

Logan and I had been texting back and forth all day and he was waiting for my text saying that I finally was home.

I texted Logan around 6 p.m. to let him know that I was home. Having eaten 1 hot dog and 2 Corona beers at the local birthday party, I was definitely a little tipsy. He came right over with his duffle bag full of sex toys. I was wearing my leather mini dress with my red lace bra and black lace panties. I was also wearing my black leather collar and leash. We did our usual routine in the Salon (kneeling, caressing him, unzipping his pants).

We talked and played and kissed for a while, then… into the Playroom. He unzipped my dress, removed my bra and tied me up to the door. He did the ice cube trick on my nipples, then attached the vibrating nipple clamps (I'm really getting used to them). Then he removed my panties and put these tiny clothespins on my private parts. I must say the tiny clothespins are one "toy" that I really didn't like. He also got a new flogger, and I loved it—it was very sensual when he moved it over my breasts. Then he turned me around on the door and used it to hit my ass. It didn't hurt like the belt and probably didn't leave marks, but I did like it. When I could no longer take it, he took me down from the door and led me to the bed, where he proceeded to fuck me, laying on my back and then laying on my stomach. I slid to the floor when he was done and was staring into his enormous cock. I couldn't resist and took it into my mouth and had my way with him.

He then began showing me some of the other new toys that he had gotten since we were together and we tried some of them. He had a very large blue dildo (which looked just like a penis) that vibrated, and he inserted it into me and turned it on. It was amazing and I had several orgasms. While he had the dildo so far into me that only about an inch was outside of me, he began kissing me and the next thing I know, I was clenching on the dildo, and we couldn't get it out. Geez, Logan can't come near me when I have something in my pussy, or it will take a tow truck to pull it out!

He told me that he had mentioned me to one of his friends in Orlando. Logan told him that he had a "sex slave" (me), and she would do whatever he wanted. When his friend asked for a description, Logan said she had a "good personality." I slapped his arm and said that was boy talk for a girl who was a “dog.” He told me that’s exactly what Carl said. Then he said he was only kidding. Then Logan said we should drive up to Orlando to meet with his friend and one of his girlfriends, who is also into women. Then his friend and his girlfriend could have their way with me. I have to say, this whole idea is very intriguing to me. It makes me hot just thinking about it. We continued playing and laughing until he left at 8:30 p.m.

While Logan was here, my landline rang and it was…Bob…again…this is the third night in a row that he’s called me. He left a message and wanted me to call him back.

***

MONDAY

Logan came over at 3 p.m. He had sent me an email with a link to a porn site. The women were wearing bras, panties and thigh-high stockings. He said that’s what he wanted me to wear. So, when he arrived, I had on my lacy black bra, boy shorts, lace panties and thigh-high stockings with high heels. Also had on my gold collar and leash. He seemed to like the outfit. We sat in the Salon for a while, and then he had me strip out of everything and leave it all on the rug and led me into the Playroom by my leash.

We spent the next 3 hours pleasuring one another, and finally, he had a massive orgasm while I was playing with myself on the bed and he was laying next to me, watching me. I then went down to his pleasure center and licked up the cum and rubbed my face in it. I was so turned on I couldn't believe it. When he left at 6 p.m. my lady parts were still tingling.

***

WEDNESDAY

I met with Peter, the cartoonist, at a coffee shop in Delray. We talked and caught up on what we were doing. I get the feeling that he cares for me as more than just a friend. He wants to see me again next week in person. He later followed up with several texts that were quite personal and endearing.

I had a dance lesson with Justin at 3:30 p.m. We both wore masks (but I must say it was difficult to dance with a mask on). We have such chemistry when we're together. It doesn't help that he's holding me in his arms and staring into my eyes, and we're inches apart. He wanted to take me to his bedroom and play with me, but I resisted. He kissed me through the mask… He asked me when I would go out on a date with him. I told him that I needed him more as a dance instructor than as a lover. After my lesson, we sat in his kitchen for a while and talked. He said I was a beautiful woman and he really wanted to have sex with me. I must admit, I was very tempted. He's tall, dark and handsome with thick black hair that you could get lost in—and a small mustache with a soul patch (he's also in his 40s). Believe me, he can carry it off—he looks like a Latin lover… We made an appointment for a dance lesson next Wednesday at the same time.

Bob called when I got home. Told me he had a real estate agent coming over on Friday to see about selling his house. I asked him where he planned to move to, and he said California. I think it was a test to see how I would react to his relocating. I didn't discourage him. He then called again at 9:30 p.m. and woke me up. He said he was thinking about me and that he thought we should be married and then I could move to California with him (don't know what he's been smoking). He said he loved me and wanted to be with me. I honestly don't know what to do with him—I've told him a thousand times that I'm seeing another man, and it's serious, but he doesn't care. I really don't understand men. Is it the chase, the challenge, the fact that they want what they can't have…who knows?

***

THURSDAY

Logan came over at 2:30 p.m. (with his black gym bag full of goodies). I had on my lacy black bra, boy shorts, lace panties and thigh-high stockings with high heels as I did on Monday, but this time, I added a white button-front sweater that scooped low in front, exposing the top of my lacy bra. I only had a few of the buttons done, so it was open at the bottom for his viewing pleasure. I thought it was a very sexy look…like I had just been ravaged and was only half-dressed. Also added my lace and silk "handcuffs." I had ordered a set of chokers with sexy sayings on them and I wore the one that said "Fuck Me." He really liked the outfit. We went into the Salon, where he suggested that I kneel in front of him on a pillow instead of directly on the rug. We talked for a while. I pleasured him (which I can't get enough of), and then we went into the Playroom to explore the contents of his bag.

He had received a second flogger with a wooden handle that he decided to leave with me. He played with the flogger (used it all over my body teasing and stroking me…occasionally striking a serious blow), and then he got the belt out from my dresser… it had been a while since he used the belt because it left my ass bruised and looking like the back end of a zebra. He meted out 6 hits with the belt on my ass and made me count out each one (a la "50 Shades"). I can't explain why, but the belt turns me on… When he does these things, he uses a different voice—very serious—and gives me orders— "spread your legs," … "Bend over," … "Turn around" … it's like I'm a prisoner, and he is the prison guard making me do these things… I have no control of the situation and must submit or face more discipline… that voice just turns me on! And then when he's finished disciplining me, he fucks me and continues to order me around… There's something about giving up my power and feeling vulnerable that's very exciting…I'm at the mercy of this delicious, sexy man and must do whatever he wants (that's HOT!!).

We fucked and played with the toys and laid next to one another and talked and laughed… I swear, I've never laughed so much with a man after having sex… He left at 5:30 p.m., and I miss him already… He really pushes my "horny" buttons… I can never get enough.

Bob called and said he wanted to take me out to dinner on Friday. I'm so tired of arguing with him that I said OKAY. Maybe if I talk to him in person, he will read my lips… "I'm involved with someone else…"

***

FRIDAY

I'm feeling a little naughty today… I think I'll play with my mailman…He told me that if I ever wanted to see him, to put up the flag on my mailbox with no mail in it and he would come to the door. So today, that's what I did.

He walked up to my front door and rang the bell. When I opened it, he handed me the mail and a package. I was wearing a sexy black lace bra and panties under my men's white shirt (I love that shirt) and nothing else. The shirt was closed but not buttoned. As he stood there with his mouth wide open, I asked him if he had been a "good boy," and he said, "Yes." I slowly opened my shirt to reveal what was underneath. His breath caught and I thought he was going to come flying through the door and fuck me right on the floor, but he controlled himself. He said, "Stacey, you're killing me! I want to fuck you so bad it hurts. Now I'm going to be driving around all afternoon with a hard-on." I apologized and said I wouldn't do it again, but he said, "Oh no, you can do it anytime. But one day, you and I are going to get together and I'm going to finish what you started." I told him that I look forward to doing that. He limped away from my front door, but before he drove off, I opened my shirt one more time and waved goodbye (I'm such a bitch!). He shook his head and, bit his finger and drove away.

After he drove away, I opened the package he had left, which was my Sex Slave outfit. I went into my Playroom and tried it on and got so horny that I got out Mr. Buzzy and had a wonderful time… Several orgasms later, I was just laying there touching myself and imagining that my mailman was standing over me and watching me….and I had more orgasms! Maybe I should wear this outfit for my next encounter with the mailman.

I wonder what my Master would think about what I did… perhaps he will discipline me for being a bad girl… how many lashes with the belt would I get? How long would I be deprived of grapes? Should I even tell him?

Logan texted me today and asked what I was doing. I had not expected to hear from him since he said he was working this weekend. I told him I had been working on my book and was about to go into the pool. He said to leave the front door unlocked, and he would be right over and meet me in the pool. (I then texted and left a voice mail for Bob cancelling our dinner date for that night.)

Logan arrived at 2 p.m., let himself in and took his clothes off in the TV room. He watched me in the pool from the patio door as I enjoyed the jet that pleasured my pussy. I was a little startled when he opened the patio door, and he just smiled since he knew what I had been doing. He joined me in the water and we talked and played and kissed.

When we had enough of the "water sports," we went inside to the Playroom and got down to some serious business. As we were talking, we got on the subject of my dating other guys when he was away. I said that I asked them to do some things to me… he asked what things… I said I asked them to smack my ass, pull my hair and talk dirty to me… Logan was shocked that I had asked other men to do to me what he considered his "moves." I tried to explain that those were things that I missed and what was the harm in asking for them. He was "furious" that I would even consider having other men do those things to me, and that deserved punishment. He made me get the belt, and he bent me over the bed and gave me 6 lashes with the belt, which he made me count out. He also used the new flogger as an added punishment. When he finished with my discipline, we laid on the bed and he soothed me and I pleasured him.

I reluctantly let him go at 6 p.m.

***

SATURDAY

Logan called. Said not to have too good a time with the Brit today (that's what he calls him). He's adorable.

Jordan arrived at 4 p.m. I was wearing my men's white shirt over my lacy black bra, boy shorts, lace panties and thigh-high stockings. I opened the door and told him that I was sorry, but I was running late and had not finished getting dressed. He didn't blink. He entered carrying two bags of what was to be our dinner and we went to the kitchen to unpack (Jordan is very cool like that—most men would have gotten a little flustered). We had drinks (Jordan had limeade and I had a glass of wine). I had been feeling dizzy all day and did not plan to drink, but I took a chance anyway. We decided that we would have dinner first and then go into the pool. He brought turkey meatloaf, artichoke salad and cheesecake mousse for dessert from Whole Foods.

After we ate, we went into the Playroom, got out of our clothes and went into the pool. That didn't last very long since a thunderstorm was approaching. We went inside, dried off and got into bed. He went down on me, and I had several orgasms (he's very good at that). I gave him a blow job, and he was moaning with pleasure. Then he pulled my ass up over his face, and we were doing the 69. Finally, exhausted, he held me in his arms, and we fell asleep for a short while.

When we woke up, I suggested that we have dessert. After dessert, he got dressed, and I walked him to the door. He left at 8:30 p.m., setting another date for next Saturday.

As I was reading back in my diary, I realized that it was Jordan who introduced me to BDSM. I had almost forgotten. It was before Logan came back from California, and I was in a learning mode. Jordan would bring over sex books, and he was the first to tie me to the door. He saw the Bondage Beginner Kit that I ordered, and we did use some of the items while we played. However, since Logan came back into the picture, I don't feel comfortable doing that with Jordan (call me crazy—but I can't be playing these games with 2 "Masters").

While Logan knows about Jordan, Jordan doesn't know about Logan. Both men say they are not jealous but I wonder if I told Jordan that I was seeing someone else regularly, what his reaction would be. Right now, I don't want to rock the boat because I'm enjoying both men. I really am a sex addict…

***

SUNDAY

I was surprised when Logan contacted me today and wanted to come over. Anyway, I'm always happy to hear from him. He asked if I was going to be home, and if so, could he come over.

Logan arrived at 1:00 p.m. I greeted him at the door wearing my naughty schoolgirl outfit with white knee socks and black flat shoes. Underneath, I had on my red lacy bra and, boy shorts panties. My hair was in pigtails, and I had one of my new collars on that said, "Daddy's Girl."

We went to the salon, where I knelt on a pillow at his feet, and we played out the father/daughter scenario. I unbuttoned his shirt and began kissing his chest and sucking on his nipples. We talked according to the "script" of Daddy and errant daughter while I worked my way down to his pants. I unbuttoned and unzipped them and released his delicious cock, which I proceeded to play with. While I could have gone on like this for hours, I wanted to see the "toys" he brought in his now oversized gym bag.

I took off my clothes (except for the white knee socks and panties), and he opened the bag and showed me some of the new things he had gotten. Of course, we had to try them. He handed me a small vibrator that goes into the panties. I tried it and had such a wave of pleasure I thought I would swoon—it was great! Then there was the "50 Shades" vibrator (just a tiny thing that is inserted into the pussy that gives a heavenly massage). There were vibrating balls that made me crazy and a vibrator that you put on your finger and rub on your clit. By this time, my panties were on the floor. There were so many other contraptions that I felt like it was Christmas morning… and Santa had come… (I wish).

He asked me what I wanted to do today. I said I didn't want to be hung on the door, but I did want him to tie me to the bed. We put on the black wrist cuffs, and he got out the purple silk rope and tied my cuffs to the rope, then tied the rope to the base of the headboard. This was much more secure than the bed restraint. Once I was restrained and laying spread eagle on the bed, he began playing with the various devices on my pussy. He was touching me all over—even with the new flogger. OMG, I was so turned on. He finally put on the finger fucker (or as I call it—Little Mr. Buzzy) and used it on me. I thought my head would explode. I had so many orgasms that I asked him to stop so I could catch my breath. He put an ice cube in my mouth to cool me off. Then I asked him to put another ice cube in my pussy to see what that would feel like. It was shocking at first since I was so hot down there, but then it was refreshing. It melted in no time, and he rubbed the water over my body. My head was screaming with pleasure.

During his ministrations with the toys, he also got on top of me and fucked me. It was so frustrating not being able to move my arms. I was totally out of control. Then he would get the new flogger and tell me to spread my legs in that voice that makes me quiver, and he would smack my body (not to hurt me but just to awaken my senses). He would then drag the flogger over and around my pussy, teasing me and getting me close to orgasm but then backing away. Geez, I was going crazy. When I would have orgasms, I screamed at the top of my lungs (if the neighbors heard, they would think someone was killing me—truth be told, he was "killing me.")

He finally untied me and made me lay the top half of my body across the bed. Then he got out the belt. He had not used the belt in quite a while since it marked up my ass so badly, but now the bruises were almost gone, so we could start again. He gave me 20 hard lashes, using the flogger in between… He seemed to get so turned on doing it, and I was so turned on receiving it.

We went on like this for hours, taking short breaks to talk and laugh, and then I got into my favorite position (laying across the bed with my head buried in his manhood—licking and sucking and kissing it).

We took a break and went into the TV room, where we sat on the sofa and talked. Then, of course, I wound up kneeling in front of him again with his cock and balls in my mouth. We continued to play and enjoy one another's bodies until he left at 5 p.m.

When I think about the evolution of my friendship with Logan, I am totally surprised and confused at how we got to this point. I met him almost one year ago. We flirted by text and phone until we finally met. When we finally met, I told him that it had been 12 years since I last had sex. We tried to do it, but it was too painful, so I paid a visit to my gynecologist. She recommended a vaginal dilator and a prescription cream and said to come back in a month. I sat down with Logan and told him I couldn't see him anymore because I wasn't able to satisfy his sexual needs. He was very patient with me and supported me through the vaginal dilation, cream, and no sex for 2 weeks. What a trooper!

Anyway, we were finally able to have sex, and it was great. He took my virginity (for the second time in my life) and opened my "Pandora's Box" of pleasure. He would come over occasionally for a "booty call," which was great, but I didn't feel satisfied. He would go MIA for weeks at a time, and my sexual urges were totally frustrated. I realized that I had to find other outlets (other than my vibrator) to get my rocks off.

I read the "50 Shades" trilogy (twice) and watched the movies on TV whenever they were on. That lifestyle really turned me on but I needed to find someone I could trust to do some of those things to me. As I "auditioned" men, I realized that it was going to be a long road before I could ask a man to tie me up and hit me with a flogger. I also read a lot about BDSM and started finding items on the Internet that I could use. The first thing I ordered was a Bondage Starter Kit. I did send a text to Logan with a photo of the Kit, letting him know that I got it but didn't know what some of the items were for. I was surprised to find out that he could identify most of the items.

When Logan finally returned after about 3 months, he gave me a DVD (The Story of O), which I really enjoyed. That was "50 Shades" and BDSM on steroids. I was so turned on I couldn't sleep thinking about the scenarios in the movie. I guess that was the green light for Logan to assume that I was really into that kind of "kinky fuckery" as Anastasia said in "50 Shades."

And that brings us around to today… I can't go for one day without thinking about being tied, beaten, fucked, fondled… by Logan… and Logan seems happy to oblige… He's such a Sexy Mother Fucker (SMF).

***

MONDAY

I've been horny all day thinking about Logan. I sent him Sunday's "Update" and got him "hot" again… We went back and forth with our flirty emails until neither one of us could stand it any longer.

He came over at 5:30 p.m., and we went at it like dogs in heat! OMG, I can't keep my hands off of him. I was wearing a T-shirt and black panties with my hair in pigtails. He brought "Little Mr. Buzzy," and we wore out that poor toy… We fucked and sucked and kissed and talked until we couldn't move anymore. He even used the belt again.

He left at 8 p.m., and my pussy was still throbbing with desire. I can't get enough of that man.

***

WEDNESDAY

Logan came over at 1:00 p.m. Since we were going to try to set up the "hanging ropes" in the living room archway, I was wearing jeans and a T-shirt. I had everything laid out to construct our project—rope, scissors, ladder, screws—Wow! Sounds like a torture chamber.

Anyway, we figured out how to engineer the device and when we had it set up, Logan cuffed my hands and tied me to the ropes. I had taken off my t-shirt, bra and jeans and only had on my panties. I was hanging there, standing on my tiptoes, totally helpless. It was looking like the scene from "The Story of O" …, except I wasn't bruised and bloody…yet.

He began by using ice on my nipples to get them hard, then rubbed the melted water all over my body and in my pussy. He then removed my panties, and now I was stark naked, hanging from the archway. Geez, I was getting hot! Then he put on the vibrating nipple clamps. He stepped into the Playroom and came back with the big flogger and the belt. He was playing with the flogger, running it all over my body and teasing my pussy, but he wouldn't let me come. Then he would hit me with it—he used it on my breasts, my ass, my clit—I was in sexual agony.

Then came the big guns—the belt. He struck me with it on the ass as I hung there, unable to move or protect myself. The pleasure/pain of the belt cannot be described. I was so turned on that I thought I would pass out. I finally begged him to let me down and he had to hold on to me as he walked me to the Playroom. My legs felt like they were made of rubber. He made me lay on the bed on my stomach and used a hand vibrator to massage my backside. It felt so good after the beating I had taken.

I asked him if he had gotten pleasure out of what he had just done to me and he admitted that it really turned him on. I was so happy that my Master was pleased with me.

We played and kissed and fucked and talked on the bed for hours. I can't even count the number of orgasms I had! We would take breaks and I would bury my head in his manhood and suck and lick and kiss his cock and his balls as if I couldn't get enough…I really love doing that!

He left at 5:00 p.m. I don't need to say the state I was in.

Logan's Response to my Wednesday Entry:

The book is getting more filled up with HOT adventures. I think we make a pretty good team coming up with NEW construction projects around the house for our sexual adventures. It was a HOT afternoon.

I love our new Hanging Hallway project. I am so glad that it gave you a new thrill. I am sure you had very nice dreams last night and, more than likely, this morning. I sometimes have to pinch myself that you are really real. Your sexuality and libido have set a new standard for me, and it is so much fun to be with someone with whom we can push our limits safely and enjoy one another so profoundly.

I have never experienced the pain/pleasure, but I am so glad you're enjoying it. As you say, we are two sides of the same coin. I think Vanilla sex is pretty much not an option for either of us anymore.

I suggest you get a magazine to read on Saturdays with the Brit. lol

The Master

***

FRIDAY

Logan came over at 10:00 a.m. We discussed his friend from Orlando coming over next Friday with his girlfriend. Logan had asked me to contact the woman to discuss our meeting.

Apparently, Logan has been telling his friend about our BDSM activities and how hot they are. With the competitive nature of men, it's going to be like, "My girlfriend is hotter than your girlfriend…she will do ANYTHING I ask…" Oh, Geez… It's not that easy to slide into the BDSM lifestyle without some preparation. Don't know how much of that we can/want to share with those two. I'm sure Logan's friend would love to watch it (it's a man's wet dream).

I'm very curious as to how far Logan's friend's date will go with this fantasy next week. If I read her text correctly, she thinks it will be more of a "swinging" situation rather than a girl-on-girl show… Sounds like she wants to have more guy action than girl action. She's thinking we're just going to kiss…Logan wants us to go all the way… I'm okay with it, but we'll see how that works out.

After a while, Logan and I went to the Playroom and tried some new toys—the clit sucker was amazing… I love all the toys my Master brings. Logan left at 12:30 p.m., and I was still more than excited!

***

SATURDAY

Logan called in the morning all chipper and asked what I was doing on Sunday. I told him my friend, Suzette, was coming over at 1 p.m. for lunch and a swim. He said he might come over later on Sunday.

Jordan came over on Saturday at 4 p.m. I was wearing my Calvin

Klein dress with the lavender teddy underneath. I made pasta with olive oil and a vegetable salad. We went into the kitchen for drinks (Jordan had limeade and I had white wine). We talked for a while, and then Jordan dug into the salad—it was very good. Then I plated the pasta. Jordan always says, "Not too much," … but I gave him a big helping anyway and said to eat what he could. Well, low and behold, he ate the whole thing and said it was delicious. He said I could make that anytime for him.

After we ate, we went into the pool naked. He sat on the bottom step leading into the pool and I was facing him with my legs wrapped around him. We talked and kissed and finally had enough and went inside for dessert. He had brought a slice of cake that we had before—absolutely delicious.

Eventually, we worked our way into the Playroom for a "nap." We did lay there for a while, then we started kissing. He went down on me and pulled my ass over his head and we were in the 69 position (which seems to be his favorite). I really got off, then I tried to satisfy him. He seems to enjoy it when I give him a blow job, but he never comes. We went back and forth for some time—rest, talk, fuck, repeat.

Jordan left at 8:30 p.m. While he was here, I heard my cell phone ping with a text. After Jordan left, I read the text from Logan at 6:19 p.m.— "What time is the Brit gone?" … I texted back at 8:41 p.m.

that "He just left." ...He said, "Are you all full of pasta?" ...I responded, "The pasta was delicious. I have leftovers. Plus, the salad was a hit. But I really miss you!!" That was SO true. No matter who I'm with, I can't stop thinking about Logan.

I cleaned up the kitchen and got into bed. At 10 p.m. my cell phone rang… It was Bobby calling to check in on me. He's someone who's been following me on Facebook (never met him). He has a TV show. He thinks he's in love with me. Has been out of commission for the last several months with Covid but is recovering. He wants to have coffee with me in a couple of weeks. Before he hung up, he said, "Take care of that beautiful face." Sweet guy.

***

SUNDAY

Logan came over at 10:00 a.m. I was wearing my Calvin Klein dress with black lace undies. We sat in the salon, and I was asking questions about our upcoming meeting on Friday with his friends. I told him I didn't want to watch him fucking the woman. He became indignant, and I said I'm not asking him NOT to fuck her…I just don't want to watch. He said, "What am I supposed to do? Go into another room?" I got into a hissy fit, and I was sorry I even brought up the subject. After all, even if he's fucking her, I'll be fucking his friend! So, at least I'm getting something out of it.

I'm really going around and around about this meeting on Friday. It seems like it's going to be more "swinging" than BDSM. I've never done that in my life and I'm not sure how it works. I think I'll need to have a lot of wine so that I'm relaxed. I'm not inhibited, but until I understand the "rules," I'm going to be insecure. I don't mind fucking his friend…it's just doing something with the woman that bothers me. Both Logan and his friend were swingers with their wives years ago, so they are familiar with switching partners. Anyway, my entry after this adventure is sure to add a blistering chapter to my book.

In the Playroom, Logan beat me with the flogger and belt to punish me for being a "brat" earlier. He really got off on it—I guess I must have pushed his buttons, and he was so upset with me that he took it out on my ass. Anyway, I did enjoy it! He left at 12:30 p.m. so I could get ready for my next guest (Suzette).

My friend Suzette came over at 1 p.m. for lunch and a swim. I reheated the pasta from the night before, and we had that and the leftover vegetable salad. I also had chocolate cake for dessert. We talked for quite some time because it had started raining and we had to wait to go into the pool. Suzette is so intelligent that she's a pleasure to talk to.

When the sun finally came out, we changed and went into the pool. Unfortunately, that didn't last long since another thunderstorm was coming our way. She left at 4 p.m., and we decided that it would be fun to do it again.

***

MONDAY

Well, I'm still angry with Logan after our "argument" yesterday about fucking his friend's date. I don't know why it bothers me so much…yes, I do…it's because I'm in love with Logan, and I hate to see him making love to someone else (of course, "swinging" isn't making love so much as just FUCKING). Anyway, I'll get over it and not mention it again if I don't want to drive Logan away from me and then REALLY into another woman's arms. One of the complaints he had about his second wife was that she was jealous and was always accusing him of looking at women when they were out. I'm trying to "counteract that effect" and am trying not to be ANYTHING like her!!! I just have to reign in my jealousy and not overreact.

Just like I had "revenge sex" when Logan was MIA, I did something I shouldn't have done today… I went on the Lesbian dating site, where most of the inquiries were from horny men. I struck up a conversation with a man named Joel from Boca. We privately texted back and forth, and he wanted to meet me. He's in love with my picture from the site (I'm dressed in my cowgirl outfit). We'll see what happens.

Joel called me several times tonight… told me he thought I was sexy, beautiful and was a fantasy woman. He said all of the things I wanted to hear from Logan. He wants to meet me in person to see if we have any "chemistry." He says he's in lust with me and can't stop thinking about me. I needed to hear that to boost my confidence before my encounter on Friday.

BTW…Logan never contacted me today…not by phone, email or text…and not in person either… I wonder if he's upset with me for my outburst on Sunday.

***

TUESDAY

Logan called me after I sent him a text saying, "Hope you're having a good day." He was all chipper. Said he was busy yesterday and needs to buy his daughter a machine for her job that costs $5K. He has his son coming over today to work with him and he went to the store and bought chicken to make for dinner.

I had just gotten out of the pool and was wrapped in my beach towel and decided to have some fun with the mailman. I stood by the front door with only my towel on when he arrived at my mailbox. He had put the mail into the box, but when he saw me, he removed the mail, turned off his truck and came to the door. He stepped inside and handed me the mail which I put on the entry table. I then opened my towel and almost gave him a heart attack as he looked at my naked body. He caressed my breasts and sucked on my nipples. Then he kissed me. He had a major hard-on… He limped back to his truck, shaking his head… I hope he went home and fucked his wife. She'll thank me later.

Bob keeps calling…

***

WEDNESDAY

Logan came over at 10:30 a.m. I was wearing a Calvin Klein dress with black underwear. We discussed what was going to happen on Friday. We went over the schedule and how the house should be set up…things we needed…all the details… we really worked well together. I'm getting so excited I can't sleep.

Then we went into the Playroom to try out the new Spreader Bar that I got. A leg spreader bar is a type of sex toy designed to keep the legs parted, with a rigid central bar and ankle cuff at each end.

He attached the cuffs to my ankles and then played with me through my panties, which we left on. He pulled the panties down to get to my pussy, and all I wanted him to do was to rip them off. We decided later that I would buy some inexpensive panties and have him either rip them off or cut them off when he has me in the Spreader…very sexy.

We set up the Spreader on the door and decided that it could also be used to hang me instead of using the rope. Then we hung a bunch of stuff on it…the flogger, the dog collar with spikes, the purple leash and the rope (for good measure). It really looked like a dungeon…so cool… I wonder what our Friday "guests" will think when they see the setup… I hope they give us a good Yelp review.

Logan left at 12:30 p.m., and I continued to prepare the house for our Friday adventure.

I had my dance lesson with Justin at his house at 3:30 p.m. I had on my black underwear, but I added a black garter belt and black stockings…I was going to seduce him today.

While we were dancing, a woman came in his door and just stood there looking at us. I quietly asked him if it was his "girlfriend," and he indicated that they were more than friends. Well, that killed the mood as far as my seducing him. While I was preparing to leave, I lifted my dress and showed him my garter belt and that took his breath away. He said we could get together at my house next week, but I declined.

Again, Bob keeps calling…

Jordan called with a "Hello Gorgeous" … we decided on our plans for Saturday. He wants me to cook pasta again with the same vegetable salad we had last week. He said he would bring dessert.

Joel called and again gushed all over me, wanted to schedule a coffee and can't wait to see me.

***

THURSDAY

I had my session this morning with my personal trainer. I told him what was going to happen on Friday with Logan's friends. He said it would be a disaster and that I would hate it. I got upset with him and told him not to rain on my parade. I was just curious and had never done anything like that before. He asked me to send him a text on Saturday with a thumb's up or thumb's down on how the date went, then I could fill him in on the details next week.

After my session, I went to BJ's and Publix to pick up food for our "party." Logan said he would stop over to help me set up and do whatever had to be done.

Logan arrived at noon, and I had most of the "staging" done. I just wanted his input in case I forgot anything. I told him what happened with my dance instructor and he was not very happy with me. He said he didn't mind if I did things like that, BUT I couldn't lie to him about it. Now, that is going to inhibit anything I might want to do in the future because I'll feel that Logan is already anticipating my moves, and I won't enjoy it.

He did use the purple leash on me to punish me and it really hurt! My ass was stinging after he left at 3:00 p.m.

Bob called me several times. He was worried that I wasn't feeling well and sent me the link for the Covid questionnaire. He keeps asking to see me and wants me to move to California with him. I keep telling him I'm seeing someone and it's serious, but he doesn't care.

Joel called several times. He says he can't stop looking at my picture and wants to meet me in person. He says he's in "lust" with me. Lord help me… I wish I knew how to control this thing I have—must be sending out very strong signals to the opposite sex.

Peter also called to tell me he was putting the animated cartoon of the photo he took of me when we had coffee 2 weeks ago into the local newspaper. He wants to see me again soon.

***

FRIDAY

Well, today's the big day. I was up at 4 a.m. THINKING… Logan and I had talked about having an "exit interview" survey form for his friends to get their input on how the day went. I created the survey and sent it over to Logan for his input. So far, I'm being very "clinical" about this upcoming meeting. I guess it's one way not to think about how nervous I am.

Logan came over at 2 p.m. to help me set up for the party. There was not much left to do, so we went into the Playroom and fucked for a while before they got there.

His friends arrived around 4 p.m. I met them at the door with big hugs and kisses. I was wearing my black Dominatrix dress with red lace bra and red lace boy shorts. We fixed them drinks—tequila on ice for her, Banana Whiskey for Logan and white wine for Logan's friend and me. We went into the living room to chat and get to know one another better. I was a little surprised at how comfortable we became with each other very quickly.

After a bit, we decided to go into the pool, and I took the woman into my Playroom to change. I showed her my drawer of toys and the tray where Logan had set up an assortment of toys that we could try. We all got naked and went into the pool.

At first, I was with Logan in the water, and his friends were together—caressing and kissing. Then, the boys encouraged us girls to get together and play a little. So, she and I started kissing—this was the first time either of us had kissed another woman (like that). Then we started playing with one another's tits and clits, and the next thing you know, we're having orgasms in the pool. I think the boys were really enjoying the show. I was surprised at how comfortable I was doing sexual things with a woman and didn't for one minute think about people watching.

It wasn't long before we switched partners, and the woman and Logan were going at it—kissing, sucking, petting. She gave him several blow jobs, which I'm sure he enjoyed. In the meantime,

Logan's friend and I are kissing, and he's finger fucking me, and I'm getting very excited. I may have gotten carried away with my kisses, but what the hell—as Logan says, "It's only sex."

The four of us were playing and cumming and making so much noise (we girls are very loud when we climax). I'm surprised my neighbors didn't call the police…

We finally had to get out of the pool because it started raining hard and there was thunder and lightning… We dried off a little, then went into the house, where we sat in the living room wearing only our towels and had some snacks and more to drink. By this time, I'm feeling no pain and am ready to do anything.

We played a game that I found on the Internet, which was hysterical—take a card with a scenario on it and respond to how you would react.

After the game, we went into my Playroom and got on my bed. The boys encouraged the woman and me to continue kissing and touching while they stood there and watched. We kissed and rubbed one another's clits and sucked one another's tits—it was so hot! Then the boys decided to dig into this pile of flesh and add some cocks to the mix. She was eating me, and Logan's friend was eating me, and I was eating her, and Logan was eating us both. OMG, it was hotter than some of the porno flicks I had been watching all week. Then while she was giving Logan a blow job, someone was playing with my pussy. There were so many arms and legs and cocks and pussies, you couldn't tell who was doing what. Then Logan's friend got on the bed and started kissing me. I closed my eyes and pretended he was Logan and my kisses became so passionate that I think his friend was surprised. I was running my fingers through his hair and caressing his face and he was getting so excited that I thought his kisses were going to completely envelop me.

We went on playing with one another like this for hours…it was so hot…my very first ORGY… Then we finally took a break and went into the living room for some snacks—Logan's friends were on one loveseat, and Logan and I were on the other—all totally NAKED. No one was self-conscious about doing that. The woman was caressing her date, and I was sucking Logan's dick while we chatted. It was total debauchery… I felt like my native Italian ancestors must have felt when they held their orgies in Rome… that's what I call going back to your roots.

While we were sitting there, Logan suggested that he hang me in the living room archway by the cuffs. He tied my wrists up to the restraints and proceeded to beat me with the flogger and the belt while his friends watched. Then he asked if the woman wanted to try it, and she was game. So, Logan tied her up and hit her (pretty lightly) with the flogger, and she got so excited that she "squirted" all over the floor. I had never seen a woman do that. It was like she was peeing, but it wasn't urine. Logan's friend tried very hard earlier to get me to "squirt" by finger fucking me, but we just couldn't make it happen. When Logan was tying up the woman for her turn at being whacked, I moved over to the loveseat to sit with his friend so I would have a better view of the "beating." He started playing with my tits, and I didn't mind one bit. Logan said later that he was a little surprised by my move to sit next to his friend and have him play with me. I really didn't give it a second thought. It was just a continuation of what we had been doing all evening.

The one thing I didn't feel was guilt about what I was doing. I enjoyed playing with another woman and with another man while Logan was watching and just getting raunchy with no inhibitions. I didn't really watch what Logan was doing to the woman as she kept screaming and squirting but continued to satisfy myself with whatever his friend wanted to do with me.

Logan's friends left around 8 p.m. (I guess to go to their hotel to continue to fuck and squirt).

After they left, Logan and I started fucking again. It was like we couldn't get enough of each other. Plus, I was so turned on by the earlier events that I didn't want the high to stop. We talked about the evening, and both thought it was very successful, and we want to do it again. We eventually wound up in the TV room listening to an "Easy Listening" station—both of us just wearing shirts with nothing else on. We talked and kissed, and I sucked his cock, and before I knew it, it was after midnight, and I didn't want it to end. Logan left at 12:30 a.m., and I was still so excited and hot that I couldn't stop thinking about what we had done and reliving the excitement of the evening.

I was so glad that Logan had suggested this experience. I feel like we are both pushing the envelope and are getting more and more turned on. I feel like I never want this feeling to go away.

***

SATURDAY

I can't believe it, but Logan wanted to come over on Saturday. He knows it's my day with Jordan but it didn't seem to matter. He arrived at 12:30 p.m. (just 12 hours after he left the night before). I was wearing my jeans and a T-shirt (I didn't even have the energy to dress up.) I had awakened with an episode of Vertigo. I was dizzy and didn't feel very well—I think it was from lack of sleep and dehydration (and maybe all that fucking).

We sat in the salon and talked for a while and then we wandered into my Playroom. I took off my jeans and panties and bent over the bed then he hit me with the flogger and fucked me, but then the whole room started spinning. He had me lay on the bed to try to recover. I was so dizzy I became nauseous. I told him that I get these episodes of Vertigo from time to time and they usually passed in a day or two. He said, "Why didn't you tell me about this?" Geez, it's not like I have a terminal illness or a communicable disease. It's just something I've been living with for years. Then we just talked and hugged and passed the time together. He left at 2:30 p.m.

Jordan arrived about 4 p.m. I had the same outfit on as I had with Logan—jeans and a T-shirt. I apologized that I didn't have a fantasy ready for him and I told him about my Vertigo episode, and he was very understanding. He brought a box full of cake—6 slices. He also gave me a "motorcycle" jacket that he ordered for me. I'm not sure where that gesture came from. He doesn't have a motorcycle and it was not something that we ever discussed, but the gesture was very sweet.

We had our drinks (Jordan had limeade and I had cranberry juice—didn't want to get any dizzier with alcohol). We started with the vegetable salad then had the pasta that I made. I don't think he really liked the pasta with red sauce, so he only had a small portion. He said he really wanted the spaghetti with olive oil that I made last week. Okay…noted.

After we ate, we sat in the TV room and I laid down with my legs across his lap. I was still dizzy. We talked for a while, then decided to get into the pool. After we got out, we sat on the wicker sofa on the patio and just talked. Then he said he was tired, so we went into the Playroom and he got into bed to take a nap. I covered him with a blanket. Then, I went to the kitchen to clean up and get the Scrabble game ready.

When he finally got up, we played a game of Scrabble—he won 426 to 249. He left at 8:45 p.m.

In between all of these comings and goings with my men, I got a call from Joel, oozing over me and wanting to get together soon because he was in lust with me.

Of course, not to be left out, Bob called. Again, with the moving to California and taking me with him. And, AGAIN, I said I was involved with another man, and there was no way we were ever going to get together. I can see creating a sub-scenario (fiction, of course) where he gets some of his "questionable friends" to kidnap me and take me to the Victorian house he's remodeling in California, where I am held prisoner in the basement. Geez… what an imagination I have. But folks… if I suddenly disappear, please don't overrule that option.

Also got a text from Logan's friend thanking me for a great evening— "It was incredible" and "I just love the way U kiss." … Another good Yelp review.

***

SUNDAY

Logan came over at 11 a.m. I was wearing jeans and a T-shirt with pretty lace undies. I had just finished coloring my hair…OMG, what a mistake… I tried a new product and came out looking like the Little Mermaid (the red hair was screaming). Logan called me Ariel but was very kind and said all the right things. At least it will be gone in a few weeks.

We went directly into the Playroom, and he laid down on the bed. I then straddled him and stayed on top of him (which is unusual because he's the Dom and I'm the Sub). But it was fun for a change. We talked dirty and got one another into a super state of excitement (which doesn't take long anymore). We then morphed into our regular roles, and he took off my jeans, t-shirt and bra and cuffed me to the door. He used ice on my nipples and sucked them until they were standing at attention. He put on the vibrating nipple clamps and then used the flogger on my body. Since I still had my panties on, he would cup his hand down there and run some ice over my lady parts. Geez, I thought I would die! He beat me with the flogger, and when he finished "beating" my front, he turned me around (still hanging) and recuffed my hands and began using the flogger on my backside. I was in agony/ecstasy… He really seems to get pleasure out of this scenario.

After I could no longer take it (my wrists were getting sore from hanging there), he uncuffed me and walked me to the bed. He bent me over the bed and continued striking my ass. When he finished, I fell to the floor, and his cock was in my face, ready to be sucked and fondled. I really love that cock. When he was satisfied, he raised me from my knees and threw me on the bed on my back and proceeded to fuck me until I screamed with pleasure and had mind-blowing orgasms.

At this point, we took a break, and he held me in his arms on the bed. We talked and laughed (my God, this man can make me laugh!) and kissed. It wasn't long before we were ready to fuck again. We went on like this for hours.

Finally, we were both spent and hungry, so we went into the kitchen, and I reheated the pasta from the night before. We were sitting at the kitchen table in just shirts. I had on his white dress shirt with nothing underneath and it brought to mind that scene in "50 Shades" where Anna was making breakfast for Christian and wiggling her ass, then turned around to see him and said, "I'm making pancakes!" That was such a cute scene.

While I was reheating the pasta, Logan dug into the vegetable salad (seemed to like it). We devoured pasta dinner and then were ready for dessert (no really… actual dessert). Logan had brought cannolis (it's our inside joke— "Leave the gun…take the cannolis"). So, we shared a cannoli, talked for a while and went back into the Playroom.

We tried a new scenario…I was bent over the bed and he was beating my ass with the flogger. He was a prison guard, and I was his prisoner. While he beat me, other guards were watching and waiting for their turn to fuck me. I was whimpering and moaning, and he was yelling at me to be quiet (in that deep voice that so turns me on). Then, I decided to throw some improvisation into the mix. I got up from the bed, turned around and pushed him away and started screaming for him to stop hitting me. The look on his face was priceless! He didn't know what the fuck was going on—did I lose my mind? Finally, when I started laughing, he realized that I went "off script" on this fantasy, and he picked up the new dialogue. We then needed another rest on the bed—more talking, cuddling, laughing, kissing.

We talked about him getting guys to come over and fuck me while he watched. That was such a hot fantasy. I swear, the two of us can be dangerous when put together…it's like Bonnie and Clyde on steroids… I even brought up that we could travel to Amsterdam and steal some diamonds and smuggle them back to the States in my pussy. Wow!

We went on and on for hours with our playtime. What a fabulous way to spend a Sunday afternoon. He left at 7:30 p.m. (check out the time, folks—how many of you had that many hours of marathon sex? If it was an Olympic sport, we would probably win the Gold).

Logan's response to the above Update:

Good Morning, my Little Mermaid. Another GREAT weekend Update...

What great FUN Yesterday. By the time I got home, showered and watched a little TV, I was hard and horny for you again. I have no idea what we would do if we spent the night together or went on a trip together. We would have to make a pact to actually get some sleep.

As always, you make it a fun day. I love our role-play, and yes, you did get me on that one yesterday, but I will be ready the next time. I did like the prison guard one. We need to get you one of those orange jumpsuits the convicts wear.

I like the ice, so I can get your nipples as erect as I can get them. Then, the warmth of my mouth feels so great on your ice-cold nipples as I warm them up, only to ice them down again. You really seem to like the vibrating nipple clamps. I sometimes forget they are on you.

I am liking beating you more and more, and I think about it when I am not there. I am often tempted to keep it up until you call out RED, I was sort of there yesterday. I love it when I can beat away your will until you crumble on the floor, having lost all sense of your previous self and become MY property. Holding on just to stay upright and kneeling in a subordinate role. It is then that I like to comfort you and reassure you that your Master loves you and that you ARE a GOOD Girl when you continually attempt to find new ways to please your Master.

I think it is that deep seeded roleplay that both of us like. Both of us depart from our normal and usual lifestyle. You, a strong-willed woman, eager to be controlled, told what to do, and feel the pain and pleasure and daily anticipation of bodily punishment. It becomes like a tonic you must have on a daily basis to balance your life.

Me, normally a nice, funny and gentle person. I find myself wanting to control you and bring out a firm but fair Master to his subordinate slave. I revel in the thought and image of you as a human belonging to me and property to do with, as I will, in our fantasy world. I do think that will expand as we continue into other areas of our lives. I sometimes wonder if we are ready for how this will continue to grow. I guess the only way to find out is to try it.

I love that you enjoy having your body used and viewed by others as well. I really loved flogging you in front of my friends. As with any other property of mine, such as a new car, I want others to see it and enjoy it. Show it off, if you will. As a sexual object, you should be seen and used. Men on dating sights have indicated that they find you attractive. I am sure they have fantasies, and we of the Oasis Gentleman's Club are in the business of making those dreams come true.

Be it a man or a woman or both, I know it will give you, me, and others the pleasure to play with and use you. I know your sexual desires will grow and grow as they have over the past few months.

Our Club could be quite an Oasis of pleasure for many. Not many people get to move forward in their dreary lives and think out of the box... to push the envelope of their own sexuality to the brink of eroticism.

I think you're getting more and more mentally prepared for it all. Flashes of desire and increased creativity. Together, we can take both of us to exciting new limits.

I will strive to find new ways to increase the pain/pleasure experience for you. We have now embarked upon a potential anal adventure. Perhaps, and hopefully, it will be enjoyable.

We move to include new additions to Stacey's Playroom of Pain and Pleasure with men who desire to simply have sex with you and women with whom you can give and receive feminine pleasures with and from.

Looking forward to seeing you again and hearing your new thoughts on Sunday's topics.

THE MASTER

***

FRIDAY

I haven't made an entry all week (shame on me!). But this week has been "all about Logan." He came over Monday, Tuesday, Wednesday, Thursday and Friday. Needless to say, all of his visits included mind-blowing sex. I can't seem to get enough! We even graduated to deciding to experiment with anal sex (Wow! Never thought I would do that!).

He brought me about a dozen pair of lace panties (plus some "schoolgirl" panties for under my naughty schoolgirl outfit), purple butt plugs (to stretch myself for easier access—similar to the vaginal dilator), rubber gloves, and anal lubricant… He also gave me a silver ID bracelet engraved with "His Angel," an Infiniti sign and a pink stone. He's so sweet and sexy—NEVER met a man like him.

After going through all of the goodies he brought, we went into the Playroom and donned some rubber gloves, lubricated them and fingered one another in the ass. Pretty hot!

We went into the pool for a while and talked about the Oasis Gentlemen's Club and all of the things we've already accomplished—T-shirts, business cards, Zoom account, special email account, and the list keeps growing. I've been trying to recruit men to join the club and had a Zoom call scheduled with a man, but it fell through and we will have to reschedule. Another man—Jason— will let me know when I can Zoom call him next week.

They are both interested in joining the Club, so we'll see what happens.

I also joined 2 other dating sites looking for women for me to play with (that's in addition to the one I'm currently on—which seems to be attracting only men).

After the pool, we went out for something to eat. We went to Duffy's (it was our second date-). It was such a shot of "normal" in our otherwise crazy lives. When we returned, we went into the Playroom and went crazy AGAIN. We really tear up the bed when we're together. The passion is more than I thought I could ever rise to. I can't believe how I totally lose control when I'm with him. I buried my head in his manhood as he was laying on the bed and I was kneeling at his feet—just sucking and licking and caressing his cock and balls and body. I got so excited that I had an orgasm (without even touching myself—twice!).

On one of his visits during the week, I mentioned how crazy I got with a former boyfriend when we smoked pot and then had sex, so he's arranging to get some as an experiment. How much crazier and out of control can I get than I already am? The man has introduced me to sexual adventures that some women can only dream about!

***

SATURDAY

Jordan arrived at 4 p.m. I was wearing black slacks and a print blouse (didn't want to dress up for a fantasy). In lieu of food, he brought me a book, "Red Shoe Diaries." We had our drinks in the kitchen and chatted for a while. We had dinner in the dining room (he had mentioned last weekend that would be nice). I made his favorite spaghetti with olive oil and the vegetable salad which is quite good.

After we ate and relaxed at the dining room table for a while, we got undressed and went into the pool. We talked, and he caressed my breasts and kissed a little, but to tell the truth, my heart wasn't in it. All I could think about was Logan. That man invades all of my thoughts.

We got out of the pool, dried off and went into my Playroom and laid down on the bed. I was shivering because after coming in from the warm pool, the house seemed unusually chilly. We got under the covers naked, and he held me to warm me up. I had already told him that there was going to be no fooling around because of my infection. He didn't argue. But I did say I would take care of him. So, after I warmed up, I went down on him and had him moaning and groaning. I knew he wouldn't climax (because he never does), but I kept it up until he moved my head up to his shoulder.

This was about the time he usually took his nap, and I took the opportunity to clean up the kitchen and load the dishwasher. After I finished, I went back to the Playroom, and he was watching TV. He asked if there was anything I wanted to see, so I tuned into a marathon of "Las Vegas," which I had been watching earlier in the day. We just laid there, him holding me until the witching hour approached, and he got up and got dressed. He left at 8:30 p.m.

Around 7 p.m. I heard my cell phone ping with a text message. It was from Logan. I answered his text after Jordan left, and we went back and forth for a little while. He will come over sometime tomorrow, and I can't wait to see him!!!

***

SUNDAY

OMG… this was a day like no other in my life! I'm still trying to figure out if it was real or if it was a dream…

Logan came over at 11:30 a.m. He looked absolutely delicious wearing his blue sunglasses… I wanted to tear into him the minute he walked in the door. He is the sexiest man I've ever encountered… He had brought some surprises—one being 2 "joints"… I was ecstatic—it had been eons since I last did that and was excited to try it again.

We sat and talked for a while… couldn't keep my hands off him…

then we went into the pool (it was either that or he would have to spray me down with the garden hose!). After enjoying the pool, we sat on the patio sofa and lit up a joint. I didn't think anything was happening then it hit me like a thunderbolt.

I noticed that Logan had hurt his foot, so I told him to sit there on the patio, and I would get the first aid supplies. I went into the house and fumbled around in the medicine cabinet in my bathroom, seemed to be distracted by the least little things, then went out to the patio to minister to his wound carrying bandages, alcohol, disinfectant spray, cotton swabs... For as long as I was gone, the poor guy could have bled to death. I had no concept of time. He watched me as I tried to bandage his foot and finally got exasperated and took over the task. After his foot was all bandaged up, he helped me get inside the house since my walking skills were a bit compromised by the pot. We went into the bedroom and began tearing into one another. It was like I was in a porno film—everything was strange… his face kept changing… even though I was buried in his crotch, sucking and licking and kissing, I felt like I was alone and couldn't find him. I don't remember half of the things we did, but I do know that everything we did was enhanced and the pleasure was double what it would normally be. I do remember having multiple orgasms, even without touching myself. My body was on fire. I couldn't get enough of Logan.

We did try anal sex again—baby steps and I'm getting used to it. I also fingered him and he liked it as well.

Don't know how long we were going at it, but I started getting the "munchies," which I did recall happens when you smoke pot, so I suggested that I get up and cook. Logan thought I was in no condition to do that and thought that I might "burn down the kitchen." So, we waited for a while then I said I really wanted to eat something. We went into the kitchen and I took out the pasta from the night before and put it in a pan to reheat it. Apparently, I forgot to turn on the stove, so we ate cold pasta! I didn't notice. He did like the salad I made and filled up with that. I also had some cake leftover from the bounty I received from the Brit last weekend, so we had strawberry shortcake.

We went back into the Playroom and got back on the Merry-go-Round one more time. He videotaped some of our sex acts—in the state I was in, I didn't care.

Hours after we began our sexual journey, I was coming down from the enormous HIGH I was on. I was still having trouble formulating thoughts and would start to make an "important" point, then forget what the hell I was going to say.

As he was getting ready to leave, he showed me some costumes he got for himself—a Prison Guard Shirt with black leather pants (he's such a sexy mother fucker!) and a flight suit (I just love men in uniform). Can't wait to use those props in another of our fantasies (and…Scene…).

He left at 8:00 p.m. Check out the time, Ladies. Can your man spend the day in bed with you and fuck your brains out for that many hours??!! The bonus about all of that "exercise" and smoking the pot was that I slept like a baby… Can't wait to do it again!!!

Logan's Response to above Update:

Additions from this story remembered from a different perspective. I did perhaps cut myself on something in the pool, and, just finished the lawsuit papers which we can turn into the insurance company for personal injury and imminent loss of blood. After spotting blood on the pool deck, Stacey went into the house to get medical supplies. Approximately a half hour later she came back with half the bathroom. Two boxes of bandages, and one huge box of surgical pads? My baby toe was injured. She wiped down my whole foot with alcohol? Telling me it's going to hurt. It did not. Then pulls out the smallest bandage in the box and could not open it. I finally got a bigger one and tore it open, then she got it stuck on her fingers and spent ten minutes trying to figure how to get it off!

Yes, after fumbling around in the kitchen, we did have pasta. She stood at the stove mixing the pasta and never turned the heat on. She did however advise that it was just like eating left over cold Pizza. I did bring up the idea of getting a pizza, and we talked about it for a half hour, but I never got any pizza. She forgot.

Sex of course was super good. Much better than it normally is. Stacey thought we had company and kept asking who was here, so I just made-up names of men. She was very happy with that as long as she knew who was there. I advised they were all here to watch and fuck her and she replied with a simple OK! I told her to bend over the bed to get fucked by us all, and she did it without hesitation, but it took her two or three trips crawling around the bed to find the right spot. I started to fuck her, and she then asked me what I was doing? I simply said we are fucking you and taking turns. She just said OK, and began to wiggle her butt and begin singing "I am getting fucked," I am getting fucked." I then decided to beat her with the flogger and I gradually flogged harder and harder while she continued to wiggle her ass. I asked her if that hurt at all, and she replied, she did not feel anything?

We started many stories, but never finished any of them as she forgot. I apparently looked like other people, which confused her some but she was happy for the company and was willing to fuck or suck them as well.

A fun time was had by all and I hope to do that again soon. but next time, smoke very little pot. I had a great time and took some great video.

***

It's been a while since I made an entry in my diary… Logan and I have been seeing one another almost every day. It's like we're both "addicts" and we need a daily "fix."

***

WEDNESDAY

Anyway, I've been looking to find members for the Oasis Gentlemen's Club. I found a man online—Jason—who I "auditioned" by phone and text and then invited him to my house to meet with Logan and me.

Jason came over on Wednesday at 1:00 p.m. He was very prompt. When he arrived, I was in awe of his size! He did say he was 7' tall, 300 lbs. (ex-basketball player), but hey, guys always fudge about the size of things. Well, he was enormous and handsome and sexy. What a turn-on!! Logan is 6' tall and Jason towered over him.

We sat in the living room talking for a while then Logan mentioned our being into BDSM and some of the things we were into like tying me up and "beating" me. Jason was intrigued and asked for a demonstration. We went into the Playroom to work on the scenario. I was wearing my black dominatrix zip front dress with sheer pantyhose (no panties) and a black lacy bra. While I stood there, Jason unzipped my dress and took it off. Meanwhile Logan started removing my pantyhose. To make it easier, Jason lifted me up off the floor like I was a doll and Logan easily removed my pantyhose. Then Jason took off my bra and Logan cuffed me to the door. I was now totally naked. Jason began playing with my body and finger fucked me while I was restrained. OMG it was so hot having these 2 handsome men all over me and I was helpless to do anything about it.

Logan got the flogger and began his ritual of beating me in front then turned me around on the door and continued on my ass and legs. Meanwhile, Jason was taking in the scene from the bed. After Logan was through, he walked me to the bed where both men were naked and they began taking turns touching me and kissing me and doing whatever the hell they wanted to me. I was so turned on I couldn't even see straight. Then I saw the size of Jason's cock and I almost had a heart attack. It was the biggest, thickest thing I had ever seen in my life! I gave him a blow job but could hardly fit it into my mouth. Then he tried to get it inside of me. That turned out to be an exercise in futility. With the size of my vagina (very small) and the size of his cock (super, super large), there was no way that was going to happen. We tried anyway and he was very patient with me…whispering to me to slow down, think of a beautiful place, relax. He was so sweet! He made me melt.

Even though total penetration by Jason wasn't going to happen, we didn't let that stop us. We continued to play—to kiss and suck and fuck… Jason was laying on the bed and I was sucking his cock while Logan was fucking me in my pussy from behind. My first menage a trois… and I loved it!

Jason said he has several friends where he “services" the wife for the husband. The thing he does that I’m sure every woman would pay money for is that he continually compliments the woman—“You’re so sexy,” “You’re gorgeous,” “You’re absolutely breathtakingly stunning,” “You’re so beautiful"… God knows he probably says that to every woman (even if she looks like a troll) but who cares…it’s what women want and need to hear… By his reinforcing a woman’s sexuality and self-image with his “love talk," she becomes even more passionate so he benefits from the results as well.

As one final gesture Jason had me kneel before him while I gave him a blow job and he played with his cock (plenty of room for both of us). Then he came all over my face and in my mouth. Like everything about the man, it was a huge amount of cum (tasted pretty good). I had it all over me including my hair but I didn’t care. I got back on the bed and just laid there trying to recover. The boys were on either side of me petting me and touching me. It was amazing—being with two glorious men… Eat your heart out ladies!!

Jason left at 3 p.m. and Logan and I sat and reviewed the day. Jason became the first "member" of our Club and he promised to speak to some friends of his to see if others had an interest in joining. I can't wait to do that again.

Logan's version of the Meeting:

Yes, it was a fun afternoon with our new friend Jason. I was a good helper as he lifted Stacey and moved her around the room. It was fun to see her tied to the door as Jason fingered her eager and wet pussy into an exciting climax and orgasm. Love to hear her scream in pleasure. I thought when I saw Stacey hopping on top of Jason it was like watching her slide a tree stump into her waiting vagina. I stood by the bed with two cans of WD 40 and blasted one on his cock and one in her pussy as she slid down the pole. I think about a quarter way down, he had filled her up. Her eyes looked like two TV Screens as they were wide open and she could barely breathe. She prayed some and called upon God many times. She did not last too long up there but perhaps he stretched her out some to make it easier for us normal sized weenies to get in, in the future. Stacey was eager to get a nice cum treat for all her work. Jason complied, with a nice creamy blast to her face. It was sort of like getting hit with a firehose. It blasted her halfway across the room, blowing her hair back, and she smiled, licking her lips and made a YUMMY sound. Not a good cherry / almond taste like mine, but good stuff in any case. Stacey is hot on the trail of getting some new pussy for our club and I am hopeful to get a gangbang for her. Always new and exciting news from the club.

***

SATURDAY

In my search for new adventures, I decided to look for a woman to play with and found Cara online. I am bi-curious. We agreed to meet today at the Lake Worth Beach at 10 a.m. She was a very sweet lady but I was soon to find out that she used to be a man. She told me about the many surgeries she had to make the transition and her story was fascinating. We spent 2 hours talking and I really liked her. I would like to see her again.

I texted Logan when I got home and told him about my encounter with Cara. He said he would stop over on his way home from the yacht. He arrived about 12:30 p.m. We talked as he watched me make the vegetable salad for dinner. It was kind of fun just doing something as normal as preparing food in the kitchen. We talked, and laughed, and fucked until he left at 3 p.m. Jordan was coming for dinner at 4 p.m. so it didn't give me much time to get ready and start preparing the Shepherd's Pie I was going to serve. This is not the first time that Logan came over just before Jordan was due and fucked me. I guess he was marking his territory.

Jordan arrived at 4 p.m. I was wearing my jeans with the beads sewn on the front and my white low-cut sweater. I had on my red lace panties and bra (the bra was exposed by the sweater—very provocative). We had dinner and dessert (he brought cake) then rested for a while in the TV room and talked. We then got naked and went into the pool. When we got out and dried off, we went into my Playroom and laid down on the bed. We started playing around…he went down on me and made me come several times. Then we just relaxed until he got excited again. I gave him a blow job then he wanted me to get on top of him and put his cock inside of me. I lubed up and did just that. He finally had the first orgasm he ever had with me. He said it was the best orgasm he ever had in his life. Score another one for Stacey! He left at 8 p.m.

At 8:15 p.m. there was a familiar knock on my front door. It was Logan! He said he was on his way home from West Palm Beach and decided to stop by and see if I was alone. I greeted him at the door wearing his white shirt with nothing underneath (which is the way I was dressed when Jordan left). He was shocked to see me like that and said that the white shirt was OUR thing and now I couldn't wear it with him (I guess he was kidding). He said he would bring me another of his shirts that I couldn't wear with anyone else.

Logan's "possessive" behavior is really puzzling to me. He says he not jealous but he seems to keep coming back to mark his territory anytime someone else enters the picture. I'm not complaining but it is a real turnaround from his usual response to what I do. Ever since the episode this past week with Jason (who was fawning all over me), Logan has taken more of an interest in me. Also, he's been saying, "I love you" to me without my having to say it first (not "love you" but "I love you").

Jason texted me this week and said that he wanted to see me again. I told him he would have to check with my "Master" which I thought would put him off. But no, he actually texted Logan and asked him if he could see (i.e., fuck) me again. Since he already told Logan what a lucky man he was to have such a beautiful, sexy, etc. woman, it was clear there was more than a passing interest in me. I guess Jason figured that if Logan was so willing so share me with him once, he wouldn't mind doing it again. We have another "date" scheduled for this coming Friday with the 3 of us.

***

SUNDAY

Logan came over at 11:30 a.m. to get ready for a visit from Rhonda on Monday (a woman who is dating one of his friends). We played until 7 p.m. WOW!!

***

MONDAY

Rhonda was scheduled to arrive around 12:30 from Orlando so Logan came over about noon. We checked to make sure we had everything ready—food, beverages, costume, fantasy, etc. She arrived around 1 p.m. and we sat in the living room and had some beverages and talked. Then I brought out the lunch—hoagie sandwiches, potato salad, coleslaw and cupcakes for dessert.

When we finished lunch and rested for a while, we went into the pool naked. First Rhonda and I started playing—kissing, touching—while Logan watched. Then Rhonda and I started playing with Logan. I know he was really enjoying that!

We went back into the house and told Rhonda that we were ready to give her a fantasy and was she ready. She said yes, and Logan tied her up naked to the restraints in the living room alcove. I went into the bedroom to change into my Mistress Camille dominatrix outfit. I wore red and black lace crotchless panties and a black lace bra with fishnet thigh highs. Over these I had on leather strappings that looked really cool and a little scary. I put on my dark brown wig and bright lipstick and even I didn't recognize myself in the mirror.

When I came out of the Playroom and Rhonda saw me in that outfit, she was very surprised. I put on a German accent introduced myself as Mistress Camille and asked if she had been a good girl and that I was there to punish her. She said she was ready. I had my flogger in my hand and began using it to caress her body and then I would land a good smack. I told her to spread her legs so I could play with her pussy with the flogger. Then I went behind her and began striking her with the flogger. (Poor baby, her skin is so tender, that even though I was not hitting her hard, I was still leaving red marks on her ass.) After I hurt her a little, I caressed her and played with her tits and her pussy. Boy was I turning myself on doing this. Whatever "taboo" there may have been in my mind about playing with a woman was completely wiped out. Meanwhile Logan is videotaping this entire scene. Then I asked Logan to take a turn beating her while I videotaped the scene. He was a little rough on her (she really was a newbie at this) and she finally said "RED" (that's the safe word to make him stop) and he stopped and took her down.

After Rhonda had enough of this punishment, we headed for the Playroom. I had asked Rhonda if I could look at her clit (since I just discovered the day before that the "thing" I thought was my clit was NOT—can you believe that I was that stupid?!?). Rhonda laid down on the bed and Logan went right for the goods and showed me where her clit was. I touched it and she started moaning. Then Logan got out of the picture and let me go down on Rhonda all by myself as he filmed the scene. I was having a good time sucking and licking her and she was moaning and writhing on the bed in pleasure. When I finally got her to come, I was beyond pleased with myself!

She and I rolled around on the bed and I kept hugging and kissing Rhonda trying some new things—like the "scissors" (which Logan suggested). When we finally got the hang of that position, we both had great orgasms. Then we cuddled again…and kissed… and touched. I'm really getting into this girl thing.

Logan joined us in bed and became the center of our attention with the 2 of us taking turns sucking his beautiful cock and playing with him. We were all so engaged in the sex play that the time just flew by. Rhonda said he had to leave by 5 so she took a shower and got dressed and we bid her safe travels.

Logan stayed so we could recap the events of the day and we played some more. He left at 7 p.m. A good time was had by all. Can't wait to do this again!

Logan's response to above update:

Another, first and fun packed afternoon was held at Stacey's Palace of Pain and Pleasure the other day.

Our friend Rhonda stopped over the other afternoon for Round Two of her on-premise slut training.

After gobbling down some sandwiches, four beers, chips and fruit, she made her way to the pool for some water sport.

It was fun to have the girls in the pool with Just ME!! Watch them play and I got to rub two pussies at the same time and have four nice breasts to play with. Stacey and I sucked Rhonda's breasts together and fun was had by all.

Stacey dressed up as a seductive Marlene Dietrich, and proceeded to smack Rhonda's ass with the flogger. There is a lot of ass there, but she made good work of it She did not yell too much until I got a chance and cracked her ass hard and she yelled something, but

NOT RED, so I kept beating her ass.

Off we went to the fun room after that, and the girls played, hugged and kissed. We put ice on Stacey's nipples which she likes a lot. Rhonda ate her pussy some which was fun to see.

We had to have a demo session so Stacey could find out where her clit was. We had watched Video's, took photos of her own clit, but she still was NOT sure where it was.

She was excited when she found out where it was on Rhonda. Then, I proceeded to have fun licking and sucking on hers. And, Rhonda licked her pussy and now that Stacey knows where her clit was, she could enjoy it much more. And I got to lay in the middle and have the girls lick my balls and suck my cock, which was great fun. I had to be the cameraman, so I got cut out of a lot of bed time as a result. As soon as we get our spy camera, I can relinquish that duty and have more bed time fun. NOT FAIR.

I tried to teach the girls some new moves. The scissors move, which I thought these two jamokes would never get down. I had to move them into position, and all they did was laugh. Santa Maria, what a group.

They finally got it after rubbing up and down on each other for a half hour, not knowing what the hell they were doing. And did eventually cum. New lessons with these two will be hard at best.

We laid around for a bit, each of the girls earned a grape or two. We finally packed Rhonda up with sandwiches and off she went. A good time was had by all.

***

THURSDAY

This was the most "normal" date I have ever had with Logan... He arrived at 4 p.m. and we kissed and went to the living room. Instead of making me kneel before him, he asked me to sit on the loveseat next to him. He gave me a necklace that he ordered with an "O" on it...it represented ownership of me. Very sweet thought. We talked for a while then we got undressed and went into the pool. We did a little kissing but mostly talked and caressed one another.

When we came inside, I asked if he was hungry and said I could make soup and grilled cheese sandwiches. I did a lousy job of preparing such a simple meal but he was patient with me and even though I burned one of the sandwiches (which I ate), we had a nice dinner. We had slices of pie for dessert, then continued to talk.

We finally went into my Playroom and laid on the bed. Of course, one thing led to another and we wound up having crazy monkey sex. We played and talked some more until he left at 8 p.m.

***

SATURDAY

Cara came over at 1:00 p.m. She is the transexual I met last weekend. She seems very sweet. I made a quiche and salad for lunch. We had our drinks (she had San Pellegrino and I had white wine) then we had lunch. After lunch we went into the pool naked. I gave her the option of wearing a swimsuit but she wasn't shy about not wearing anything. I must admit I was very curious as to what she would look like after all her surgeries to become a woman.

Once we were in the pool, she came close to me and started kissing me. I responded and we touched one another and talked and had a good time. We stayed in the pool for quite a while getting to know one another. Then we decided to go into my Playroom. We got on my bed and continued kissing and caressing. She went down on me and I had a wonderful orgasm. I asked her where I should put my fingers to give her an orgasm and she directed me and I was successful in making her cum. This whole scenario was very erotic. While I did play with Rhonda on Monday, she was very inexperienced and didn't help me with any direction. Cara, on the other hand, since she's been a male and a female, was teaching me a whole lot of things.

It seems like she's no stranger to BDSM and told me that one of her neighbors came over and tied her up and hit her with a flogger and she liked it. I asked her if she would be willing to do a threesome with me and Logan and she jumped on that. She said one of her fantasies is sucking on a man's cock with another woman. I also asked if she would do a foursome with Jason and she agreed to do that as well. She's really not shy and has certainly been around the block a few times so I may be able to learn new things from her.

She showed me some vibrators she brought—3 of them! She also brought some pot but we didn't smoke any of it. She said it makes her very passionate. I told her it just makes me crazy and I lose my thought processes. We played and talked until she left at 5 p.m.

I got ready for bed—I was exhausted. Then at about 8 p.m. there was a familiar knock on my front door—it was Logan! He just wanted to stop by and find out how things went. I filled him in on my day and told him that Cara was interested in a threesome with us as well as a foursome with Jason. Logan didn't seem thrilled with the thought of having a former man suck his cock. We'll see what happens. He left around 8:30 p.m.—he was very tired.

***

SUNDAY

Logan suggested inviting Cara over in the afternoon for a swim so that he could meet her. She arrived about 5 p.m. dressed in a leather vest, short shorts over a leather frontless bra with chains on it. She had on a leather spike collar and high heels.

We sat in the living room with our drinks (they had San Pellegrino and I needed a glass of white wine) and talked for a while. I then suggested that we go into the pool. We all took off our clothes and went into the pool naked. Logan was standing at the very end of the pool, Cara was on the right side and I was on the left side. I decided that it was bit uncomfortable trying to decide what to do so I waded over to Cara and she put her arms around me and started kissing me. Logan watched for a bit then waded over and joined us. We were all holding one another, and kissing and touching… it was quite erotic.

After we "pruned up" we got out of the pool, dried off and headed for my Playroom. Cara and I got on the bed and started playing and kissing. Again, Logan watched for a bit then joined us on the bed. We told him to get between us so that we could suck his cock and Cara and I were head-to-head taking turns sucking on his "head." I don't think he was enjoying it as much as he should have (probably because he kept thinking that a former guy was sucking his cock!).

We played on the bed—Cara went down on me and I had a great orgasm. I played with her until she had an orgasm. Then we just laid on the bed relaxing and touching one another. Cara tried some nipple contraption on me that was supposed to make my nipples larger…I didn't love it. I asked Logan to hit us with the flogger which he was happy to oblige. Cara took it like a trooper. She left around 8 p.m. and Logan stayed to do a recap of the afternoon.

Logan left around 9:30 p.m.

***

FRIDAY

Today was the second scheduled "menage a trois" with me, Logan and Jason. Logan arrived first and Jason arrived at noon. I know I've done this before but I was a little nervous this time. I took a couple of tokes from the MJ (slang for pot in case you are a newbie) cigarette to relax myself.

I wore my naughty school girl outfit with white knee socks and my hair in pigtails sucking on a giant lollipop. I greeted Jason at the door with a "Hi Uncle Jason, so good to see you. Uncle Logan is already here." He had a good laugh at my costume.

I had sandwiches for lunch served in brown paper bags with our names written on them (just like in school). Also had chips and juice boxes and other beverages to choose from. Jason said he found a couple that we could play with and was going to follow up with them to see if they would be interested in our Club. We also made him my Bodyguard. He said he wouldn't let anything bad happen to me. Very sweet.

We had a nice lunch but got right down to business since Logan had to be in West Palm Beach for the yacht around 3 p.m.

I sent the boys into the Playroom while I set up the remote spy camera (which, by the way, didn't work!) and then I went on the patio for a couple more tokes of the MJ.

The boys were already naked on the bed when I entered the room…what a site…two gorgeous men just laying there waiting for me. I took my time getting undressed—first I took the elastics off my pigtails so my hair would just flow down. Then I slowly unbuttoned my "uniform" and slipped out of it. That left me in my red lace bra and boy shorts. The boys were getting excited. I crawled up on the bed (like a feral cat) and sat there looking down at my prey… then the touching began. They slipped me out of my bra and panties and while I was sucking Jason's cock, Logan was behind me fucking me in my pussy… Geez, it was so HOT!! Then the second tokes of MJ kicked in… Things began getting a little fuzzy and the boys had to take over the direction of the production.

With the help of the MJ for courage, I asked Jason to try to penetrate me (once again). We tried but I thought he was going to tear my pussy in half. I felt so bad and apologized that I couldn't satisfy him. He was very gracious and said it was okay.

I guess I must have asked to have Jason cum on my face because the next thing I know, I have a giant standing over me as I lay on the bed playing with his dick while I wiggled into position to receive my "treat." Logan was filming the entire scene—WOW! Jason came all over my face and I was covered in cum—licking it and sucking on his dick. It was quite tasty—vanilla (unlike the sex we were enjoying).

I don't know how long we played but I do remember laying between my two handsome gentlemen and talking and having them play with my body (which I loved!).

Jason left around 2 p.m. (he never overstays his welcome) and Logan and I had some alone time before he left for the yacht. I was finally coming down from my high so things were becoming clearer to me.

EARLIER IN THE DAY ON FRIDAY

Since the working title of my book was "Diary of a Sex Addict," one of the things I wanted to do was to contact Sex Addicts Anonymous to see if they had any meetings and possibly get more details for my book. I found a listing for a group that meets by Zoom on Wednesdays and Fridays. So, I contacted the leader of the group and got the information to join the meetings.

The SAA meeting began at 6 p.m. on Zoom. I was the only female in the group of 14 men. I introduced myself, "I'm Stacey and I'm a sex addict." I didn't "share" at this meeting because I wanted to see what the other participants were going to say. I didn't think it would have been appropriate to say, "Well guys, I just had my second menage a trois this afternoon with 2 burly men…they fucked my brains out...couldn't get enough of their cum…" So, I just listened.

It seems like most of them had some addiction to watching porn, lying to their spouses and cheating on them with other women, paying prostitutes for sex, masturbating like monkeys, etc. So, with that being said, I guess I AM a sex addict (and so is Logan). Momma Mia, Santa Maria.

I put the meeting on my calendar for next week as well. The leader said he wants the newcomers (one other guy and me) to give the meetings a chance before we bug out.

***

MONDAY

It's Labor Day and Logan was coming over at 12:30 p.m. (He was taking a break from writing movie scripts. (Did I mention that he's a screen writer in addition to being a Yacht Captain?). I decided to give him a BDSM fantasy that woke me up at 3 in that morning. I had been thinking about it all day long.

I wrote a note on a post-it and taped it to the front door saying, "Please come in and lock the door." Inside there was another post-it on the table where he puts his keys, etc. saying, "Go to the Playroom." On the closed Playroom door, there was another post-it saying, "She is your sex slave… Do what you want to her… she's wearing tear away panties."

I was laying on the bed wearing only panties. My ankles were restrained by black cuffs and bound together. My wrists were also bound with cuffs behind my back. I was basically helpless. Logan slowly opened the door and looked in… He burst out laughing when he saw me… then he realized that I was unable to move.

He came over to the bed and began touching me and playing with me. He turned me over and began spanking me with the flogger and with his hands. He tore off my panties and played with my pussy. He got undressed and got on the bed and made me suck on his cock. I was so frustrated because I wanted my hands free to touch him all over. Eventually, he undid my wrist cuffs and I was able to enjoy touching his beautiful body.

I continued to pleasure him and do whatever he wanted me to do. He then undid my ankle cuffs and I was able to mount him and fuck him in the ass with my pussy. I kissed him all over—in every opening—I couldn't get enough of him.

After we played for a while, we cuddled and talked. He said it would have been very funny if this was a regular day and the mailman came to the door and saw all of the post-it notes and HE wound up in the Playroom… We both got hysterical.

He left at 3 p.m. to go back to work and I felt very satisfied—I had my BDSM fix for the day

Logan's Response to the above Update:

That was so much fun to see all the notes stuck all over the house and then to see my subbie all tied up in just her panties. It was fun to rip the panties off of her. We definitely need to do more BDSM. Sometimes, we get busy with other stuff and forget that this is the area we want to focus on. I love when my subbie kisses me all over, and she has her own spot between my legs to lick and suck. I love it when she gets a sensation overload and lets herself go entirely into another gear. HOT, HOT, HOT. I love that red hair all over as she sucks and licks my cock and balls all over her face. She loves it when I call out dirty names and encourage her more. Pull at her hair and shove her face deeper into my crotch. I love when she becomes a wild slut, whore, totally intent on pleasing her master. Which, of course, she does. We are definitely both going to miss our sexual encounters over the next few weeks, but we are going to tape a session so she will have something to watch and listen to while she plays with her pussy for a few weeks. The Master

***

TUESDAY

I had the 2 vaginal ultrasounds done on Friday. Jason has checked with me daily to see if I got the results. When I hadn't heard from the doctor as of yesterday, Jason asked if he could come over to visit. He arrived at 12:30 p.m. (his lunch hour—he's a property manager) and said he didn't want lunch, just wanted to be with me. He told me not to worry and that no matter what the doctor said, he would stay by my side and get me through it. He knew I was upset and just hugged me and kissed me. We went into my Playroom and laid on the bed—him holding me and reassuring me. He told me he loved me many times (not the "love you" but the "I love you"). He said we had a very strong connection, and I agreed. We are old souls who were together at another time and have now been brought together again.

We talked about Logan, and I told him that as much as Logan meant to me, it bothers me that he doesn't mind "pimping" me out to other men. I told him that I wanted the "50 Shades" relationship of Christian and Anastasia, not "The Story of O" relationship of Renee and O—the difference being that Christian loved Anastasia and wanted to keep her to himself, whereas Renee was happy to pimp out O to other men even though she loved him. Jason understood that and said I should talk to Logan about how I felt. I told him I couldn't do that. Then he asked if I wanted him to do it. I emphatically said NO! I also said that we should probably not have another session with Logan/Jason/Stacey because the feelings he and I have developed for one another might become obvious to Logan. He admitted that after the second session, he felt that Logan sensed that Jason had feelings for me and was feeling threatened. The main thing I admitted to Jason was that I didn't TRUST Logan. Because of his track record, I still assume that during his 2-week trip, he was screwing around with someone/anyone. Lack of trust is the kiss of death in any relationship.

Jason left at 2:30 p.m. and called me one minute later, saying he missed me. He continued to text me for the rest of the day, saying very sweet and positive things.

I did call the doctor's office yesterday afternoon and they said they didn't have the results of the tests. I told them that when I called the day before, the nurse said the results were there, but the doctor was not in the office to evaluate them. I'm sitting on pins and needles, waiting to find out what's wrong. I'm still having pain (not as severe as before), and I just want to know what's wrong down there.

Even though Logan has kept in touch (either by text or phone) almost every day of his trip, I still feel like I've lost some of my intense passion for him before he left. I realize that there is no future for us because Logan is severely damaged emotionally, and I don't think he's capable of giving me the love and affection that I'm seeking. I'm not looking to live together. I just want a companion I can count on, and I don't think he has the emotional maturity to provide that.

I also don't see a future with Jason. He will be a part of my life if I want him there. I know he loves me in a way that Logan never could, and I love him for being the kind, sweet, empathetic, gentle soul that he is. But I don't see anything more permanent occurring.

Logan called yesterday and said he should be back late Friday night and would like to come over on Sunday (he knows Jordan comes over on Saturday). I wonder how I will feel when I see him in person again. Perhaps he met someone during his trip and doesn't feel the same about me (again, that TRUST issue). Also, my noon trysts with Jason will be jeopardized once Logan returns to town. How will that play out? Will Logan sense a difference in my feelings towards him? Will he say anything? He did ask me if I had heard from Jason, and I said we texted and he was looking for some women for me to be with.

I feel like a ball of emotions all tied up in a bow… don't know where any of this is going… I guess I just have to sit back and try to enjoy the ride.

***

WEDNESDAY

Well, today was an interesting day…to say the least! I've been very bummed out since I found out that I'm going to have surgery to remove a growth in my uterus. The doctor wants to make sure it's not cancer. So, I've been moping around the house, feeling sorry for myself.

Logan has been away for almost 3 weeks bringing the yacht back from California. He returned this weekend and was supposed to come over on Sunday, but he got sick (vomiting) and couldn't come over. I was concerned about seeing him again because it seems that every time he goes away for an extended period, his spell over me is broken. Before he left, we saw one another almost every day, and the passion was through the roof. Within that 3-week hiatus, I cooled down (and frankly, I assumed so did he). When he came over on Monday, he acted normal, and we played for 2 hours (no intercourse, but we did everything else). Although we texted, I didn't see him on Tuesday, so I assumed things were cooling off.

I've been in constant contact with Jason throughout Logan's 3-week absence. We even got together twice for a kissing and cuddling session. Jason and I both know that intercourse is out of the question because of our anatomical differences (he's too big to get inside me!). Since I was feeling blue (Logan was not very supportive about my health issues, and Jason was), Jason asked to come over during his lunchtime on Wednesday.

So here we are on Wednesday…Big Surprise… Logan texts me and says he wants to come over this morning… I told him I was having lunch with my sister and would only be home until 11:30 a.m. He said that was fine. So, at 10:30 a.m. he shows up. We head for the Playroom and proceed to get naked and play on the bed. I give him several blow jobs, and we have a kissing and cuddling session. He then ends the session using the flogger on my ass…which I like… He leaves at 11:30 a.m. and tells me to have a nice lunch with my sister. He also said, "Love you." I then text Jason and let him know that Logan has left so we are on for our nooner.

Jason arrives at 12:30 p.m., and we go into the Playroom. We get naked and kiss and cuddle. Again, he knows that's about all we can do. After talking for a while, I asked him if he wanted to play "50 Shades," he said that would be fun. We go into my toy chest and get out cuffs and a blindfold. We put the cuffs on me and tied them behind my back. Then he puts the blindfold on me. He begins teasing me with a feather, then his hands, and he puts his enormous cock into my mouth. He's playing with my pussy as I'm giving him a blow job. Eventually, he comes all over my face. He removes my cuffs, and we lay next to one another on the bed and cuddle and talk. After a while, I realize he will need to return to work so we go into the shower together. He sits on the built-in seat in the shower, and I wrap myself around him while we kiss under the steamy water. It was like a scene from “50 Shades.” We get out, dry off, and return to bed to cuddle more. He keeps telling me how much he loves me, and, God help me, I love him too. He also tells me not to worry about the surgery…that he will stand by me through the whole thing. He says he will never leave me as long as I want him in my life and that I am a part of him…so romantic!!! Anyway, he leaves to return to work at 2:30 p.m. I now have to get dressed because my dance instructor (Justin) is coming over for a lesson at 3:30.

Justin arrives at 3:30 p.m., and I fill him in on my upcoming surgery. He offered to take me to the hospital and take care of me if I needed it. I explained that I would stay at my sister’s after the procedure until I felt up to going home. (BTW—just to be fair… Logan and Jason both offered to take me to the hospital.) We had a good session, and as always, we kissed during our dancing. We never made it into the Playroom. I’m a little nervous about doing that since Logan could show up anytime. Justin looked up the procedure on his Tablet and was surprised at what was involved. He also said he loves me.

I now realize that I'm not just a "sex addict" but also a "sex, love and romance addict." Look that up…it's a thing. I withdrew when Logan was gone, even though it was like pulling teeth to get him to say he loves me. But just a day like today, with 3 handsome men expressing their love for me… got my endorphins flowing.

I reiterate that I'm not looking for a permanent relationship with ANY of them, but I need them ALL in my life for the individual things they give me.

Jason knows I'm with Logan and that Logan "owns" me but still wants to be part of my life. Logan knows that I go out with other men, but since he "owns" me and I return to him, he's okay with that. And Justin knows about ALL this and still wants me in his life.

Now Jordan the Brit knows nothing about this (although I suspect he assumes I have been seeing other men). He said the last time he was over; he was happy that he could share 1/7th of my life. I asked him what he meant, and he said that since he sees me one day a week, I probably see 6 other guys the rest of the time. I also think Jordan would be very comfortable doing the BDSM thing, but I'm not quite ready to have him share that with me.

As it is, I've moved Logan to the dark side (he's never done the BDSM thing before me), and today, I did it with Jason (he's never done the BDSM thing before me), so why not Jordan?

Whatever happens with this surgery, I'm not going down without a fight, and I'm not giving up my sex toys and sex boys! I've waited too long for this chapter in my life and want to keep it going as long as possible.

***

I can't sleep…thinking about my surgery and thinking about my social life.

Logan and I were going hot and heavy before he left to pick up the yacht. We were together almost every day…sometimes twice a day. Since he returned, it hasn't been the same. I think he either met someone on the trip or rekindled a relationship with someone he already knew. Perhaps it's my guilty feeling since I "fell in love" with Jason during Logan's absence.

But I miss talking with Logan about the Oasis Gentlemen's Club and our plans for parties and socials. I know Logan is a self-centered man, and maybe he's pulled away because of my upcoming surgery.

If all he wants from me is sex, my surgery and being out of commission for at least a couple of weeks would put him off. I always thought that even before Covid, we rarely went out, and whenever he came over, it was just a "booty call." But I was willing to accept that because I was crazy about him!

You might think that if I am now "in love" with Jason, what difference should Logan make in my life… But Logan keeps breaking my heart!

The problem with Jason is that he has so many other obligations…his wife (whom he's been trying to get separated from), his parents (whom he adores and who adore him), his job, his friends (too many to count), so where do I fit in? He admits he wishes to give me more time but can't.

I don't see a future (living together, marriage) with either of these men, but I want a companion I can count on. Jason texts me daily to let me know he's thinking about me. But Logan…not so much.

I don't know why I'm letting the feeling that Logan's slipping away get to me, and I guess I may be accusing him of what I've done while he was gone…projection… But he's been a part of my life for over a year, and we had something special. He took my virginity for the second time in my life, and it formed a bond for me. We were able to talk about everything and laugh and make love. I feel like if he's not in my life, it's like suffering another death.

You would think that having Jason be really into me would be enough, but Logan was the love of my life for so long it's hard to let him go. I don't want to rock the boat, so I've got to learn to live with whatever he can give me.

I have enough other men "in love" with me, so you'd think that would be okay. But somehow, it's not. When Logan told me he loved me, it made me soar. I couldn't have been happier. But how can someone turn love on and off like a faucet? He said that he felt so lucky to have found me…someone who was so adventurous sexually and who would bring him to new sexual heights. How could this change in 3 short weeks? He said he didn't cheat on his second wife while they were married for 3 years because she gave him everything he wanted. Then she dumped him for another man, and he hasn't been the same.

Since I met Logan on a dating site, I assumed he was looking for someone and probably didn't have anyone special then. I hate myself for obsessing over him. He doesn't deserve this much of my attention. But without him, I feel like my heart isn't whole. That is such a sad admission!!!

Today is Thursday, and I haven't SEEN Logan since Sunday. If I can get him to come over today, I would like to talk honestly with him. I don't want to be accusatory, but I need to know what's going on. He knows I'm seeing other men, and although I said I didn't want to know about his seeing other women, I just want to know if he's working me out of his life. If these other women are just flings, I can deal with that, but since he's shown that even with all of his "flings" while married, he had 2 other families that he kept at the same time. That means that he likes to have a relationship—his wife and children in one city and his girlfriend and her children in another city. He did this TWO times during his marriage. It's like being a bigamist. Knowing he's capable of that has pushed my mistrust button on him. That's why the least little thing that changes can mean that he's about his old tricks again. AGAIN, I "cheated" on him with Jason while he was getting the yacht, so I have no room to talk. I guess it's the uncertainty and unknown that is getting to me—probably sparked by the surgery that I am facing with an unknown future (cancer?).

Maybe I'm letting my upcoming surgery bring these thoughts to the forefront of my mind because when all is said and done, I do want someone around, especially when I'm sick and vulnerable. I've got to get a handle on these feelings, or I'm going to make myself crazy.

***

Logan came over yesterday at noon. We talked…he had asked me if I got lonely the last time we were together. I cavalierly said no, I enjoy being by myself. After rethinking that, I realized that just wasn't true. So, I asked him why he asked me that question and did he ever get lonely. He said that he did, and he also gets depressed and doesn't want to engage with anyone. I admitted that I, too get lonely, especially when I'm not feeling well. It's like taking baby steps with him to have a serious conversation. I don't think he's ever had a relationship where they did discuss serious topics. I tried to open the door slowly so he would feel comfortable talking to me about his "feelings."

I told him I worried when I didn't hear from him, and he was surprised. Why in the world would anyone "worry" about him? God, this man is damaged! Anyway, he apologized for his "radio silence" and said he would be more thoughtful in the future.

When he left at 3:30, I felt nothing but love for him. But…I didn't tell him I loved him. He's coming over on Sunday afternoon after he works on the boat, and hopefully, we can continue to break down the barrier to intimacy in his mind.

I realized that even though I had Jason fawning all over me, my life didn't seem whole without Logan. That is sad on so many levels.

***

FRIDAY

Jason came over today at 12:30. He was going to replace the light fixture in my laundry room. When he checked it, he discovered that it was not the fixture—just one of the bulbs—and that I should return the new fixture and buy 2 new bulbs. Whew!

After the light diagnosis, we entered my Playroom and got undressed (down to our underwear). I was wearing my black lace bra and black lace boy shorts, which he thought was very sexy. He was wearing Calvin Klein briefs. We just laid on the bed and hugged, kissed and cuddled. Then I asked him to tell me more about himself, which he did… He told me that he met the love of his life in high school, and when they went away to college, they lost touch for a while, but then they reconnected. Unfortunately, she was diagnosed with leukemia and passed away. He said it tore him apart for the longest time and he never wanted to feel like that again (which explains why he has so many women chasing him with no commitment on his part). He said he only told 5 women in his life that he loved them and I am one of them (WOW!!). That floored me. He said there was something so special about our relationship, and he feels we've been together in another life. He said he thinks about me all the time.

We stayed in bed (with no sex) until he left at 2:30 p.m. He told me he loved me dozens of times. He's so sweet—such a gentle giant. I apologized that I was not able to have sex with him (because of our physical differences), but he said that didn't matter. He just wanted to be with me and hold me. Geez, where does this man come from?

I sent him away with a brown paper bag with a sandwich, chips, cookies, and a juice box since he missed his lunch hour. After he left, he texted me photos of his lunch in his car and couldn't thank me enough for being so thoughtful. It's really easy to be thoughtful to a man like him.

We did talk a little about Logan. I told him Logan wasn't jealous. He said Logan WAS. I told him Logan wasn't possessive. He said Logan WAS. I guess guys can tune into one another and see signals that aren't visible to women. Anyway, neither one of us wants to rock the boat at this point.

This "thing" with Jason has been going on for a very short time, and I'm wondering how much more it could escalate and what happens if and when it does. Again, all my boys know there is no permanent future with any of them, so we shall see how all of this plays out.

***

SUNDAY

Logan came over at 2:30 p.m. directly from the yacht. He was tired and cranky. I emailed him a few days before, letting him know that I changed the menu from pizza to baked pork chops and potatoes, but I never heard back. Apparently, he never read the email. He reluctantly accepted the change in menu but kept bitching about wanting pizza (talk about a brat!).

Anyway, I popped dinner in the oven, and we went into the pool. This was his first time in the refurbished pool. When we got out, we had dinner, which he ate, and then he chattered at the dinner table for about an hour. FINALLY, he said we should go into the Playroom and lie down. We did our thing, but it wasn't great (for me, at least).

When he was getting dressed to leave, he said why don't we have a sleepover… I was floored. He said he hadn't asked me before because he was worried about the neighbors but honestly, that ship has sailed. So, I said it was a great idea, and he said we should plan on it after my surgery.

The funny thing about this suggestion was that I told him that the Brit wanted to take me to Miami for dinner and stay overnight at his daughter's house in Miami. Logan doesn't think of these things. They become subliminal messages then they pop out of his mouth. Perhaps I'm wrong… but when I told him I like Jason talking romantically, Logan tried to do it as well (he failed miserably but tried). He left at 6:30 p.m.

Earlier in the day, I got my first text from Jason at 8:01 a.m. Here's how it went:

Jason:

Good morning, my sexy hottie redhead lover!!

Happy Sunday Fun Day!

Stacey:

Good Morning, Lover, I Just got back from Home Depot—returned the light fixture and bought 2 bulbs…easy peasy…Thinking of you, as always

Jason:

WOW. Someone wants the early bird worm.

Did you check out Fetlife and see all the different sexual avenues? Heterosexual. Bisexual. Pansexual.

Stacey:

I don't think I'm ready for Fetlife…baby steps…I've only been doing this for a short time…

Jason:

No worries, my love!!

Stacey:

I'm counting on you for guidance

Jason:

A whole new world for my LOVE!!!

I will never let you down.

Stacey:

I trust you with my life

Jason:

So do I, my love

***

THURSDAY

I went to Justin's house (my dance instructor) at 10:30 a.m. because I wanted him to color my hair (he's also a hair stylist). I brought my box color. When I got there, we chatted for a while, and he gave me a wheatgrass shot (very healthful) and got caught up on all my "boys." Justin knows about all of them.

Anyway, he gave me a birthday card and hugged and kissed me. I did have sex with him quite a while ago, and I will probably do it again when I feel better (I'm such a slut!!). He still wants to stay in the line-up of my lovers. WTF! I will never understand men!

He colored my hair, and we chatted for a while, but I had to get home for a client Zoom call. He said he loved me, and I walked out the door.

***

FRIDAY

Jason came over at 12:30 to celebrate my birthday. I planned a fantasy for him… I had a sign on the front door that said, *"Welcome to the Oasis Gentlemen's Club. Please come in and lock the door. Proceed to the Playroom. Madame Camille."* When he got to the Playroom door (closed), another sign said, *"Welcome to the Oasis Gentlemen's Club. Your hostess today will be Anastasia. She will be at your service for all of your desires. Please knock and enter. Enjoy!!"*

He followed all the instructions, and when he entered the Playroom, he started smiling when he saw me… I was lying on the bed in a short, see-through lace mini. I had my faux mink blanket wrapped around me. He handed me a "preserved rose" that would never die and the most romantic birthday card I ever received.

He was very excited by the scenario and took me in his arms and kissed me passionately. He got undressed, and we kissed, hugged, and cuddled on the bed for hours. He knew that we couldn't go any further than that until I got clearance from my doctor… He kept telling me how much he loved me and missed me.

He stayed until 3 p.m. I missed him before he walked out the door. What am I going to do with this man?

***

SATURDAY

Jordan came over at 2 p.m. He had a Trader Joe's shopping bag filled with candy and cookies for my birthday. I told him if I ate all of that, it would put me into a sugar coma for a week! But it was a very sweet gesture.

He wanted pizza, so I prepared a basic cheese store-bought pizza and added onions, anchovies (we both love them) and pepperoni. After dinner, we watched TV in the family room.

We then continued to watch TV in the Playroom. We kept our clothes on but we kissed and hugged and cuddled. He left at 5 p.m. He's a very sweet guy, and I enjoy spending time with him, but he doesn't make my heart flutter.

***

SUNDAY

Logan came from the yacht at 3:30 p.m. (I honestly did NOT expect to see him). When he called to tell me he was on his way, I asked if he was hungry, and he said he was, so I quickly threw together a jar of tomato sauce with frozen meatballs and spaghetti. I was running around the house, getting everything ready and getting dressed. When he arrived, we sat and talked while I prepared the meal. After we ate, we sat and talked at the table for a while. I was asking him about all of his indiscretions with other women and why he cheated on his first wife. Of course, he eventually got on the subject of his second wife, who left him for another man. He said it was probably Karma for what he had done all his life. Then, he got a little depressed and quiet.

I suggested that we go into the Playroom and lie down, and that's what we did. He knew that sex with me was still out of the question since my surgery, but we kissed, hugged and cuddled anyway. I finally brought him out of his mood, and we began having fun and laughing. He did mention that we hadn't heard from Jason in a long time, but I quickly changed the subject so I wouldn't have to lie to him.

BTW, I had mentioned to Jason when I saw him on Friday that

Logan really likes to spank me as part of the BDSM scenario and sometimes gets carried away. Jason said that if Logan ever hurt me, he would kill him… So, I was not surprised to find a text from Jason on Sunday night asking, "Was Logan easy on you?" I texted back that Logan was a "good boy" and he was "tired," and his response was "Glad to hear that!!" Geez, my bodyguard.

Logan invited me to dinner on Monday night to celebrate my birthday. He wants me to dress up sexy. I have a black, short, very tight dress—I call it my "slut dress" that I said I would wear. That got him excited.

When we were in the Playroom, he seemed like the old Logan—loving, kind, sweet…but we both know that he swings with the wind… He left at 6:30 p.m. during a raging rainstorm, and I was a little sad to see him go. That man knows how to scramble my brain!!!

Can't wait to see how our dinner date goes.

***

MONDAY

Logan came over at 4:30 to pick me up for our dinner. We had 5:30 reservations at Mario's in Boca. It's a really nice restaurant, and I was so excited to be going out on a "date" with Logan (we've had so few of those since the Covid quarantine). I wore my black "slut dress" that barely covered my ass, and when he came to the door, his eyes popped out of his head. He told me how sexy I looked, took me into his arms, and kissed me. We sat in the living room for a while, then decided to head to the restaurant early to sit at the bar and have drinks (he said he wanted all the men to watch me).

He brought me a beautiful, romantic birthday card, a carrot cake and Ben & Jerry's ice cream for when we came home.

On the way to the restaurant, he had his hand on my thigh and was moving it up and down, lifting my dress to my crotch… it was very hot (a la 50 Shades)! When we got to the restaurant, the bar was full, so we went inside, got a table, and ordered drinks. We sat in a booth beside one another, and he couldn't keep his hands off me. He was rubbing my thigh, kissing me, telling me how sexy I was and how much I was turning him on (Magic Logan was back!!).

When we were leaving the restaurant, we passed a table of about 10 seniors (men and women) …the men couldn't stop looking at me and smiling, and the women just scowled at me… Logan thought it was hysterical.

After dinner, we walked to one of the stores nearby, and he bought a shirt and a belt, then we headed home. We had some cake and ice cream then went into the Playroom. We both got undressed, and even though I couldn't have sex yet, we had a great time. We played, kissed, and hugged; he even said, "I love you." WOW! Shocker! He said he wanted to have a sleepover with me. This was not the first time he flew that trial balloon. I said it sounded like a good idea.

He left at 8:30 p.m., and my head was spinning… It's amazing how this man can turn me on and turn me off like I'm some sort of an appliance. It will be interesting to see how long his attention span lasts this time.

***

FRIDAY

Jason was scheduled to come over today at 12:30 p.m. I hadn't seen him since last Tuesday. I was beside myself with excitement. At 12:15 p.m., Logan called me. He said he was going to the boat and wanted to stop by. Normally, I would have jumped at this opportunity, but not today! I was so flustered that I said I was waiting for one of my girlfriends to come for lunch. He asked which one. I said Suzette. He said, "Great, I'll stop by and say hello." (Since he knows her). I panicked and talked him out of coming over (geez, that made me feel guilty). I told him I would see him on Sunday after he returned from the boat. He seemed a little put out at my rejection (and possibly a little suspicious).

Then a funny thing happened…Suzette called me…I told her about the lie I told Logan and wondered how I would explain if he questioned me on Sunday about why I didn't want him to come over. She told me to say that she was having problems with her teeth (which she is—her new dentures don't fit) and was self-conscious about seeing anyone since she has no teeth. (That's what friends are for.)

Anyway, back to Jason… when he got here, I wore my black mini dominatrix dress and fishnet thigh highs…underneath, I wore my red lace bra and red lace boy shorts…Also had a temporary tattoo above my lady parts that said "Sex Goddess" with roses around it. His eyes popped out of his head when he saw me. Since we only had a couple of hours before he had to return to work, we went into my Playroom. We stripped down to our underwear and just laid there holding one another and kissing. He said that was enough for him and that he had NEVER done that with any other woman. He said being with me in my Playroom was his safe place with no drama or stress. (I work very hard to keep it that way.)

I asked him questions about how long he was married (12 years) and how long after he was married, he started to cheat (on his honeymoon). Wow! At least I waited a couple of months before I started cheating on my marriage… I then talked about the saga of my various affairs during my marriage and how I would feel very guilty and vow never to do it again… but we all know how that turned out. He admitted that he could never be monogamous, which disturbed me initially. Then I realized that even if we were to be a "couple," I would cheat on him as well (especially since we can't have intercourse). Also, even though he may have tens of dozens of women chasing after him—which he does—he is powerless to say no to a beautiful woman. BUT the number of women who are built to take in his "organ" is not in the majority… Even his wife has never been able to have intercourse with him (hence, the cheating).

I need Logan and Jordan to be able to have normal intercourse, and no matter how much I love Jason and how much he loves me, we need our sexual outlets. My God…I think like a man in a woman's body!!

He stayed until 2:30 p.m. I missed him when he walked out the door.

***

ON ANOTHER MATTER:

This man—Bobby, a TV producer—has been following me on Facebook for years. Recently, he began calling and texting me, asking me to help work on his TV show. He calls me many, many times a day and texts like there is no tomorrow… He says he fell in love with me (Mind you, we've NEVER met in person! Who am I kidding—remember Christopher Logan? —I never met him either, and he wasn't even REAL, and I fell in love with him!!).

I told Bobby that I date and have several 'friends' I see weekly. He said he was fine with that. However, he had a total meltdown on

Friday and started texting me at 3 a.m., saying he was so angry at me… I had told him I had dates on Friday, Saturday and Sunday with 3 different men. He seemed okay at first, then I guess he stewed about it. When he finally calmed down, he admitted that he was jealous, and that caused his overreaction. I told him I would not give up my 'friends', and if that bothered him, I was sorry. I also told him that I don't play games and all my "friends" know that we are not exclusive and I see other men. They all seem to accept that and want to continue to be in my "orbit." I swear that as long as I live, I will NEVER understand men. They want to be able to play the field, and when a woman does the same thing, they get crazy.

Anyway, Bobby wants me to be part of his new TV show, and he's headlining me and I will be the "Ed McMahon" to his host. He's scheduled a taping in early February and has all the talent lined up. He posted it on Facebook, and there is a picture of me as part of the show… this guy is like a runaway train.

***

SATURDAY

Jason and I shared our daily texts, but I felt something was missing this morning. I asked him if we were okay and if I said or did anything to change things the day before. It was probably my guilty conscience knowing what I did to Logan (lying to him).

Anyway, this was Jason's response:

WHAT??

No way will my feelings for you change. Like I said yesterday. Till the Day I die, you will always be my LOVER!

If we just sit and chat

Stop being a worrier!!

I LOVE YOU

Jordan the Brit came over at 2:00 p.m. (each week, he's coming over earlier and earlier). He said he almost didn't come because he had "damaged" himself over last weekend (I had no idea what he was talking about—it turns out he stepped on some bougainvillea thorns when he was gardening, and they were stuck under his feet). I didn't wear a sexy outfit since I had no idea where this "damage" had occurred, and I didn't want to tease him.

His birthday was last Tuesday, so I decided that I would have a little celebration for him. I made what he had requested—linguine primavera, and I had cupcakes for dessert—I even had a candle, sang Happy Birthday and had him make a wish. I also bought him a bottle of Tommy Hilfiger cologne, which he was very surprised about. He said he never had a birthday party growing up because he was in boarding school, and they didn't give a crap about the boys' birthdays. So, this made it kind of special to me. But he's such a "Brit"—never shows emotion, cool as a cucumber, a bit aloof at times.

After dinner, we went to my Playroom, and he got naked on the bed. I stripped down to my undies and got into bed beside him. We just cuddled and kissed a little. Then, I decided to take over since he was not making any moves to do anything. I took off my undies and started kissing him and turning him on, and we had great sex. He was very surprised. He never initiates these moves because he thinks a woman should be the one to decide whether she wants sex or not (always the gentleman). He started talking about having a "sleepover," and I said that no one had ever slept over since my partner passed away. He wanted me to think about it… We played until he finally left at 7:30 p.m. BTW, that was some kind of a record for us…He's never stayed that long before.

Bobby had asked me to call him on FaceTime after Jordan left to discuss the TV show, which I did. We were online for about 30 minutes (8-8:30 p.m.), but he saw I was tired and let me go. He thinks I'm "gorgeous beyond gorgeous," and I have his heart. Oh boy! This was the first time he saw me "in person." He wants me to be the Executive Producer of his TV show (I have no idea what that means), and we will have a Zoom call next Saturday with some of his colleagues to discuss moving forward with the show. I have no idea if this is a pipe dream or if any of this will happen.

***

SUNDAY

Logan said he would stop over when he returned from the boat. He texted me at 3 p.m. and said he was on his way. He arrived at 3:30, and I was wearing jeans and a sexy blouse. I had put a pizza in the oven (that's what he said he wanted). We sat and talked until the pizza was ready, then relaxed at the table for a while after we ate. He was talking about his past, and I just let him reminisce.

BTW: Logan never mentioned anything about my having lunch with Suzette on Friday (and blowing him off). He did ask me questions about my date with the Brit.

Eventually, we went into the Playroom and got undressed. Since I had been watching '50 Shades' all day long, I was horny for some BDSM activity, and I told him so. He handcuffed my hands behind my back, threw me down on the bed on my stomach and began to beat me with the flogger and then the belt. I was screaming while he was doing this, not because it hurt so much but because it was so exciting. He got so excited watching me writhe on the bed and scream that he 'came' all over my ass without even penetrating me. He seems to get off beating me. Then he untied my hands, and we both got on the bed and began kissing and hugging, and I started sucking his cock…he was getting even more excited. He was flogging me and talking dirty to me while I was lying between his legs with my head in his crotch. I was beyond excited myself and had multiple orgasms while I kissed him and crawled up his body to get to his lips.

We had passionate sex until we were both spent. No matter how frustrated I get with Logan for his MIA actions and inconsistent presence, I still LOVE it when we have rampant SEX.

He left at 6 p.m. Boy; I needed that…then I went back to watching the “50 Shades” marathon and getting excited all over again…

When I checked my phone after Logan left, there was a text from Jason:

How was your beating?

Hope you’re fine.

And didn’t need your safe word.

Jason knows that Logan and I play with the BDSM lifestyle, and he doesn’t like it. He has threatened to hurt Logan if he ever hurts me. I must say that sometimes Logan scares me when we do this because he gets so excited that I'm not sure I could stop him if I wanted to (so maybe Jason is right to be concerned). Obviously, I can never let Jason know how far Logan goes during this role-play.

As I read these entries again, I realized I wouldn't change a thing!!! I LOVE, LOVE, LOVE all of my men!!!!!

***

TUESDAY

Today, I was scheduled to go over to Justin's house (my dance instructor/hairdresser) to have him color and cut my hair. I got there about 12:15 p.m. We talked for a bit then he had me take off my t-shirt and put a cape over me to begin the process. We kidded around and flirted as we always do.

When he finished with my hair, we started kissing, and he led me into his bedroom. I took off my jeans, my shoes (flip-flops), my bra and panties. Then he got undressed, and we started kissing and playing on his bed. He took out some lotion and massaged it all over my body. He got excited pretty quickly and put on a condom. We were going at it full blast, and we both had orgasms when he suddenly jumped out of bed and left the room.

I didn't know what had happened then I heard loud talking coming from the living room. Apparently, his girlfriend came home unexpectedly, and he met her at the door—he was naked and still wearing the used condom. She raced into the bedroom and saw me on the bed—also naked—and started screaming at both of us. The funny thing was that he kept telling her that we had NOT had sex (even though we were both naked in his bedroom and he was still wearing the used condom). She said she thought he loved her…didn't he sleep with her every night…didn't she walk his dog…and on and on…

Then she directed her anger at me and came running at me, grabbed my legs, and pulled them apart. Don't know what she was looking for…Justin came over and dragged her away from me before she got more violent.

Then they walked over to the other side of the bed, where she found my lace panties on the floor and shoved them in his face, and said, "Who do these belong to?" Then she ripped them up and threw them at me. Meanwhile, I'm still on the bed—naked—and they are still arguing about the fact that he and I didn't have sex.

I then quietly grabbed my jeans from the bottom of the bed and walked out of the room, where I retrieved my t-shirt, which I left on the dining room table when I arrived. Thank God I did that since my lace panties were in shreds in my pocket, and my bra and shoes were still in the bedroom with the maniac woman.

She came out of the bedroom holding his used condom, and threw it on the floor in front of me, and tells me to take it with me. Then she storms back into the bedroom and slams the door. I follow her, open the door, and ask if I can get my shoes. She screams at me to go and get my shoes, then opens the patio door, and throws my shoes and bra into the pool! Meanwhile, I hear the shower running, and Justin is in the bathroom taking a shower!!! I step out of the bedroom, close the door, and grab my purse from the living room (thank God I left it there, or it would also be in the pool).

I got in my car and got the hell out of there before she ran after me and tried to kill me. She was that mad!!!

Shortly after I got home, I got a text from Justin saying that she had broken up with him, and he was very sorry for what happened. I told him I was also sorry, but if she really loved him, she would come back. (I hope I NEVER see that bitch again!!!)

Looking back at what happened and recounting the story makes it sound funny. But I have to say, while it was going on, I was terrified. She had murder in her eyes, and she was ready to beat the living crap out of me until he pulled her away.

***

THOUGHTS ABOUT MY LIFE

I have way too much time on my hands. I'm down to 5 clients (from 10) and am not motivated to do anything for them… All I can think about is my "social life."

I currently have 4 "boyfriends" (I used to have 5 until my dance instructor screwed up—literally). Anyway, let's go through them.

LOGAN

He's the one I've had in my life the longest. I was totally infatuated with him for the longest time. He was the first man I had sex with after 12 long years of celibacy, so it was like he took my virginity for the second time in my life. A girl doesn't forget that! Logan is charming, endearing, and attractive. He's also a "horn dog." If you don't know what that means—it means he will fuck anything that stands still. He's incapable of monogamy!

During our relationship over the past year, he would go MIA without contact for weeks. Whenever he came over, I felt like it was just for a "booty call." But since I had such strong feelings for him, I kept seeing him.

Now it's true that when he was gone, I was seeing and fucking several other men (until Covid), and then my social life seriously diminished!

One of the things that I brought into Logan's life was BDSM (which I picked up from 50 Shades of Grey). He had read the trilogy, so he was familiar with the story. Of all the crazy things he had done and the crazy women he had slept with, he had never been involved with that kind of sex.

Then he shared a video with me—The Story of O—which was like 50 Shades on steroids. However, unlike 50 Shades and Christian Grey, the "hero" in "O" was Rene, and also unlike 50 Shades (where Christian loved Anastasia and wanted her all to himself), Rene would pimp out "O" to other men.

So here we have Logan—he says he's not jealous (and I believe him), but he's willing to share me with other men for sex. I go along with this to make him happy, but I still long for the relationship with "Christian," where he wants me all to himself.

Logan was a Swinger back when that was the rage, and I had NEVER even known about the lifestyle! So, he started introducing me to that part of sex play. We began with a foursome with one of his friends and his girlfriend. It was the first time I ever "played" with a woman. It was the first time that I was in a bed with 3 other people having an orgy. I enjoyed it and found it exciting.

Not only did we have the foursome, we also had 4 menage a trois—Logan, me and Jason (twice), Logan, me and Cara (a transexual), and Logan, me and Rhonda (the woman who came down for the foursome—she came back for an encore alone).

He also wanted to invite some of his friends over to "gang bang" me and have me suck their cocks. Now, don't get me wrong, it all sounded pretty exciting to me, and I am an exhibitionist, but he was just like Rene in "The Story of O"—pimping me out! By the way, the "gang bang" never happened!

So, check him off the list for being my Christian Grey!

JASON

Jason came into the picture recently. I had gone online to find someone to "play" with, and he responded to the posting. He was looking for couples he could play with. I "interviewed" him by phone and text and invited him to my house to meet Logan and audition for us.

Jason is 7' tall and is gorgeous (a former professional basketball player)! He's gregarious and sweet and really turned me on (but I didn't let on to Logan—after all, I'm incapable of being monogamous). I had a lunch prepared for the 3 of us. We talked for a while, then wound up in the bedroom.

Jason turned out to have such a big cock that no matter how hard (tee hee) we tried, he couldn't get it into me. He was a very good kisser, but I felt he was holding back. So, I just gave him a blow job while Logan fucked me from behind. We had a good time and decided to do it again next week.

The same thing happened in round 2 with Jason—meaning nothing as far as him getting inside of me. I was frustrated, but I wasn't giving up.

Logan had to go on a trip to the West Coast for a few weeks (where I'm sure he fucked his old girlfriends in LA), so I took that opportunity to invite Jason to the house where we could have some time alone.

I told him I thought he was "holding back" when we were with Logan, and I was right. He was loving and passionate and a great kisser. We met alone a few more times while Logan was away and the next thing I know, he's telling me he's in love with me. And you know what? I felt the same way.

Unfortunately, he is married…they were married for 12 years and had separated, but she moved back with him because she lost her job and apartment. That was a bit of a fly in the ointment. He told me it was just temporary and that he wanted to get her to leave as soon as possible.

We continue to see one another on the sly because neither of us wants to rock the boat. He texts me daily, telling me how much he loves me (this is something I wish Logan would have done).

Again, I'm still looking for Christian Grey, and while Jason isn't pimping me out to other men, I'm not sure about his ability to be monogamous.

You may think…well, you're not monogamous either, and you may be correct. However, if I were with a man who was faithful and devoted to me, I would give up every other man in my life.

So, I'm still looking for my Christian Grey.

JORDAN

Jordan the Brit is a sweetheart but is a typical "Brit." He's attractive in a Prince Charles way, and I've been seeing him for about a year. He's not warm and fuzzy. When he comes to my house, I greet him at the door in some sexy outfit, and you would think I was wearing flannel pajamas. I've tried to get him to be passionate, but it isn't easy. He allows me to get passionate with him and has told me I am, but I guess it's not in his "wheelhouse" to be that way.

I want to keep him in my life. He's my Saturday date, and we enjoy being together. We do fuck, and he's not bad. He's very good at oral… But he's not my Christian Grey!

He also enjoyed the swinger lifestyle (since he's about the same age as Logan) and said he would take me to swinger clubs. He said when he was with his live-in girlfriend for many years, they would go to Fort Lauderdale to the clubs (the same ones Logan went to with his wife). I asked him what he did there, and he said that it was up to his date what and with whom she wanted to fuck. Didn't sound like he played much of an active role in the swinging scene.

Jordan has involved me more in his life than Logan or Jason can. He took me to meet his daughter and granddaughter in Miami several times. He doesn't contact me regularly (like Jason), but our date on Saturdays is something I look forward to.

Jordan is not my Christian Grey, either.

BOBBY

Bobby is not really a "boyfriend." He's relatively new in my life. He's been following me on Facebook for a year, and then he started calling and texting me, asking me if I would do PR work for him. I'm always willing to consider new clients, so I continued our communication.

Bobby is a TV producer; he had his own TV show, but…he has Parkinson's and is now in a rehab center in Boca trying to get healthy again.

He comes on very strong and is extremely persistent. He texts and calls me often daily, but we have never met in person. I've only seen his photos online.

He also has proclaimed that he's in love with me and wants to be with me. Again, he's no Christian Grey, although he tries to provide some of the criteria I want from a man. We'll see what happens with this relationship. He tries my patience sometimes, but his heart is good.

So now I'm 4 and 0, looking for my Christian Grey.

***

NOW WHAT?

So, I'm sitting here, frustrated and wondering if my quest for a Christian Grey wannabee is realistic. I've said this before, and it's become my mantra:

THEY ALL GIVE ME SOMETHING…BUT NO ONE GIVES ME EVERYTHING!

That's why it takes so many men to satisfy me. Maybe I'm picky, but I hope that out there somewhere is a man who will love me, want to be with me and be faithful to me. I would give up all of my "boys" just to have that relationship before I die!!!

***

WEDNESDAY

In the "Are you freaking kidding me" category…I received the following text from Justin (my dance instructor/hairdresser):

Hola darling. How are you? Missed our lesson today. When can we start up again?

Talk about men having a passing relationship with REALITY…you would think the scary situation with his girlfriend never happened!! I'm not getting back to him. We'll see how long it takes for him to acknowledge that he's a dirtbag for not defending me against his deranged girlfriend's attack!

***

FRIDAY

Jason came over today at noon. We were supposed to go to Dunkin' to meet a couple who wanted to play BDSM games (he found them online). When he walked in, he said they canceled. Truth be told…I was really happy. I was going along with it to show him I was up for anything (and truly I AM), but during this Covid situation, I'm not interested in getting together with strangers. So that left us with time alone until 3:00 p.m.

We went into my Playroom and got undressed down to our undies… We proceeded to kiss and hug and cuddle…but I wanted MORE…I had been using my vaginal dilator for weeks now, trying to stretch my lady part, and now it was time to test drive my equipment.

We lubed up and started very slowly. He penetrated me, and there was lift-off… We tried several positions to get the most comfortable and the one that worked best… Since he's so large and my vagina is so small, he didn't have to go in very far before he hit my G-spot… I screamed, and he was afraid that he was hurting me, but I said it was just the opposite. I'm a screamer when I have an orgasm, so until I said the "safe word"—RED, he wasn't to worry about his hurting me.

We took a rest and stayed in one another's arms, and then we did it again…Same result—screaming orgasm… And for another encore—we did it a third time!!! OMG, I couldn't believe it. I was so afraid that I would never be able to satisfy him sexually, and he said that was okay with him…but it WASN'T okay with me!!

He controlled himself and only came a little while he was inside me. Then I was laying on the bed giving him a blow job, and he was getting more and more excited… P.S. He came in my mouth… I have to say, his cum takes delicious (unlike some men). We then basked in the afterglow of sex, and I brought in a silver tray with cookies, grapes, and green tea for us… until he left at 3:00 p.m.

One little fly in the ointment… I had texted Logan in the morning, saying I was going to my sister's for lunch so he wouldn't decide to drop in to see me on his way to the boat. He asked me what time I was going, and I said 11:30 a.m. ..... so that would give him no time before Jason arrived at noon. He said he didn't know if he would be back in time on Sunday to come over. I told him we would play it by ear. I've gotten to the point with Logan that I expect NOTHING from him. I don't count on seeing him, and if I do—fine, and if not—that's fine too.

Of course, Bobby continues to text and call me a hundred times daily, professing his love and adoration for me.

***

I analyzed my relationships with the 4 men currently in my life and realized that each one has something that I want, but…as I've said before, none of them gives me everything that I need:

Logan—Handsome, funny, great in bed, likes to play BDSM with me, BUT although he's a bachelor, he's unavailable emotionally and personally, and he's a horn dog (fucks anything that walks—so I don't trust him).

Jason—Handsome, great in bed, professes his love for me every day, BUT he has a wife he's still living with, and I don't like having to sneak around to see him.

Jordan—Handsome, good in bed, very controlled in his emotions (he's a Brit—what can I say?) BUT he doesn't make my head spin when we're together. Don't think he's a horn dog, but who knows?

Bobby—Since I never met him in person, I don't know what he really looks like…he professes his love for me every day by phone, text, and email, BUT he's got Parkinson's and is living in a rehab facility.

Now an amalgam of those 4 men is my Christian Grey: I want a man who is handsome, funny, great in bed, healthy, professes his love for me every day, is NOT married, is into BDSM, doesn't want to pimp me out, and wants me for himself alone and will be faithful to me. Hey Universe…Is that too much to ask???

***

SATURDAY

Jordan arrived at 2:30 p.m. He brought spaghetti with Bolognese sauce and cake for dessert. I was wearing my black Dominatrix body suit. We had dinner and dessert and then went into the TV room. We started playing the game he brought last weekend, which was fun. Then we watched the BBC news. As we were scrolling down the TV guide, I saw that "50 Shades of Grey" was playing. So, we tuned into that.

After a while, we went into my Playroom to continue to watch the movie. Jordan got undressed and got into bed. I kept on my undies. We cuddled and watched the movie. He remembered seeing this one before, so I put in the next episode that I had on DVD. That version was unedited and more graphic than the TV version. One thing led to another, and we started kissing and having sex.

I like Jordan, but he doesn't blow my mind when we have sex. He always tries to take care of me—and he does—but it's not magical like it is with Logan and Jason.

I asked him what he was doing on Christmas (next Friday), and he said he was hiding from the world. So, I invited him to come over and have lunch/dinner with me. He had to think about it but finally said he would. I asked him what he would like, and we settled on a "comfort food" menu—meatloaf with gravy, mashed potatoes, and roasted Brussels sprouts.

I decided to do this because Logan would either be on the boat or with his ex-wife and kids, and even if he said he would "stop by," I would have to sit around all day waiting for him, and he might not even show up. Also, Jason will be with his wife and parents and could not get out. So that left Jordan. I was not about to sit around ALONE on a holiday while my "boyfriends" were with their families. Jordan left at 7:00 p.m.

***

WEDNESDAY

Jason came over today at 11:30 a.m. I wore a black lace bra, black lace boy shorts, and black thigh highs. Over that, I was wearing my black mink coat. When I opened the door, he was speechless. He walked in, took me in his arms, and kissed me. I led him into my Playroom, where he got undressed. I kept my undies on.

We talked for a while, then started kissing, and it got totally out of control, and the next thing, he was fucking me (going inside of me—I never thought that would happen!!). We took short breaks and then did it again! We had sex 4 times this afternoon!!!! He left at 2:00 p.m.

***

Well, Happy Day After Christmas…

Yesterday, Logan sent a Merry Christmas message to Jason (it was a Peanuts cartoon that just said Merry Christmas).

Jason responded with: *"Hey Logan, Merry Christmas! Buddy!! Where r u in the Caribbean on the boat??"*

Here's the rest of the dialogue:

Logan: *"No, wish I was for sure. We're all stuck here in Florida but hopefully better for all of us in the new year."*

Jason: *"Yes. That's for sure!! How's sexy, Stacey? U still playing?? I have been soooo busy at work!"*

Logan: *"She is great. Yes, but the Covid thing has slowed things down"*

My 2 worlds are colliding…

I would like to hear Logan's version of this exchange if I see him on Sunday after the boat. Also, will my 2 boys continue their dialogue???

BTW Jason shared all of these texts with me… it probably took all of his self-control not to say to Logan, *"Yes, Logan, Stacey is great …I've been fucking her for weeks…"* LOL

***

WEDNESDAY (TWO DAYS BEFORE THE NEW YEAR)

Jason was coming over at noon to take me to meet a woman we could "play" with. We were supposed to meet her at Dunkin' across the street, but neither of us received a confirmation text from her, so we decided to skip it and go into the Playroom.

Our Playtime has been getting more and more erotic and sensuous. He can penetrate me, and we do it several times during our session. I can't believe he can get inside of me. He was kidding me about how when I have sex with Logan, he will just slip out because the opening has been stretched (LOL). We played, talked, cuddled, laughed, and just enjoyed one another. He keeps telling me how much he loves me. I love to hear that! He left around 3 p.m.

I walked Jason to the door in my black lace panties, wearing one of Logan's white shirts with nothing else on. After he left, I straightened up the house and dressed in my jeans and T-shirt. Thank God…you'll see why in a minute.

Not 15 minutes after Jason left, my phone rang, and it was Logan. He's been on the boat since last weekend. I asked him where he was, and he said he was IN MY DRIVEWAY!! Oh shit! I raced around the house, looking for clues that someone else had been there when he appeared at the door.

We sat in the living room and talked for a while. He was acting a little subdued and was just jabbering on about nothing. I kept waiting for the other shoe to drop and for him to ask me who I was seeing since they probably passed one another on the road (Geez, I hope not). He didn't indicate that he would put me on the spot, and I played it very cool.

We started playing in the living room. Then he undressed me, leaving my jeans and t-shirt on the floor, and walked me into the Playroom. He got undressed and got on the bed, and we started kissing… He is a good kisser!! He asked me if I deserved to be flogged, and I said, "Yes." ... I felt so guilty I did need someone to flog me. He got into the flogging and got this strange look on his face, which frightened me a little. (He was enjoying it a little too much!) After he flogged me, we had sex in every position we could think of. I think he was a little surprised at how "wet" I was and how easy it was for him to penetrate. We went on like this until he left at 6 p.m.

Now people…looking at the timeline from Jason coming over at noon…then a short break…then Logan taking over until 6 p.m. I think I deserve some kind of a medal for my stamina!!!

I haven't done anything like this since I was separated from my former husband. Frank had taken me to dinner, then he came up to my apartment, and we had sex. After he left, Brian called me drunk and came over, and we had sex. Then, after Brian left, JG called me (he lived in the building), and he came over for sex… Three in one night was my record!

And just for the record, when Logan was here, my cell phone was ringing off the hook—it was Bobby checking up on me (5 times). Also got a call from Peter (the artist), and he left a voicemail… My "boys" must be in heat… or maybe they know I'm in heat and want some action (LOL).

After the incident with Justin and his insane girlfriend, you would think I would be a little more careful. But the fact is that Logan goes MIA with "radio silence," so I can't anticipate where he is or what he will do. He runs hot and cold. When I know Jason is coming over, I usually text Logan in advance to explain why I won't be available on that day and time so something like this doesn't happen. But this time, since I hadn't heard from Logan, I had no idea that the boat was back… and that he was going home to get more clothes, then back to the boat for the weekend… Oops!

To be honest, I don't regret anything that I am doing. I should have done this decades ago, but I want to experience all of this NOW. Everyone seems to enjoy the ride, and even though Jason thinks Logan is "using me," I'm also using Logan. After all, a vibrator can only do so much…and I've already broken 3 of them in the last year (LOL).

So, ladies (and gentlemen), don't give up on sex…It appears that you can do it forever if you want… Just enjoy the ride and have a HAPPY NEW YEAR!!

***

THURSDAY

Jason came over today at 12:30. I was wearing a sheer nightie with black lace boy shorts underneath. He had called me on his way over to say he wanted to shower at my house because he was coming directly from work. When he arrived, he was all sweaty and dirty (still turned me on). He went into my bathroom to shower and came out smelling all sweet and delicious.

He got on the bed with me, and we played and kissed. It wasn't long before I was out of my nightie and panties, and we were rolling around on the bed, making passionate love. We even put my butt plug in my ass while I was holding my vibrator on my clit, and Jason was fucking my pussy. Geez, what an experience! Then we tried it again, but this time he put his finger in my ass instead of the butt plug. He's the only man I've ever let get in my back door.

We went on like this for hours—he penetrated my vagina 3 times!!! I had so many orgasms I stopped counting!! I can't believe we've come this far in a relatively short time. I told him we've done everything and he assured me there was a lot more. I told him I couldn't wait to discover what else I'd missed. He left at 3 p.m., and I missed him immediately!

***

FRIDAY

I hadn't seen Logan since last Wednesday. He said he was sick after he left the yacht on Sunday and was staying home until he felt better. I really don't know if I believe him. Anyway, he said he would stop over today on his way up to the boat. He arrived at 1 p.m. looking fabulous—was he really sick? We sat in the living room and talked; he was very reserved. I remember when he couldn't keep his hands off me for 2 minutes. That's why I feel like something is going on with him—he met another woman, having an affair with one or many of the stews on the yacht—who the hell knows???

He asked me about the woman I was supposed to meet to play with and asked to see her photo. We went into my office, and I showed him her picture. We sat and talked for a while—he was on the sofa, and I was at my desk. He asked me to come over to him and give him a blow job (which I did). It was very unsatisfying for me. I pretended that I was playing with myself and was having an orgasm just to please him (what a schmuck I am).

He left at 2 p.m. and I was feeling very used and unappreciated!!! I have no one to blame but myself. Logan has been using me for a long time, and I continue to let him. Unfortunately, whenever I think he's broken the "spell" and I can take or leave him, my feelings for him come back. I think I've loved him since I met him, and, in the beginning, he was so romantic, but he has the attention span of a flea, and then he moves his attention to the next victim. He's been doing this all his life, and I don't know why I would think he could change at this point.

He told me that the only time he didn't stray or cheat was when he was married to his second wife…he said it was because she gave him everything he wanted —youth (she was 26, and he was in his 50s, so she made him feel young—even when people thought she was his daughter), sex, adventure...so he didn't have to go elsewhere.

I've been turning myself inside out, trying to please him sexually, emotionally, and in every other way I could. I never said no to anything he wanted to try. He did tell me at one point that he couldn't believe that I was real and that I was so exciting and sexually fulfilling. What happened??? Again, I think he's keeping me as a sure thing for his sexual needs but keeps looking for younger versions (with bigger tits) to play with.

I SO wish I could get him out of my system. I thought having Jason in my life, with all his romantic gestures telling me a million times a day that he loves me, would break the hold that Logan has on me. But right now, I really want Logan—God help me!!!

I really need to find my Christian Grey. Maybe he can break the spell once and for all. I feel like a drug addict who just can't break the habit, and it's killing me!!!

***

SATURDAY

Jordan arrived at 2 p.m. He brought a whole chocolate cake. I was wearing black jeans and a black sweater. I made mac and cheese with prosciutto with a green salad for lunch. We had a drink while I prepared the salad and then headed for the dining room to eat. He seemed to enjoy the mac and cheese, and we had a relaxing talk.

He showed me some information he brought on a swinger's club he wants to take me to in Pompano. He wants to take me there and watch me interact with other men… I swear all of the men in my life right now are voyeurs and/or pimps… I don't understand them at all. So, I asked Jordan why he wouldn't be jealous of his woman being with other men (either in front of him or just knowing they were playing with other men). His answer was the same as all of the other men I asked—"I'm not worried because I own her/you, and I know she/you will be coming back to me." I asked him, "What happens if she falls in love with someone she is with?" (Like what happened with Jason) And he didn't seem to think that would happen… (Ahem…it can, and it did—but I didn't tell him that!)

Somehow, the subject of my dance instructor came up (Jordan's a dancer), and I told him we had a falling out. He pressed me for details, and I told him the story of the girlfriend walking in on us while we were having sex. This perked him up. Men get excited about the strangest things.

After lunch, we went into the TV room, and he put on a Rugby game for a while before we had our chocolate cake for dessert. After dessert, while I was cleaning up the kitchen, Jordan disappeared. He wound up in my office. He called me to come in there. When I got there, he asked me to turn on my computer. My computer was asleep, and I just touched the mouse, and it came to life. He went to a porn website and was scrolling through some of the videos that were available. I asked him what he was doing, and he said he wanted to find out what my sexual preferences were.

As we watched some of the videos (which were very provocative), I began getting very excited. He watched me as I reacted to the various videos and scenarios. Finally, after watching an assortment of porn, we went into my Playroom and got undressed. He looked at the assorted sex items I had hanging from the door and the things in my bedside chest and selected a pair of cuffs and a small flogger. He then went into my lingerie chest and took out my vibrators (all 3 of them). He was ready for business.

He bound my hands behind my back with the cuffs, bent me over the bed, and stood behind me. He began playing with me with his hands and the various instruments and wound up inserting the penis-shaped vibrator into my pussy. He used the other vibrators as well and bent over me so he could play with my tits. I swear, he was like an octopus. I was writhing around on the bed, having multiple orgasms, and finally got to the point where I couldn't take it any longer and said the "safe word"—RED (MANY TIMES!). He ignored me and kept on with his machinations.

Finally, I worked my hands out of the cuffs and pulled away from him. I turned over on my back, facing him. He stood over me, smiling, and penetrated me from the front with his penis while I was laying on my back. I pulled him down on me so that he would stop, and he got on the bed and took me into his arms. I was totally surprised at this side of him. He had never acted so aggressively in the past.

We kissed and caressed and talked, and then he got hard again, and I was on top of him. While I was sitting there, he wanted me to tell him again about the details of the encounter with my dance instructor. As I recounted the story, he was getting more and more excited. We played for hours (which was unusual for us) until he left at 7 p.m. I was totally exhausted!!

***

SUNDAY

I invited Cara over for lunch today. She arrived at 1 p.m. She was wearing a black skirt and a white blouse. I was wearing black jeans and a black sweater. I served the leftover mac and cheese with a salad and Jordan's chocolate cake for dessert. We talked about a lot of personal things, and I told her my concerns about Logan, how he was making me crazy, and my newly formed relationship with Jason. She shared that she had some conflicted feelings about her former partner but wouldn't let them get to her.

Around 3:30 p.m. I got a text from Logan asking if Cara was still there and, if so, he was going to stop over. In the meantime, Cara and I got undressed down to our undies and put on white men's shirts (as if we had been playing all afternoon). Cara asked if I had any pot, and we both had a couple of tokes.

When Logan arrived at 4 p.m., he saw both Cara and I walking around in our men's shirts, and he assumed we had been playing all afternoon (which we hadn't). He didn't say anything, but I invited him to sit down at the dining room table and have a piece of chocolate cake. He seemed a little nervous/preoccupied, which wasn't like him. We talked for a while, and I could see he wasn't pursuing going into the Playroom. So, I got up and said why don't we go play. He said you girls, go ahead. This was all very strange for Logan. Usually, he would be the first one to jump on a threesome.

Cara and I went into the Playroom and started playing (we took off our shirts but still had our undies on—then we got naked). I asked Logan to get my cell phone and take some pictures. He was happy to do that. He stripped down to his underwear but didn't go any further and began filming our activities. Finally, I suggested that Logan join us. He took off his underwear and got on the bed between Cara and me, and we started playing with him.

After some time, he got out of bed and took the flogger from the door, and told me to stand on the side of the bed and lay across it while he beat my ass. Cara was on the bed facing me, and she and I were holding one another's arms. Logan was really flailing into me. Then he went over to Cara and started on her. He was having too good a time! I almost had to signal the safe word—RED.

After he finished beating us, he flipped me over and fucked me while Cara came over and was playing with me and kissing me. Then we all got on the bed. Cara and I played with Logan, which he seemed to enjoy. Then everyone was writhing around on the bed, and there were legs and arms and hands and mouths all over the place—the pot was making everything much more surreal.

After we played for a while, Logan was in the middle of the 2 of us with his arms around us, and he started telling some of his stories (about his second wife and the wild things they did—YUK!!!). Then he said, "Let's put Stacey in the middle and play with her." So, we switched places, and Logan and Cara started kissing me and playing with me. One thing I want to note—I tried to kiss Logan (one of our deep kisses) and he wouldn't let me. I asked him why he wouldn't kiss me, and he said he didn't feel like kissing today. RED FLAG…RED FLAG… What the fuck is going on with him. If he's seeing someone else and didn't want to see me, why the hell didn't he just say he was working on the boat late and skip the threesome??? The other thing about him is that since he's been fooling around in his relationships ALL his life, he should be a better actor when it comes to lying so his partner wouldn't get suspicious. After all, how do you go home to your wife on the weekend and act natural after spending the entire week playing house with one of your whores!!!

After a couple of hours of playing, Logan got dressed to leave. He left at 6 p.m.

After he left, Cara and I talked, and I told her there was something wrong with him tonight. I just have a sick feeling in my stomach…WHY IN THE WORLD CAN'T I GET THIS MAN OUT OF MY SYSTEM SO THAT I DON'T CARE WHAT HE'S DOING OR WHO HE MIGHT BE WITH?????

After Cara left, I texted Logan, asking if he was upset with me or something I did. He gave me a lame excuse that he had a headache and didn't want to complain about it.

Meanwhile, I received a couple of texts from Jason asking what was going on. I told him Logan had stopped over, and he said he was pretty sure Logan would. BTW before Logan left, he said that we should do this again with Cara and maybe invite Jason over to join us…both. Cara and I looked at one another with a knowing glance (since I had told her how my relationship with Jason had evolved). When I told Jason about what Logan said, he said he would love to be with Cara and me but NOT with Logan. He REALLY doesn't like Logan.

Then, I composed this letter to Logan:

Dear Logan,

I've known you for over a year, and it has been great. There was a time when we couldn't be apart for more than a day or so. Now, things seem to have changed. I understand that you need to work to make money, but something else seems to be going on.

I know from your background that you need to find sexual fulfillment from a number of sources. I do, as well. But I feel that you are either satisfying yourself with someone else, with someone from the boat, or with someone you met through your other activities. I know I told you that I didn't want to know about your sexual exploits with other women, and that still holds true. But my imagination can develop scenarios that are possibly more intense than actual reality.

I've told you how I feel about you, and because of that, it hurts me that I cannot seem to satisfy you anymore. At one time, you said that you couldn't believe I was real because I seemed to satisfy your sexual needs AT THAT TIME.

Because of your past escapades, I thought you would be able to hide your indiscretions from your current partner more discretely. I don't know what to say to you except if you are merely staying with me so that I remain your "booty call," that's not fair to me.

If you have to force yourself to see me or if you have to try to fit me into your life, I am not that special person anymore, and I will find someone to make me feel special.

As I've told you, I do NOT want another permanent relationship at this time. I just don't like to feel that your attentions have moved on, and you don't want to be with me anymore, but you are afraid to tell me.

I'm not making an ultimatum here... you and I are both free, and if we seem to be drifting apart, everything will happen naturally. I have really enjoyed my time with you, and I do love you, but I keep having my heart broken by trying to make you happy and letting you have your space.

No matter what happens, I will always treasure the time we've had together and the fact that you introduced me to some very exciting and mind-blowing sexual activities. It's been a blast. You do not have to respond to this letter. We can continue to go on as we have, or you can go on without me.

Love,

Stacey

***

VALENTINE'S DAY

This year's Valentine's Day was very special. With 3 lovers, I was not sure what to expect—perhaps nothing—but I was pleasantly surprised.

JASON

Jason picked me up at 10:00 a.m. on the Wednesday before Valentine's Day (Wednesdays have become OUR day to meet). He gave me a set of parameters to follow for the 'surprise' he was planning:

1. *Be ready to be picked up at 10 a.m.*
2. *Pigtails Or Ponytail if easier*
3. *Casual clothes that can get dirty*
4. *Bring the mountain bread. If none is left, I will get some on the way over. Just let me know*
5. *Sunglasses*
6. *Prepare to have some FUN!!*

I obeyed each of those requests and waited for the scenario to unfold. Jason picked me up exactly on time in his HUGE blue Jeep. He buckled me into my seat and then began to drive. He didn't say where we were going, and I didn't ask. We wound up at a park in Delray Beach. I had never heard of it and didn't even know it existed. The park was virtually empty as we drove through. When we got to the end of the park, we stopped at a facility where men were flying model airplanes. We got out and walked over to the sheltered area where they were preparing their miniature aircraft to take off, maneuver, and then land.

I, of course, began chatting with the men, asking them questions about their planes, and they were very friendly. Some of the feats they put their planes through were truly amazing! After watching this 'show' for a while, we had lunch. Jason had brought a cooler with the ingredients for a picnic—peanut butter and jelly (our favorite). I made sandwiches, which we enjoyed, and then had some cookies and fruit for dessert. It was such a 'normal' day—we were able to hold hands and kiss in public—just like a "normal" couple.

After a couple of hours, we returned to my house and into the Playroom, where we both got out of our sweaty picnic clothes and began playing. Because of the size of Jason's organ, we usually begin slowly in order to stretch my pussy. We go from his entering from the front, then we rest. Then we go to his entering from behind, then we rest. And finally, we go with my sitting on top of him. This is usually the greatest penetration, so we approach this position carefully. BUT this time, I wanted to START with that position. Mounting this handsome, sexy man is a challenge (I've told him that he is wider than when I tried to mount my horse). Anyway, he was laying on the bed, and I slowly sat on top of his enormous cock and slid down until I thought my eyes were going to pop out of my head. I started moving around and had, I don't know how many orgasms, and then I collapsed on top of him. I felt like I was in another world. Everything seemed surreal.

He is so adorable. He took me into his arms, held me tight, and told me to relax and catch my breath. He asked if he hurt me, and I said no…he didn't hurt me, but our sex act was so amazing that I almost passed out from the emotions I was experiencing. After resting for a while and coming back down to earth, we proceeded to engage in every other position possible. When he left at 4 p.m. I was totally spent. My God, I love that man!!!

He did leave me a Valentine's card and asked me not to open it until Valentine's Day. It said, "From a Heart that LOVES YOU!"

LOGAN

Logan has been a little elusive lately (big surprise), and I hadn't seen him for over a week, and that was just to meet him for Pizza and then we both went our separate ways. I didn't call or text him, but I did respond to his texts (after waiting for a while). He had asked to come over on the previous Wednesday (when Jason was planning his Valentine's surprise), but I told Logan that I was busy and couldn't see him. I figured that would push him further into his MIA mode. But he called me on the Friday before Valentine's Day and asked if he could stop by on his way to the boat. Since I wasn't busy, I agreed.

He arrived at noon bearing a dozen red roses, a huge box of chocolates, and a beautiful card. Now brace yourself for what the card said:

On the cover of the card were 2 cartoon characters (s'mores)…one said 'Love You', and the second said 'Love You, S'more' ...cute, huh!?!? But INSIDE the card, it said, 'Love You Most' ...Now I don't want to read too much into that since it was the card talking, BUT he did write in 'Huge hugs for a very Happy Valentine's Day, Love, Logan XO'.

We went into the Playroom and had fun until he left at 2:30 p.m. On his way out the door, he said, "Love you." I said nothing.

Anyway, he knew I was going out with Jordan on Saturday night to a sex club, and he texted me all weekend wanting details on the date. As I answered his questions about what happened at the club, he got more and more horny and curious. He wanted a chapter and verse description of what happened. Who fucked me? Did I have sex with a woman? And as I answered his questions, he got more and more interested in me. (Men are pigs!)

I swear to God, I do not understand Logan. He runs hot and cold, and I never know which Logan it will be.

JORDAN

Jordan knew I was curious about sex clubs, and he found one in Pompano. He asked if I wanted to go for Valentine's Day, and I thought, 'Why not?' He suggested we have dinner before we went to the club (which opens at 9 p.m.). He picked me up at 7:30 p.m. and took me to a very nice restaurant in Boca. We had a leisurely dinner, then headed to the club a little after 9 p.m.

We arrived at the club and signed in (Jordan bought a Membership and signed us up as a couple). We went inside the club, and the music playing was deafening and very primal, with a drum beat that overshadowed even the music itself. Since it was a BYOB, we gave our bottle of wine to the bartender, who kept it there so we could come for refills throughout the night. I walked around to get the lay of the land. There was the main room with seating arrangements and a large bar. Through one corridor was a locker room. I was told this is where you put your clothes when the sex part of the evening begins. Then we went into another large room with a bar and wall-to-wall beds. There were also smaller rooms with beds and doors if you wanted privacy.

We went back to the main room, and I drank my wine. They kept passing around Jell-O shots (I guess laced with Vodka). Anyway, we listened to the music and watched the crowd of half-naked women bouncing around the dance floor. I felt totally overdressed. I had on a sexy black dress studded with rhinestones, and I wore sheer pantyhose. About an hour into watching the outfits the women were barely wearing, I went into the locker room, removed my panties and pantyhose, and put them in my purse.

When I came out, I hiked up my dress, straddled Jordan, who was sitting on a sofa, and gave him a lap dance (to his surprise). Then I started kissing him. People were watching us, and it made me even more excited. Then I sat beside Jordan on the sofa, and he began running his hand up my leg to my private parts. It was so sexy doing all this in public. (I'm an exhibitionist!)

Eventually, it was time to go to the 'bed' room…Jordan and I took off all our clothes, put them in the locker, and retrieved 2 towels from the locker to wrap around us.

We walked to one of the unoccupied 'beds' in the main room and put our towels on the bed to lay on. Jordan put me on the bed and began going down on me. As I was laying there groaning and moaning and eventually screaming with orgasms, a small crowd had gathered to watch us. I think they were waiting for Jordan to give them a sign for one of them to continue playing with me (which he did not do). He moved me up on the bed, got next to me, and held me in his arms to keep the wolves at bay. Between the 6 Jello shots and the 3 glasses of wine, I needed someone to protect me.

It was fascinating to watch what was going on around us. The place was filled with naked people doing every sex act you could imagine. Across the aisle from our bed were 3 couples (who obviously knew one another), and they started with girl-on-girl while the men watched, playing with their cocks. Then, the boys stepped in. They were fucking the girls while the girls were giving blow jobs to some of the men, and then it was like a leapfrog event with one right on top of the other. It was like being in the middle of a porn movie.

Couples who were not fortunate enough to get a bed were sitting on sofas having sex—women giving blow jobs, men going down on women, and multiple couples playing and fucking and sucking. Meanwhile, the music was blasting in this room. It had a jungle-beat. Everyone seemed to be in a frenzy. No one cared about who was watching. Partners were switching. Women were screaming with orgasms. It was the most savage display I've ever seen, BUT I was so turned on I couldn't stop watching.

Jordan and I watched and played all night long. He brought me home at 3:00 a.m. I have NEVER stayed out that late EVER in my life. What a trip!!! I definitely want to do it again. But this time, I know the rules.

First of all, when we arrive, we need to talk to and meet some of the couples in the club…find out a little about them and see if we would want to 'play' with them later in the evening. Since we didn't do that, I didn't feel like fucking a stranger that just happened by.

Aside from the dinner and clubbing event, Jordan also gave me a beautiful Valentine's Day card. He wrote on the card, 'Love you and everything about you—Jordan.' Now, mind you, Jordan has never expressed any emotion (like love) in the past, so this was a bit of a surprise!

I have to say that this was one of the best (and longest-lasting) Valentine's Days I've ever had.

***

FRIDAY

Logan came over at 11:00 a.m. on his way to the boat. I hadn't seen him in over 2 weeks! I hadn't planned to have sex with him, but one thing led to another, and I did.

Jason had contacted me earlier by text and said he might stop over on Friday (knowing that Logan might appear on his way to the boat). Logan texted me and confirmed he would be over, and I let Jason know. He said to let him know when Logan left, and he would come over. That was a surprise since I usually don't see Jason on Fridays.

Logan left around 1 p.m., and the first thing I did was take a shower. I texted Jason and said that Logan had left. Even though he knew Logan was coming over at 11 a.m., he said he drove by my house at 12:30, saw Logan's car here, and went to the CVS parking lot to wait.

When Jason arrived at 1:30 p.m., he was obviously upset, and I assumed it was about Logan. He came in, and we sat on the sofa in the living room and he said he was upset because I lied to him on Wednesday by holding back what I was thinking. I was surprised because I didn't even feel that he was upset when he left, AND I didn't know what he thought I was holding back.

He acted hurt and distant and said that if it was anybody else, he would never see them again because he thought I lied. Honest to God, I didn't know what he was talking about. I got a sick feeling in the pit of my stomach.

He knows I get upset because Logan comes and goes as he pleases, yet I continue to see him. I KNOW Logan has many flaws, but I deal with it. Believe me, I don't feel this bad when I don't see Logan as when Jason is acting so hurt and upset with me.

I told Jason that what I was "holding back" was about him and his life. I said that the day before, my trainer said that men and women cheat for different reasons…men cheat just for sex because they are DOGS, but women cheat to find something they don't have at home. My trainer said not to trust ANY man because they are incapable of being loyal. I did tell Jason about that conversation when we were together on Wednesday.

I thought about what my trainer said all day Thursday and decided that I was ready to share what I thought with Jason. I asked Jason how long he had been married (16 years), and he confirmed that he had gotten married because he thought he was in love with the woman even though he KNEW that there would be a problem with intimacy in their marriage. He said that in their 16 years of marriage, he had not been able to penetrate her. Every time he tried to have intercourse with her, she would scream in pain. I guess he felt that would justify his fucking other women. I said that his going outside the marriage for sexual fulfillment, given the facts, was understandable. That he stayed married and protected his 'roommate' from knowing about his infidelities was a good thing, and I understood he was a 'good man'. Many men would have just gotten a divorce and moved on, but he continued to stay with her and protect her as he does now. **THAT'S what I was thinking about on Wednesday, but I had not thought it through enough to verbalize it then!**

One thing that Jason said that stuck with me, and I'm not sure if I understood him correctly, was that he was the 'boss' at his job and could come and go as he pleased. I wasn't sure if he was dangling the fact that he could actually spend more time with me or if he was just stating a fact. I didn't pursue it because I was so upset; I wasn't thinking straight. But in retrospect, I probably should have followed up on what he meant.

I know many things go on in Jason's life with his roommate (wife) that are both good and bad BUT he never shares that with me.

Because I don't know about them and he doesn't complain about them, it doesn't make them less true. And yet, I don't consider his withholding these facts from me lying to me! The more I thought about it, the angrier I got because I felt I was truly misunderstood.

Clearly, Logan has become a part of my life (like it or not), and just like Jason is not going to get rid of his roommate (wife), I'm not ready to push Logan out of my life. I guess it's my fault for sharing how angry I get with Logan for his MIA and radio silence moves. I should just keep that to myself (just like Jason keeps anything to do with his roommate to himself). When I complain, Jason wonders why I keep Logan in my life if he makes me so miserable.

Jason asked me what I wanted out of life. I told him that when I started dating, all I wanted was friendship from the men I was seeing…that was before Covid when I was free to come and go as I pleased. I dated several times a week and was very busy with my physical activities (gym), volunteer work, and business, so all was well with me. Then, all that changed for the past year with the quarantine and lockdown. The only men I kept in my life were Logan and Jordan. Then Jason entered the picture. I told Jason that it was lonely watching TV at night by myself. I said I wanted more of a relationship and someone to share my life with. I did NOT want a live-in or a marriage (GOD NO!!!), but someone I could count on to be there for me on a regular basis. If I had that, I wouldn't be looking outside the relationship for fulfillment.

I'm reluctant to share this update with Jason. Lord knows how many things I've already said here that could hurt him or push him away. He seems to be reading much more into what I am doing than is there. By the way I'm feeling, I KNOW that I truly love Jason. But now I feel that I have to guard what I say to him because either by verbalizing or withholding my thoughts, I will give him a reason to doubt me and maybe drive him away.

It's Saturday morning, and I woke up at 3 a.m. thinking about all this. Still have a sick feeling in the pit of my stomach. Still ambivalent about having a further discussion of my feelings with Jason. I'm now afraid of saying things to him (that's NOT good!!). I thought we had an honest and open relationship, but I feel very insecure about what I can talk about without setting off alarm bells. Jason said he would rather I told him everything and he wouldn't get angry, and I believe him. I just feel that my judgment is impaired when it comes to my relationships, and I may blunder into another confrontation. God help me; I don't know what to do.

***

SATURDAY (Sharon and Richie)

Sharon and Richie came over at 6:30 p.m. (Jordan arrived at 5:30 p.m. to check everything and see if we were missing anything.) Sharon was wearing a black tunic dress, and Richie was wearing casual slacks and a shirt. They also had a big duffle bag. They gave me a bottle of red wine and a homemade cake (a very nice gesture). Sharon also made "mask holders" for Jordan and me with our names in beads!!

I had an antipasto set out on the coffee table in the living room with dessert and Jello shots on the sideboard. BTW, they both refused the Jello shots because Richie had gotten sick the last time he tried them.

While I was getting drinks (Richie was helping me), Sharon sat down next to Jordan on a loveseat. Richie and I served the drinks then he sat on the opposite love seat. I sat on the chair adjacent to the loveseat. We started talking, but before long Sharon got up and took her dress off and was wearing a lace body suit, open in front and back (so basically, she was naked!). She sat back down and started rubbing Jordan's cock through his pants. He looked over at me, and I almost burst out laughing. He had that pleading look that said, "Are you seeing this?" I ignored him and kept talking. Then Richie invited me to sit next to him on the loveseat, which I did.

Sharon was pulling stuff out of the duffle bag—G-strings, panties, toys, drugs, lube, you name it, she had it… it was like a magic box full of erotic implements. They started passing around the pot pipe and then shared some pot gummies and pot chocolate…The world began to get very warm and fuzzy for me after that… Any inhibitions that I might have had disappeared (which was the point, I guess).

We sat there watching Sharon unzip Jordan's pants and give him a blow job right on the loveseat. Then Richie put his arm around me and started caressing my tits. At this point, I suggested we go into the Playroom since things were getting pretty hot in the living room. In the Playroom, we all undressed, and Richie went through the duffle bag of goodies again, took out a giant vibrator, and set some lubricant on the dresser.

After settling in the Playroom, Sharon and Richie pushed me up against the wall by the door and pulled my arms over my head. Each of them began sucking on one of my nipples while they fingered my clit and pussy and kissed me all over. Jordan was on the bed watching this scene. I don't know how long those two were at it, but I must have had a dozen orgasms. My legs felt like rubber, and I could hardly stand up. For the first time in the evening, I had to shout 'RED' since they were beginning to hurt me, and having multiple orgasms is exhausting and takes my breath away. The second time I had to say 'RED' was while I was on the bed and Sharon and Richie were doing all sorts of things to me and I couldn't breathe, hence the 'safe word—RED.' Sharon thought it was funny that I couldn't breathe and said it was similar to autoerotic asphyxiation (I saw that on an episode of Law & Order, and the person died—so WTF already!!!)

On the bed, Sharon and I played with one another. I went down on her. She went down on me. We did the 69 position. And then we took the giant vibrator and set it between both of our clits while I was laying on the bed and Sharon was hovering over me kissing me. They wanted to see if we could cum together. The vibrator did its job, and both of us had many screaming orgasms.

As far as I can remember, we performed every combination available—girl-on-girl, girl-boy-girl, boy-girl-boy.

Sharon kept Jordan to herself. He went down on her and played with her, fingered her, but she wouldn't let him enter her. She said it was because she had been playing with her big vibrator during the week, and her pussy was sore.

Richie kept me all for himself (yikes!). He said he loved my body… *"Hey, Sharon, don't you love Stacey's body?"* Sharon responds, *" Yes, she has a beautiful body."* Then he starts playing with me—touching my tits, fingering my clit, saying how beautiful I am… *"Hey Sharon isn't Stacey beautiful?"* Sharon responds, *"Yes, she is, "…* and then the subtext *("Wait 'til I get you home, you horny bastard"…* LOL).

We went on like this until Sharon decided she had enough (around 10 p.m.). Richie didn't want to leave, but she said that they needed to leave Jordan and me alone (wink, wink).

As they were getting ready to leave, Richie asked if we wanted to get together again next weekend. Sharon didn't jump on that, and neither did I. I think we can be friends and even play together, but they are exhausting as a couple!

After they left, Jordan and I got dressed and did a post-mortem of the evening. He said that Sharon was jealous of me. I asked him if she said anything, and he said she didn't like how her husband was acting with me, talking with me, complimenting me, and kissing me. I thought she was getting quieter as the evening progressed, but I didn't know why. Since Jordan spent the entire evening trying to satisfy her, he was in the best position to judge her mood… We'll see how she acts the next time we're together if there is a next time.

***

SATURDAY (Pam and David)

Jordan and I interviewed Pam and David via Zoom last Sunday. He found them on a swinger's website. They seemed nice enough people, so we accepted when they invited us to their home the following Saturday.

Jordan arrived at my house at 7:00 p.m., and we ate a bite before heading to Pam and David's house. We got there about 8:30 p.m. I was wearing my black transparent dress with my lace bra and lace boy shorts underneath.

Pam and David greeted us at the door. She was wearing a white blouse, unbuttoned to her waist, with black slacks that were cut open up the sides. BTW, the "boys" were just wearing regular clothes.

We went out to their patio for drinks and snacks and sat by their beautiful pool. We talked to get to know one another a little more, and then David suggested we go into the heated pool (that was a welcome suggestion—since it was pretty cool that night). We took off our clothes, left them on the chairs and went into the pool naked. It was heavenly—about 80 degrees. Pam began running her hands up and down my body and said, *"You're so skinny."* Just for the record…Pam was slightly plump, and her breasts were soft and sagging.

While in the pool, I asked Pam if I could kiss her because Jordan wanted to see me do that, and we did. She's a VERY good kisser. Then we split off—Pam corralled Jordan and was kissing and touching him all over. David was doing the same to me. David kissed me, and as good as his wife is, he is a terrible kisser. He just stuck his tongue in my mouth and left it there. There was no passion (at least on my part). He was playing with my tits and fingering my pussy, trying to turn me on (and still—nothing!). It could be that he was short, overweight, balding, hairy (his back was like a fur coat), and he had a small dick... he just wasn't doing it for me.

On the other hand, Pam couldn't keep her hands off of Jordan… he is 6'2", full head of grey hair, nice size cock, and very handsome. The more I thought about it, the more I thought that the reason they are swingers is that Pam gets to play with and fuck other men (much more attractive than her husband), and tonight she lucked out with the grand prize of Jordan. As far as David…he lucked out as well…not to be too immodest, but since I work out and exercise, I'm very trim, and my body is ripped—my abs are sculptured, and my tits are round and firm and fully packed.

Anyway, after a while, Pam decided she wanted to get out of the pool. So, we all exited, dried ourselves off, and headed for their bedroom. We got on the bed, and Pam went to town on Jordan. David went to town on me. Since it was a Queen-sized bed, Jordan and I were at least in visual range of one another. While Pam was giving Jordan a blow job and David was going down on me, I looked over at Jordan, and he leaned over and kissed me passionately while caressing my body. He later told me that by doing that, he got more excited under Pam's ministrations.

After a couple of hours of playing, we stopped and got dressed. We went into the kitchen to talk and snack and drink. Jordan got me home about midnight.

***

SUNDAY (Faye and Eddie)

Jordan also found this couple on a swinger's website. I spoke with them by phone, and again, they seemed nice enough, so I set up this meet and greet at my house. They had accents, so I knew they were from a foreign country. I thought perhaps Iran, but they were from Lebanon.

Jordan came over at 6:00 p.m., and they arrived around 7:00 p.m. When they came in and I kissed Eddie, I smelled his cologne. I asked him if it was Dolce & Gabbana *The One,* and he said, *"How did you know that? I'm so impressed that you recognize that fragrance."* Well, it wasn't that hard—that's Logan's signature fragrance, and I even have a bottle he left on my perfume tray in my bedroom.

I had prepared hors d'oeuvres, and we sat in the living room. They brought Grey Goose vodka, which they had with cranberry juice. Jordan had limeade, and I had white wine.

We sat in the living room and talked. Unlike Sharon and Rich, who sat on opposite loveseats so they could play with us individually,

Faye and Eddie sat on the same loveseat and held hands (very sweet). I was wearing a blouse with black slacks, and she was wearing a blouse and jeans. Since we didn't know them, I didn't want to wear anything provocative.

They talked about how long they have been in the lifestyle and some of their experiences. It was interesting how they perceived that the lifestyle had helped their marriage of 30 years. Again, my philosophy is that the 'lifestyle' gives a couple the opportunity to 'play' with other partners without the guilt of cheating.

Faye was attractive but slightly plump, and Eddie was about 50 pounds overweight. He was obviously self-conscious about it because he apologized and said he was trying to diet to lose weight. His face was attractive, but with the extra weight on his belly, he looked pregnant. I found it a turn-off.

As things were going along, I think Eddie wanted to see if the evening would wind up in the Playroom. He said he would bet me that he knew the size of my nipples. If he loses, I have to kiss him. So, he made a circle with his fingers, and I said it was incorrect. So, he got up and walked over to me and planted a wet kiss on me—full tongue and all. What is it with these guys? Do they think that sticking their entire tongue in your mouth is a turn-on? Perhaps if it was going into your pussy, it would be effective. But I prefer a soulful, dry kiss on my mouth with a surprise flick of the tongue.

Anyway, no clothes were removed or moves made for the Playroom. I mentioned that I had an early morning (having to be at the hospital to volunteer at 7:30 a.m.), so they took the hint and decided to leave. They left at 10:00 p.m.

After they left, Jordan and I had our post-mortem to go over the evening. I said that I liked them. I asked him if we should see them again. He said no. I asked why, and he said that Eddie was too fat and unattractive and that I deserved better. He said he wanted to rethink the parameters of the couples he was looking for online. He wanted the men to be in shape and handsome and be able to turn me on. Jordan is really so sweet!!

***

MONDAY

I received a text from Pam asking if I was exclusive with Jordan. I told her that I saw other men. Then she invited me for a threesome. I asked who the 3 would be, and she said—me, her and David. I thanked her and told her I would think about it. I'm not sure how that came about because she only kissed me on Saturday. We never went any further, so I thought maybe she wasn't into playing with women. Perhaps David wanted another shot at me and figured this was the way to go—with a threesome. Who knows? Not sure what I'm going to do. Stay tuned.

***

SATURDAY (Months later…)

Well, it's been a long time since I made an entry in my diary…Jason's Dad passed away on December 24 (Christmas Eve), and he's been in a tailspin ever since. His Mom has turned out to be quite a handful and demands that he spend time with her EVERY DAY!!!

We haven't had sex in months, and I'm not happy about that at all. I feel that if he really loved me, he would carve out at least an hour here and there to see me. He did drop over for an hour or less a couple of times, and all we did was talk, but he's become paralyzed with his own situation.

I've been feeling so neglected, and I've been trying to be understanding, but I'm running out of patience. I feel worse than when Logan was ignoring me!

I wonder if Jason even considers what we had discussed in the past…that he would never have been able to take me away from Logan if Logan had been taking care of me…Now the situation is reversed, and Jason is not caring for me, so I need someone who puts me first!!!

I went online and responded to 2 ads (which turned out to be the same guy). We made a connection, and I'm pursuing this 'relationship.' I also contacted Logan by text, and he responded immediately. He won't be back in the country for months (still taking the yacht around the world), but he wanted to see me when he came back.

I feel like Jason and I have already broken up, but neither of us will cut the final cord—all we have now are texts and phone calls…I feel like telling him not to contact me anymore, and we can try again if and when he gets his life together. But the thought of cutting off the phone calls and texts would be like going off drugs cold turkey. My stomach is in knots thinking about it. I feel like I would rather have a small connection to him than no connection. I'm addicted to him!!! And I love him more than anyone I've ever been with!! God help me!!

Honestly, I almost think it would be a relief for him if I broke up with him! Then it would be one less stress in his life. But what happens to him when things settle down again? He will return to sneaking around with women to add to the "trophies" on his phone. But the one thing that would be different would be that he would

NEVER feel about another woman the way he felt about me. He will go through the motions, but it will not satisfy him.

***

THURSDAY (Again, months later…)

Well, here I am back again, and my head is fucked up…I haven't seen Jason for over a month and only for a 45-minute 'drive-by,' which means we only talked…I'm still horny as hell!!! Remember, the last time we had sex was months ago!!!!!

I've been busy since my last entry, but nothing has satisfied me. I had dinner with Brad, the Pilot, went to Haulover Beach (a nude beach) with Barbara and Cara, and had lunch with Cara and Barbara at "Ace's" house (a friend of Barbara's). I hated him…he was a total douchebag.

Anyway, tonight I'm going to a social given by one of my business groups and I invited the guy I met online—Will—to meet me there. He's into BDSM and swinging. Sounds like the perfect guy to keep my mind off Jason's neglecting me!! But that's not happening. I'm feeling guilty and angry that this is the route I'm taking to deal with Jason. And I'm projecting my 'cheating' on him as to how I would feel if he was cheating on me, and the feeling sucks!!!

I've stopped asking Jason when I'm going to see him. Also, I'm not prompting him to think about his relationship with his wife. The other day, he started a conversation that a couple they had dinner with over the weekend would probably stay friends with the wife rather than him if they divorced.

I am so addicted to Jason that I can't think of anything but him. I need to get some perspective because I can't see how his relationship with me can ever work. Between his Mom and his wife, he's afraid to upset either one of them. And I'm the one who is left out.

Logan texted me last night, said he missed me, and said to "get rid of 'Skippy" (that's what he calls Jason). He's right, but I feel sick thinking of not having Jason in my life.

If I did break up with Jason, he would probably just stay with his wife forever and go back to cheating on her and fucking random women.

We'll see how tonight goes with Will. I'm not planning on anything happening except to get to know him a little in person. Our only contact has been texting and a phone call. He doesn't need to sweep me off my feet…just offer me an alternative to being alone and possibly having a playmate until Jason can give me more time (or not). Details to come.

Unfortunately, Will was a one-and-done guy, so chalk another one up!

***

I've been begging the angels to send me someone who could take me away from Jason as Jason took me away from Logan, and there may be a candidate—Peter.

He's a retired firefighter with blond hair, blue eyes, 6'1", adorable, sweet, sexy, SINGLE, and drives a Jaguar…the complete package.

I invited him to meet me at the Green Market yesterday morning, and he was there bright and early. We walked through the market holding hands. He's very touchy, feely…and we kissed as we walked around. It was so normal. We were not looking for someone who would recognize us (like with Jason).

I invited him back to my house for a snack, and one thing led to another, and we wound up in bed together. He's so thoughtful…he uses foreplay…he's a great kisser, and I really like him.

I know that it was 'revenge sex' on my part, but I was so angry with

Jason—and I still am angry with him!!! He continues to hurt me…I should never have started this with him!

Even if I move on from Jason, I have never loved anyone else with the intensity I love him (NOT EVEN LOGAN), and it would hurt me to my core…But I need to think of my own feelings…which obviously, he is not thinking about!!!

I've already started acting cool towards Jason (and he's noticed) by only texting him a few gifs in the morning…and when I look at the gifs I've collected to send to him after I read them, I don't feel the same way, and I can't send them to him.

What to do? I can't see just saying I never want to see him again…His situation pretty much takes care of seeing him regularly anyway. And I don't want to use Peter because I don't want to hurt him…So, as the saying goes, 'Be careful what you wish for.'

***

JASON BROKE THE SPELL

It has been months since Jason's Dad passed away, and he seems to be getting more and more depressed. He can't move forward. He can't make decisions. He just seems to be floating along, allowing circumstances to drive him.

He's not the man I met and fell in love with. That man was tough, took charge, and had confidence. This new man is a child who can't seem to get out of his own way. It makes me so sad. We had such plans before his Dad passed. He was going to be a motivational speaker. He even had business cards printed up, created a website, and I was going to help him with his new career. Now he has no plans, no ambition, no love of life!

But as the day wears on, I realize that I hurt so badly thinking of his not being in my life that I can't concentrate on anything!! He has no idea what I'm thinking…and that's how I will keep it. He thinks all is well.

Jason came over for a visit and laid on the bed, and we just started talking…I could tell that he really wasn't in the mood to talk, but I kept him going anyway. I asked him about his first wife, the women he slept with, and how many he said he 'loved.' It came down to 5 out of dozens.

One thing he said that really struck me was that when he left his first wife, he had been seeing a woman (he said he couldn't remember her name), and she went with him when he moved to North Carolina. That was news to me. I had heard that story about how he just walked out on his first wife but he made it seem like he was alone.

That made me think that the only way he could do it was to have another woman waiting in the wings. So, aside from his being so involved with his Mom after his Dad passed away, he's not planning to rock the boat with his wife (even though he has me) because he may not be sure of my sticking with him.

I honestly don't think he's ever going to leave his wife. He will stay with her forever unless she leaves him (which she never will). I told him about our mutual friend, saying that his wife knows he's cheating (which he knew), but she won't leave him because she wants part of his trust fund. Jason said she couldn't touch the trust fund. Also, his wife threatened to kill herself if he ever left her. She tried it about 10 years ago, so he knows she's not kidding. What a terrible threat he has to live with.

If I walked out of his life tomorrow, I believe he would be devastated, but in my heart, I don't think he would put up much of a fight for me. He would just stay comfortably married, be VERY nice to his wife, and continue to cheat on her until they both died.

He also told me that the reason his wife left him (for 2 weeks!!) almost 3 years ago when we first met was that she found out that he was cheating, and she said she didn't want to live with a 'cheater,' and she would teach him a lesson. She crawled back 2 weeks later and said she forgave him and they should go to therapy (which he refused to do).

I told him he has a 'Superman' complex and thinks it's his job to fix everyone's problems…His wife's girlfriends, his friends, hell, even total strangers.

I told him he needs to control this urge to help everyone because it overwhelms him, and he can't handle all those decisions, so he ignores some important ones.

***

MONDAY

I am the most insecure female on the planet!!! Jason and I haven't fucked for quite a while…we're on the way to setting another record after his father passed away.

In the meantime, I've fucked Peter 4 times and the pilot Brad once (which was awful). You would think that with all that revenge sex, I would feel better.

When Jason called me last week, I mentioned that I had the "fireman" help me put together my new patio furniture, which I had asked Jason to help me with, but he didn't have the time. Although he was trying to act cool, I could tell he was a little …annoyed…upset…pissed... who knows? Anyway, as with any toddler, he's playing tit for tat and not telling me as much as he used to. He usually sends me his schedule in the morning… "going to Mom's, shopping, balloon job, etc."

While he still sends me the morning gifs…BTW, the morning after I told him about the fireman and the fact that we were going to a Gala on Saturday, he only sent 1 GIF and claimed to have had a 'rough night.' (He usually sends at least 5 gifs.)

I HATE all this game-playing. Real life is difficult enough without him acting like a petulant child. I'm doing exactly what he's done to his wife for almost 20 years. If he can't satisfy my sexual needs, I need to find another outlet.

The real kicker is that Logan is back in town until July and asked me for lunch last week. He had to cancel because he made an appointment with an eye doctor. So, I'm waiting for him to contact me this week. Now, this would be the real deal-breaker if Jason knew that I was in contact with Logan, but again, REVENGE is in my heart for the way Jason seems to be pulling away from me!!!

The problem with this situation is the lack of communication. As with any relationship, you will fill in the blanks if you don't know what the other person is thinking. And whether or not that is their true feelings, it affects your own life.

I've said before that I don't see a future for Jason and me, but the thought of not having him in my life makes me sick! I'm fucking addicted to that man!! (Just like I was addicted to Logan—What is wrong with me???)

I thought that Peter (the fireman) could be my transition to freedom from Jason, but he just seems to want a casual sex relationship. And while that would be fine, I'm curious that Peter isn't smitten with me (like most men). And again, I'm being used as a sex toy (just like with Logan). My own fault. I keep looking for Romance, and it keeps running away from me.

I thought I could think like a man and just fuck for the fun of it, but I've said this before, I need and want to be IN LOVE WITH SOMEONE!!! And as long as I'm in love with Jason, I'm wearing blinders for anyone else.

***

SUNDAY (Months later)

I've spent the last 2 days editing this manuscript and have some learning to do! I keep making the same mistakes over and over again. And the only one getting hurt is ME! As far as an update on my dating is concerned:

JASON

He is still in my life—with only texts and phone calls. The in-person visits have dwindled to virtually nothing. Between his mother and his wife, he has no time for anything or anyone else. I can't imagine not having him in my life (even though we are 'just friends' at this point). We haven't had sex in months! I don't know how this will turn out, but we shall see. But I'm still madly in love with him. (Kill me now!)

LOGAN

He texts me when he has time and invites me to lunch when he's in town. No more sex with him.

BRAD THE PILOT

He invites me to lunch or dinner when he's not traveling.

JORDAN

He's been texting me from time to time. We have lunch and dinner occasionally, but he is not a "regular." However, there is a new development on this one…He recently texted me to ask me if I wanted to join him on a date with a "swinger" couple and if I wanted to get back into the lifestyle. What do you think I said? I jumped at the chance. So, we shall see how that goes.

PETER

My relationship with Peter was going just great. He's an amazing lover. He's into role-playing, and I even had him sleep over one night. That was a first in my life!! I say 'was' going great because he bought a house almost 2 hours away from me. The reason was that his landlord was selling his condo unit, and it was too expensive to find living accommodations locally. At first, I thought I had lost him forever because of the distance, but he showed up on my doorstep one day unannounced, and I was so glad to see him that I dragged him into the house and fucked his brains out. He continues to make time for me. We saw one another last week, and our sex session was so vigorous that he hurt his back and has been out of commission. He says he will be back. I certainly hope so. He says he wants to continue seeing me, even though he now lives so far away.

GENE

He's someone I've met through my business connections. We've flirted at business functions, and I really like him. I had lunch with him last week, and we hit it off splendidly. We had a lot in common, and I felt a very deep attraction to him. Since he's a bachelor, that works in his favor. He's attractive, intelligent, and successful. If he pursues me, I will definitely respond.

I've met other men online, but they didn't show any promise, so I let them slide.

Most of the other men in my life have fallen by the wayside (and I've let them).

***

I'm now working on a photo shoot, which was originally supposed to be a Boudoir Series, but since then, and after talking to the photographer, I will pose in some of my many costumes to create a "Sexy Calendar." I'm preparing a plan of what I will wear each month when we schedule the shoot and what I will do with the finished product. I would like the Calendar to tie in with this book when I get it published.

***

When I began writing this—oh so long ago—I was looking for my Christian Grey (from 50 Shades of Grey). Someone who would love ME, someone I could belong to and with… unfortunately, it hasn't worked out each time I think I've found him.

But I will continue looking for love, sex, companionship, and ROMANCE, and trust that I can find those elusive qualities. It would be perfect to find them in just one person!

But I won't give up and will keep looking, ladies (and gentlemen). There is someone out there for all of us, and hopefully, we won't have to share them with another person.

May love and happiness be in all of your futures. Best of luck.

END (For Now)

Palm Beach, Florida

About the Author

Camille Dunhill owns a public relations firm in Palm Beach, Florida. After the death of her long-time partner, she began looking for a romantic relationship and started documenting her experiences and adventures in pursuit of this quest. This is her first attempt at a book of this genre.

www.ingramcontent.com/pod-product-compliance
Ingram Content Group UK Ltd.
Pitfield, Milton Keynes, MK11 3LW, UK
UKHW021932200726
13853UKWH00010B/491